Praise ₁

MW01129129

"Baton has crafted the kind of novel that makes you feel like you've had a ten course meal when you've finished reading it. Layers upon layers of truth fill in the craggy crevices peppered throughout our limited understanding of interactions between Christians and Muslims that are often created by ignorance and prejudice. Baton's writing style sheds light into the dark places where few dare to tread. It's clear he's lived what he writes about, and that brings an element of authenticity to the plot and a depth to the characters that make you want to read late into the night to find out what is going to happen next."

Michael J. Webb, author of the *Giants in the Earth* trilogy, *The Oldest Enemy*, and *Infernal Gates*

"As an American Muslim, A Violent Light *resonates with me on several levels.* A Violent Light *offers a perspective into the plight of religious discrimination felt by an array of faiths. This novel hit very close to home.*"

Hanadi Doleh, Inter-religious Community Builder in New York City

"This book carries an extremely important message for us today, particularly as it relates to our assignment on the mountain of religion. Great job, Jim Baton!"

Johnny Enlow, founder of RISE, author of *The Seven Mountain Renaissance: Vision and Strategy through 2050* and *Rainbow God: The Seven Colors of Love*

"...all I could do was wipe the tears from my face and say, 'Wow!'"

Roger Bruner, author of *The Devil and Pastor Gus.*

A VIOLENT LIGHT

JIM BATON

A VIOLENT LIGHT by Jim Baton
(Peace Trilogy Book 3)

Printed by Amazon KDP

Scripture quotations taken from the King James Version of the Bible which is public domain.

The song lyrics in chapter 5 are translated from *Dengan Menyebut Nama Allah* off the album *Raihlah Kemenangan* copyright © 2004 by the Indonesian band Gigi. Used by artists' permission.

Cover design by Oliviaprodesign. All images used by permission.:

Library of Congress Control Number: 2016918347
International Standard Book Number: 1539776603
ISBN-13: 978-1539776604

This book contains factual references to actual atrocities and references to actual peacemaking organizations doing amazing work around the world. However, all characters and events in the story are fictional. Any resemblance to actual persons, living or dead, is purely coincidental.

First edition

Acknowledgments

Thank you to the outstanding peacemakers who added insights to this book—Robert Pope, Jared Holton, Juwon Park and Elisebeth Doty. Thank you, Joy Park, for your excellent editing skills. And a special thank you to Michael J. Webb, Hanadi Doleh and Johnny Enlow, not just for your kind endorsements, but for your extraordinary lives that model for us a better way.

I dedicate this book to my wonderful children, Evan and Alisha. We raised you to love everyone, regardless of their race, religion, or social status. Now we pray that you can lead your generation into a new era of peace that we have only dreamed we'd see.

List of Characters

YOUTH FOR PEACE FRESH START INITIATIVE PARTICIPANTS

Sari, Ismail—from Indonesia

Jolly, Rebecca—from the United States of America

Daud, Fatimah—from Palestine

Usman, Zoe—from France

Taj, Nandita—from India

Danilo, Yasmin—from the Philippines

Imam, Nadia—from Jordan

Alex, Katja—from Bosnia

Kareem, Lotanna—from Nigeria

Bol Hol Hol, Asmina—from South Sudan

YOUTH FOR PEACE FRESH START INITIATIVE EVENT ORGANIZERS
Aliyah Mahmudi, Jack Porter, Congressman Louis Staunton

CAMP STAFF
Henry, Abagail, Rev. George, Curt, Larry, Jeremy

DAY 1

Chapter 1

Everything was pitch black.

Sari thought she'd opened her eyes, but maybe she hadn't. She closed them—darkness; she opened them again—nothing changed.

Was she dreaming? The pounding pain in her head felt very real. She could feel the pillow under her neck. She was lying on a bed.

But where am I?

Her home in Indonesia was never this dark. Even when the electricity failed, which happened fairly often, eventually her eyes would adjust enough for her to stumble from her bedroom to the kitchen and light a candle. Or she used the flashlight in her cell phone to guide her.

Her cell phone! She always kept it on the floor next to her bed at night. She reached down over the edge of the bed and whacked her knuckles on—the floor?

Confused, she slowly ran her fingers along the edge of her bed, but the floor around her, which she'd expected to be much lower, was empty. She checked the other side of the bed and discovered it was the same. And her cell phone was nowhere to be found. Goosebumps rose up on her neck. Sari shuddered.

Sari's brain was a dense fog, and it was hard to think. She rubbed her forehead, hands unseen, trying to focus on something, anything that made sense.

Where am I? Come on, remember!

Sari relaxed her head on the pillow again and closed her eyes, searching her memory.

The last time she had awakened was in her own bed in Banjarmasin. Her adopted father, Pak Abdullah, had touched her shoulder long before dawn. "Sari, let's go," she had heard him say.

Fuzzy recollections of hugging Pak Abdullah goodbye at the airport, taking Garuda Airlines to Jakarta, then meeting Ismail for the first time, another airplane ride to America, landing in Atlanta…

Atlanta! She remembered the huge airport, and her feeling of giddiness at her long-dreamed-of first trip overseas. She was gathering with young people from all over the world—ten Muslims and ten Christians attending a conference on peace. They climbed aboard a bus. A kind African young man with a rhyming name had helped her with her bag. Some of the faces and names floated through her consciousness. And a handsome American named Jack was directing them.

A wave of nausea washed over her and she had to change her focus to keep from retching. She rolled onto her side and pulled her knees toward her stomach. Her hip could feel the hard surface beneath what must be a thin mat. Was she sick? Was this a hospital? Was it a morgue? Everything was so deathly silent, except for the breathing.

Sari suddenly realized she was not alone. Panic stirred the nausea again and it was all she could do to hold back the bile in her throat. *Who was out there?* Her imagination called up fearful images from her past and she shuddered again.

When the nausea passed, she pushed the fog and the fear back as far as she could and told herself again: *Remember!*

America. I must be in America.

The bus had dropped them at the Sheraton Hotel, where the twenty youth had eaten together in a meeting room. The excitement she'd felt at that moment lingered, so she decided to focus on it and remember all she could.

She had been sitting at a round table with a white tablecloth and a red and orange flower centerpiece. On her left was an Iraqi-American young man named Jalil or Jalal—he said to call him "Jolly." His brown hair was long, his face had a five o'clock shadow, and he liked surfing in California. She remembered how

2

the petite Indian girl with a gold stud in her left nostril had blushed when Jolly leaned over and whispered something in her ear. Sari wished she could remember the girl's name.

Across from Sari was a Nigerian young man named Kareem whose forehead seemed constantly furrowed, lips stretched tight above his goatee, worried about the animals he had left behind at the wildlife reserve where he worked. From his wallet he'd flashed small photos of lions, tigers, elephants and baboons.

Mrs. Aliyah, one of the organizers of this peacemaking event, had sympathized with Kareem. She'd called herself a Persian-American, a Georgetown graduate, and a worrywart. Sari recalled her beautiful paisley head covering tied on the side of her face and dropping over her right shoulder, and her equally beautiful smile. She felt more peaceful inside as she focused on Mrs. Aliyah's face.

The last person at the table, on her right, had unsettled her at first. Alex, from Bosnia, had a spiky red and gold mohawk on top, with the sides of his head shaved into some triangular design Sari didn't recognize. He had three studs piercing the top of his left ear and a stud in his lip. Thinking of him drumming his fingers rhythmically on the table brought back her nervousness. She'd always admired rock stars, but meeting one up close was kind of scary.

She turned her attention away from her table to the rest of the room. There were five other tables, each with young people like her attending the peace conference, accompanied by either a conference organizer or guest speaker. At the front of the room was a stage with a black backdrop, and a large video screen with potted trees on either side. Above the screen hung a banner: YOUTH FOR PEACE FRESH START INITIATIVE.

The mayor had been the first to speak, welcoming them to Atlanta. He told them that Atlanta had the busiest airport in the world, servicing nearly 100 million passengers a year, and shared a local joke that whether you end up going to heaven or hell, you'll have to connect through Atlanta to get there. Jolly's laugh had echoed around the room.

Next a large African-American congressman had shared about the need for peace in the world, and the role this young generation had to play. He seemed like a very caring man, kind of reminding her of Pak Abdullah, though her adopted father didn't enjoy public speaking very much.

The nausea returned and she fought to keep her thoughts focused. She remembered everyone getting back on the bus and driving at least two hours with Jack up into the Appalachian Mountains. It was after eleven o'clock when they had arrived at the camp. Jack had gone to talk to the camp staff while they were all ushered into cabins, five participants to a cabin. She and one of the African girls—was her name "Latina"?—that wouldn't make any sense—and her new Indian friend, a Jordanian girl named Nadia, and an American girl named Rebecca with brilliant red hair had dropped their bags on the floor and gone straight to bed. One of the camp staff, a towering white man, had told them to sleep in their clothes as they'd be wakened before dawn and needed to be ready to go. The girls had been so tired no one had changed.

Something was still gnawing at Sari's brain. Now that she remembered falling asleep on the bottom bunk under Nadia, why couldn't she reach down to her cell phone on the floor? She tried reaching up to Nadia's bunk and couldn't touch it. She sat up and reached higher—nothing.

Come to think of it, the bed she felt last night was more comfortable than this too.

This isn't where I fell asleep. Unless I'm still asleep and this is all a dream.

The fuzziness of her brain was starting to lift, replaced by the adrenaline rush of panic. Was she still with the other girls, or was that breathing she heard from someone—or something—else?

Sari was terrified to leave her mat and discover who else was there. Her mat felt like her safe place. But was it? Was she safer alone in the dark, not knowing anything?

Screwing up her courage, she called out softly, "Nadia? Rebecca? Anyone?"

No one answered. But if she listened carefully, she still heard the breathing. It was slow, much slower than hers. Maybe it was one of the girls still asleep.

She kept her knees on her mat, but crawled on her arms toward the breathing, feeling in the dark for what she hoped was her roommate. Her hand bumped up against a body. Tentatively she let her fingers work upward to find a shoulder. She felt long straight hair, and gave the shoulder a squeeze.

"Nadia?"

"Let me sleep, Mom," a deep voice mumbled.

Sari jerked back. It took her a minute to identify the voice, but she was pretty sure it was Jolly's. What was he doing in their room?

She crept back to her mat and sat with her knees to her chest, her head throbbing, her stomach doing gymnastics, and worst of all, her mind spinning wildly, unable to answer such a simple question:

Where am I?

Chapter 2

Sari had no idea how long she'd sat there shivering in the dark when she heard a rustling on the other side of the room. A frantic voice cried out, "Ahh...Mum? Dad? What's going on?"

Hoping it was one of her roommate's voices, Sari called softly, "Nadia? Rebecca? Who's there?"

"Nandita," the voice said. She matched the voice to her Indian friend with the nose ring.

"It's me, Sari. Remember me?"

"Oh, yeah. How come you're way over there? God, I feel sick."

"Me too."

"I gotta go to the toilet," Nandita moaned.

"Wait!" Sari called. "Be careful leaving your bed. You might not be on the top bunk anymore."

"What do you mean?" Sari heard a thump and an "Ow!" Then Nandita whined, "I don't understand. What's going on, Sari?"

Another rustling off to Sari's left. A grumpy male voice spoke, "Where the lights? Who cover the window?" It sounded like the voice stood up to find the light switch. Sari heard two steps, then a thump, a cry, and another sound like the standing person had fallen on someone.

"What the heck? Get off me, jerk!" More sounds of bodies rustling.

"Sorry, man. Looking for the lights."

Now more rustlings, more confusion all around her. Sari was beginning to understand at least part of the picture—all twenty of them seemed to be in the same room, most likely sleeping on the floor.

She heard someone softly crying and wanted to go to her, but didn't know how many sleepers were between them.

Then she heard someone vomiting. It dawned on her that no one would be able to see it to avoid it either.

She decided to try and bring some order into the chaos. Raising her voice, she called out, "Everyone, be careful! We're not in the beds we had last night. Now we're on mats on the floor. Don't walk around or you'll trip on the others."

Another voice spoke, "This is Bol Hol Hol speaking. Does anyone else feel sick?" Several voices answered in the affirmative. "Since we can't see, if you need to vomit, please take your pillowcase off your pillow and use that. We don't want to vomit on someone else." Bol Hol Hol…the guy who had helped her with her suitcase. *Always thinking of others.*

"What happened to the lights?" someone asked.

"Anyone got a cell phone? Cigarette lighter?" another voice added.

Sari could hear people searching around them, confused and concerned, some angry. No one produced a cell phone.

"This is Bol again. Can anyone feel around you and find a wall?"

"I can. This is Zoe." Sari heard the French accent and remembered seeing the cute blond girl flirting with Jolly on the bus.

"Me, too. It's Alex."

"Anyone else?" Silence. "Okay, how about if Alex and Zoe, you stand up and face the wall. Both of you move to the right, feeling along the wall for any light switch, door, window, etc. and let us know what you find."

"Okay," they both answered. Sari could hear their feet shuffling, their hands brushing along the wall surface. Surely in a few moments they'd find the lights and this confusion would all be over.

Someone else vomited and mumbled, "Sorry."

"Feels like a steel wall," Alex commented. "It's smooth, and cold. I'm at the corner now, continuing around. No light switch yet."

"Zoe?" Bol asked.

"Hold on, I think I found a door," she replied. Happy murmurs filled the room. "I'm trying the latch, but it won't open. I think it's locked."

"Let me try." Another French accent, but male. Sari tried to match it to a face, and remembered the tallest of their group, an Algerian-French man with a large afro, but she'd forgotten the name. "Keep talking, I'm coming to you."

Zoe chattered on about the door. More rustling, bumping and apologizing. Finally the male voice spoke again: "She's right. This is Usman speaking. The door is locked from the outside."

"What kind of door is it?" Bol asked.

"Steel." Usman knocked on it. "Sounds solid. Let's keep searching the wall. I'll help Zoe."

"Hey, there's a door over here, too," Alex announced excitedly, "and this one opens!"

A cheer echoed around the room. They could hear the door squeak open, but no light came in.

"Ow!" Alex exclaimed.

"Ow what?" asked Jolly.

"My knee found the toilet. Can't find a light switch though. Very small room, steel walls like the other, no sink or mirror. That's it. I'll keep following the wall."

Sari heard a collective groan.

"Wait, what's this?" Zoe kicked something. Sari strained to recognize the rustling noises across the room. "It's a pile of shoes. I'll keep going."

Another minute went by, and Sari recognized the voices on the wall had returned to roughly where they had started.

"No light switch, no windows, one door," Zoe concluded.

"Same here," Alex confirmed.

"What's going on?" a female voice, scared.

"Look—" started Usman.

Jolly interrupted him. "Look? Come on, bro, you can do better than that."

"Cut the jokes, this is serious. We need to make sure everyone's here and try to figure out what's going on."

"Good idea. Let's make sure we're all here. I'm Bol. In my cabin was Kareem…"

"Here."

"Daud…"

"Here."

"Taj…"

"Here."

"And Alex, we know is here. What about your cabin, Usman?"

"I heard Jolly already, right?"

"Sure, bro."

"Who else was in my cabin?"

"I was with you. My name's Imam."

"Ismail. Me too."

Everyone waited.

"Come on," Usman urged. "Who was the fifth guy?"

"I believe it was our Filipino brother, Danilo."

Usman called, "Danilo?"

No answer.

Usman continued, "Everyone feel around you and see if Danilo is still sleeping."

A knot formed in Sari's stomach as they searched. What if they'd lost someone? She breathed a sigh of relief when Kareem announced, "He's here. Come on, wake up, Danny boy!"

A nervous voice slurred, "Whoa, it's dark." Several voices laughed. "What's going on?" Danilo asked. "Is someone pranking me?"

"Ya, I wish, Danny boy," Kareem said. "We all here with you in the dark. Now wake yourself up."

Zoe and then Rebecca accounted for all the girls.

"Does anyone have any idea what's going on?" someone asked.

"Maybe we should all sit down and talk this through," Bol suggested.

"Like how's that gonna work, bro?" Jolly queried.

Sari spoke up. "What if we all reached out our hands and moved towards the others' voices. When you bump into someone, take their hand until we're all holding hands with two people, then we can sit down."

"Good idea," Bol agreed.

"Uh…don't come toward me," Rebecca said, embarrassed. "I, uh, puked over here somewhere."

Jolly jumped in: "Just stand next to the puke and call out 'Unclean! Unclean!'"

"Come this way," Usman called.

Little by little, they each stumbled forward until they found someone to grab on to. When everyone held two hands, they sat down. Two representatives—one Muslim, one Christian—from ten different nations. In the dark, Sari couldn't tell who wore a head covering and who didn't; who was black, white, Asian or Arab; they were all just *voices*. No one could see how pretty Zoe or Rebecca or Lotanna were, or take notice of Sari's own disfigured hand she'd tried to keep hidden under her long sleeve. Sari smiled to herself. *At least this way we can focus on what people are saying instead of how they look.*

Usman took charge. "First thing, starting with me, say your name and country, then bump the person to your left so we can get a mental image of where everyone is and match voices to names. I'm Usman from France."

"I'm Yasmin from the Philippines."

They went around the circle. Sari tried hard to concentrate and pick up unique qualities in each voice so she could remember who said what later.

When they were back to Usman, he said, "Okay, none of us knows what's going on here, right?" No one answered. "And since there's no one here to explain it to us, I guess we have to figure it out for ourselves. We're in a locked room with no lights and a lot of us feel sick. What else do we know?"

"All our cell phones are gone." Sari recognized Zoe's French accent.

"My watch is gone too," Bol added. "Anyone else here know what time it is?"

There were several murmurs about missing watches. No one had any idea what time it was.

10

"Did anyone trip over a bag in the dark? Our bags might be gone too," offered Fatimah sitting just left of Sari. She remembered Fatimah's exuberance bouncing around the bus introducing herself to everyone, her large gold earrings bouncing along with her. The Palestinian girl's voice still reflected that positive energy.

"Or a guitar case?" Alex chimed in.

More murmurs. No bags. No guitar case. The rock star sounded pretty upset.

"Anything else we know?" Usman asked.

"These are not the sleeping facilities we were promised," Yasmin complained.

"Duh," Katja responded.

It was quiet for a moment. Then a high-pitched voice spoke up. "This place is air-conditioned."

"Is that Taj? Why do you say that?"

The small Indian prodigy explained. "The air in here doesn't smell stale or moldy. It's cool. Probably a vent in the ceiling."

"And how does that help us exactly?" asked Katja

"What Taj said *does* help," Usman argued. "It means we aren't going to die from lack of oxygen. It also means if the vent is large enough to climb through, it could be a way out of here."

"Before we start planning how to get out of here, I think we should be asking why we're in here," Bol offered.

"Is it conceivable we are prisoners?" asked a guy to Sari's left.

"Who said that?" she whispered to Fatimah.

"That was Imam, from Jordan," Fatimah whispered back.

"It's only our first day here," Rebecca countered. "They told us we'd be up before dawn."

"Maybe we woke up too soon. Let's go back to bed." Danilo yawned loudly.

"Yeah, they told us this would be like no other event before, with plenty of surprises," added Fatimah. "Probably they just want to see if we'll come together or rip each other apart."

There were a few chuckles. "Some surprise," Katja groused.

"I'm sure they'll open the door eventually and explain everything," Sari said. "So why don't we use this time to get to know one another? Maybe by doing something constructive, we'll show that we passed the test."

"Do we all agree with Sari?" Usman asked. She felt good that he knew her name. "Anyone object?"

"Well, it's not like I can put on my makeup," Zoe joked.

Sari could feel the tension in the room lessen. She'd heard before of team building camps that did strange activities to help break the ice, maybe this was just one of those innovative American ways.

"So what should we talk about, Sari?" Bol asked.

She felt put on the spot. "Uh…maybe whatever we want to say. If you want to tell why you came to this event, or how you're feeling sitting in the dark, or whatever, just say what's on your mind."

"I'm happy to start," offered Usman. "In France, I'm in the master's degree program at the IAE Aix Graduate School of Management in Aix Marseille University. In my free time, when I'm not playing football or watching Olympic Marseille football matches, I advocate for economic justice for Muslim immigrants, and help new Muslim immigrants find jobs and integrate into French culture."

"Cool, bro," said Jolly, "But I'm guessing you mean soccer. You wanna play some real football, just let me know."

Usman mumbled something in French. Bol segued beautifully. "All right, tell us how you got interested in peace, Jolly."

"No problem, bro. Though I hate to be such a downer. I was just a surfer in San Diego when a few years ago my neighbor, Mrs. Alawadi, was murdered. She was Iraqi, like my family, just a housewife. I played with her kids. One day I come home and there she is, like, her head is smashed in, with a note next to her body, calling her a terrorist and telling her to go back to Iraq. It wrecked me, man. I mean, I was chill with all kinds of people; I just didn't get where that hate could come from. So when I finished my bachelor's, I signed up for the Peace and Justice M.A. program at University of San Diego. Dude, America doesn't need that crap."

"Don't nobody need that crap," Kareem agreed. "The white man always talking 'bout human rights, don't mean he doing it any better than anybody else."

A female voice grumbled. "I'm Katja, from Bosnia, and what I want to say is, this is a sucky way to start a day. Someone's going to get an earful from me when the lights come on."

A few supportive murmurs expressed the anxiety they were all feeling.

"I have a question." It was Ismail, who had flown with her from Indonesia. He'd been quiet so far. "Depending on how long we're stuck in here, how do we know what time we need to *sholat*? And which direction to face? And where will we get water for *wudlu*?"

This started several voices commenting on how the Muslims could do their ritual five-times-a-day prayers facing toward Mecca. Sari knew how important a part of their faith *sholat* was, and felt bad for them.

In the end, Usman advised all the Muslims to just agree to do it together whenever one of them felt it was time, and to do their best to face the same way, and surely Allah would understand. Once the door opened, it wouldn't be a problem anymore anyway.

Just as they were deciding this, they heard a scraping noise and the door opened.

Chapter 3

Blinding light burst forth all around them. Like everyone else, Sari covered her squinting eyes with her hands. She only caught a glimpse of a large figure standing in the doorway. After the outcry because of the light had died down, she heard a gruff voice speak.

"Everyone drink some water. We'll start our day's activities in thirty minutes."

She heard the door slam shut.

As their eyes slowly adjusted to the brightness, they all began to look around at their environment.

Sari guessed the room was about ten meters squared, giving plenty of space for all their mats on the floor. The mats were blue, about five centimeters thick. There was no other furniture in the room. She looked around at the steel walls, the main door, and the smaller bathroom door, which Nandita was now opening, allowing her a quick glimpse of the simple toilet inside. She looked up at a high ceiling, maybe as much as four meters high, with four brilliant light bulbs, and spotted what Taj had deduced—there were four small air conditioning vents too small to squeeze a basketball into, much less a human.

She took a look at the other participants—wrinkled clothes, messy hair, not too many smiles and a lot of worried expressions. If this event was supposed to teach them how to get along in difficult circumstances, well, they'd started off with a bang.

Bol had immediately gone to check the door. It was still locked. He lifted up something that had been left by the door—a two-liter bottle of water. He unscrewed the lid and poured a couple swallowfulls into his mouth being careful not to touch his lips, then passed it to the nearest person.

"Drink up," he said.

Zoe took the bottle. "What, no cups?" she asked, peering around Bol toward the doorway. She shrugged and imitated his method of drinking, then passed the bottle on to Kareem. Eventually everyone got at least a taste of the water, some more than others.

Yasmin asked, "Does anyone have a hairbrush? Or a comb?" She got no responses. "How am I supposed to do my hair?"

"That's why Allah made fingers," Jolly quipped, running his fingers through his long hair. "Want to borrow mine?"

Yasmin made a face and turned away. Sari self-consciously patted down her own hair. With no mirror, how would she know how she looked? She reached out to Fatimah who was still next to her.

"Hey, how about if you fix my hair and I'll fix yours?"

Fatimah smiled and used her fingers to brush through Sari's hair and pat down the parts that stuck out, then Sari did it for her, both girls giggling. Other girls started following their example. Bol's head was shaved on the side, but curly on the top and out of control. Sari watched him turn to Alex and Usman.

"I knew I should have gone for the mohawk or the afro." Bol grinned. Usman grinned back. Alex still looked worried.

"What's wrong, man?" Bol asked.

"That was a concert guitar. They'd better be keeping it in a safe place for me."

"Don't worry. You heard the man. In a few minutes this'll all probably make a lot more sense."

"Hey, bathroom time limited to two minutes!" someone called out. Sari could see that only one toilet and no shower could create a lot of tension in the group. She wondered when the camp staff would return their bags so she could brush her teeth, brush her hair, and get a change of clothes.

She was wearing her favorite high-waisted blue jeans and a new long-sleeved cotton wine-red top that Pak Abdullah had bought her just for this trip. While she smoothed it out she tried to imagine what adventure the day ahead might hold.

Except for the line outside the toilet, most of them had returned to sitting on their mats and chatting, the fear of the dark night dissipating into a curiosity of what was to come, when the scraping sound echoed through the room again and the door opened.

Five white people, four men and a woman, filed into the room and stood in a straight line blocking the door. The men all wore white collar shirts and blue jeans, except for the oldest who wore navy polyester slacks. The lone woman wore a similar white shirt with a long denim skirt. None of them smiled. A hush fell over the room, as though both sides were waiting for the other to speak first.

Then a sixth person entered, a towering white man with flaming white hair brushed back from his forehead and a nose as large and red as a *jambu* fruit.

"Good morning," his voice boomed. "Welcome to a camp like none you've ever experienced before. For those of you who survive," he smiled teasingly, "I guarantee you will never be the same."

Chapter 4

"**M**y name is Henry," the large man continued. "I'll be your camp director. I would like—"

"Where's Jack?" Usman interrupted.

Henry turned toward Usman, staring at him for a few seconds before continuing. "I will answer your questions in a moment. Now as I was saying, I would like to introduce you to the members of my team.

"You've already met Curt, I believe." Henry pointed out a younger man, nearly as tall as him, with a shaved head, bulging muscles, and a steely gaze. "Curt is in charge of the animals.

"Next to Curt is Jeremy." Jeremy didn't look any older than Sari. He had a thick shock of blond hair brushed over one eye, his thin lips pouting. "He's in charge of cleaning.

"That is Larry," Henry continued. Larry was tall and lean with short brown hair and a goatee, and seemed antsy, like standing still was a torture for him. Larry grinned at them, but it wasn't a friendly grin—it reminded Sari of the Hindu idols in Bali that she had always felt looked like demons. "Larry is in charge of gardening.

"Our senior member is the Reverend George." He had to be in his seventies, Sari thought, a small, balding man with thin white hair forming a crown around his head, and tiny round glasses. George glowered at them. Henry didn't mention what George did.

"And finally, my wife Abagail is in charge of the kitchen." Abagail was probably sixty, Sari thought, similar to her husband. But she was small and thin, with stringy brown hair down to her shoulders, and a wrinkled face like a pug dog. She didn't smile either.

This is the least friendly group I've ever seen.

"I will be in charge of this two-week program. We have planned out every detail for this time to have its maximum impact. You may direct any questions to me." Henry surveyed the group.

"Where's Jack?" Usman asked again.

"Ah, yes. Unfortunately, Jack was called back to the city temporarily."

"When is Mrs. Aliyah arriving?" Sari asked.

"She also has been delayed in the city, but not to worry, they told me to continue as planned until they can join us. Now, any more questions?"

"'Sup," Jolly began by raising his chin and eyebrows in greeting. "This question is for Jeremy—"

"I thought I was clear all questions are to be directed to me," Henry interrupted.

"Fine with me, dude. I was just going to ask if we could get a cleanup on aisle seven." Henry looked confused, until Jolly pointed to the vomit on the floor. "You said this was Jeremy's scene, but hey, you're welcome to tackle it yourself..."

Henry looked at Jeremy and jerked his chin toward the door. Jeremy scowled, but disappeared and reappeared with a bucket and mop. While he worked, Henry continued.

"You will be split into teams of two. Some teams will wait here for their shift, while the others follow one of my staff to their assigned workplace. When you hear a whistle, the staff will escort you back here for your rest, or for lunch. Always stay with your partner and with the staff assigned to you. Do not wander around. We don't want you to miss anything."

Henry began pointing out teams of two boys or two girls, then instructing them to put on their shoes and follow a staff member out or wait for their shift. Sari and Asmina were told to follow George and Henry to the film room first, then later they would join Curt's team, if not working with the animals, then digging a ditch.

Sari said goodbye to some of the girls staying behind, grabbed her white Converse sneakers and followed Asmina out the door.

They passed a set of stairs heading upward, then at the end of the hall with doors on the left and the right, they entered the right one. Inside Sari saw what felt like a living room, with two black

18

vinyl couches and a glass coffee table, a large oak desk with some scattered papers in the corner, another door on the opposite wall, and a video camera sitting on a tripod pointing toward a two-meter-long American flag on the wall to her right.

George took his place behind the camera. Henry motioned for Sari to sit on the couch, and told Asmina to stand in front of the flag facing the camera. She adjusted her head covering nervously and asked Sari if she looked okay.

"You look beautiful," Sari smiled, straightening Asmina's beaded necklace. "You'll do great."

Henry explained. "Please look straight into the camera. Tell us your name, age, country of origin, and religion. Tell us why you came to this camp and why peace is so important to you. Ready?"

Asmina nodded, swallowing hard, then smiled at the camera.

"Hi, I'm Asmina. I'm nineteen. I'm from the South Sudan. I'm a Muslim. Soon I'll have my diploma in Design at the Upper Nile University in Kartoum where I also volunteer at the SSWEN, that is, the South Sudan Women Empowerment Network. The SSWEN encourages women of different religious backgrounds to join together for women's rights to health, education, and gender advocacy. Uh, let's see, what else? I started my own design business training and employing young women who couldn't finish high school. Umm… I'm a Nubian in a brand new nation with several different ethnic and religious groups all doing our best to learn how to build a positive civil society together. That's why I accepted the invitation to this peacemaking event, to learn how to work with those who are different than me. And why is peace important to me? Well, peace is important to me because our nation is trying to recover from the pain of a civil war, and our only hope for survival is to live in a nation that knows how to resolve conflict peacefully."

She paused, then turned to Henry and asked, "How was that?"

"Just fine." He smiled. George gave a thumbs up. "Have a seat. Your turn," he looked at Sari.

Sari smoothed her hair and took a deep breath. "Can I ask why you're taking these videos?" she asked sweetly.

"Just recording the event from start to finish," Henry answered. "You have to know where you're starting to see what progress you've made, right?" He smiled, and Sari smiled back. "Ready?"

"Okay." Sari took her place in front of the flag, smoothed her shirt, hid her disfigured right hand behind her back, and smiled at the camera. George pointed a bony finger at her and she began.

"My name is Mayangsari, but everyone calls me Sari. I'm twenty years old, a Christian from Banjarmasin, Indonesia. I'm a Political Science major at UNLAM—that's the University of Lambung Mangkurat. I'm also one of the leaders of Peace Generation Banjarmasin. We take a curriculum with the values of peace into schools to teach the youth a way forward that celebrates our differences. My city, well, even my own family, has experienced violence and terrorism, and I believe that working together across religions for peace is a much better answer than responding to violence with violence. That's why I'm here." She tilted her head and smiled for the camera.

When George looked up, she asked nervously, "Was that okay?"

"Very nice," Henry smiled. "So you've seen firsthand the destruction Muslim terrorists can do?"

"Yes."

"And you want to stop them without violence?" The camp director sounded skeptical.

"Otherwise we never get out of the cycle of violence killing each other," Sari answered.

"I see. You want to end the cycle of violence." Sari nodded. "On that, we completely agree." Henry smiled warmly.

Sari asked, "Can you tell me how you got interested in peace?"

Henry leaned back on the desk with a faraway look and a long pause before he answered. "I love my country. I have sacrificed everything for her. When she groans, I groan. When she weeps, I weep. I've dedicated these later years of my life to help America to find true peace."

He seemed lost in another time and place. Sari held back from interrupting his reverie.

Finally Henry turned back to Sari with a softness that surprised her. "God bless you, my daughter, for caring enough about an old man to ask." As his eyes gazed into hers, she sensed a deep sadness. Then the moment passed.

"The Reverend George will walk you back to your quarters now. When the whistle blows, please join Curt's team outside."

As they walked back, Asmina whispered, "That 'Reverend George' makes my skin tingle. I once knew a witchdoctor who looked at me exactly like that."

Sari was surprised. "Really? He seems like a gentle old grandpa to me. Hey, you said you started your own business? That's so cool! Tell me more about it!"

Asmina had just started explaining when George opened the door to their room where half of the others were waiting inside.

"What happened?" Bol asked. "I want to hear every detail."

Chapter 5

At the mid-morning whistle, Sari and Asmina joined Bol and the others on the second work shift. Curt led the two girls plus Taj and Imam up the stairs and out a trap door. Behind them came Larry with his team of two. When all of them were outside, Curt grabbed two large rectangular bales of hay and tossed them over the trap door as if they were pillows.

Taj stepped toward the hay to take a closer look, attracting the attention of Larry.

"Hey, skinny little fellow. Try to pick up that hay bale." Taj ignored him, leaning down to inspect the twine that tied the hay together.

"I'm talking to you, kid!" Larry advanced toward Taj threateningly until he towered over the small Indian boy. "Pick up that hay bale."

Taj looked up at him curiously through his thick glasses, and answered, "I can't."

"You give up so easy? C'mon kid, try!" Larry wrinkled his nose and ran his upper teeth over his lower lip. Taj shrugged, then grabbed the twine and gave a heave. The bale didn't budge.

Larry cackled, "Don't worry, kid, I know how you can pick that hay up." He whipped out a knife as long as Sari's forearm, causing Taj to stumble and fall backwards on his rear. Sari gasped and held her breath.

With a quick slash the blade tore through the twine. Larry kicked some of the loose hay down on top of Taj and laughed again.

"See, now you can pick it up, one piece of hay at a time." He bit his lower lip, face lunging sharply at Taj. Taj threw up an arm to protect himself, but Larry was just teasing him, and cackled again.

"Great, Larry, you made a mess," Curt growled.

"No, Crush, I made a *point.*" Larry stabbed the air with the knife, then put it back in the sheath on his waist. "C'mon," he called to his two workers and set off for the garden.

Imam helped Taj get up and dusted the straw off his back. Sari breathed a sigh of relief that he was all right and took a look around.

They were in a large building with a very high roof, made of wood. Inside were bales of hay on both sides of the trap door, but past the hay going one direction was a chicken coop and a pen with goats; past the hay the other direction was a pen with pigs in it. Asmina followed Sari's gaze and at the pigs, the African girl had to clap her hand over her mouth to stifle her disgust. Sari had never seen a live pig in Banjarmasin, a Muslim-majority city, and knew how all her Muslim friends found them offensive.

Sunlight streamed through windows high up on the building's walls. Though it wasn't quite as humid as her native Indonesia, Sari realized it was just as hot, and with little air flow down low, the building felt like a sauna. It smelled terrible too.

"You two," Curt pointed at the boys, "pick up that shovel and that empty bag. The animals have already been fed in the morning shift. Now you need to collect the chickens', goats' and pigs' dung and save it in that bag for fertilizing the garden. You two," he pointed at Sari and Asmina, "grab those two shovels over there and follow me."

They grabbed the shovels and followed Curt to a set of large double doors at the end of the building past the chicken coop. As they exited, Sari glanced back and noticed Imam and Taj still hadn't moved. She hoped they'd be okay.

Once outside, a slight breeze washed pleasantly over them. All around them were vibrant shades of green—thick green grass, a green vegetable garden shaded by several trees, and behind that a vast forest of thick trees unlike any Sari had ever seen on her island of Borneo. She imagined this must be the home of one of her favorite movie characters growing up, Bambi, and she smiled. Whatever their job, at least they were outside in glorious nature.

Asmina seemed to relax a bit too, once the pigs were behind her. She gave Sari a half smile as they followed Curt about thirty paces away from the door where a ditch had been started. So far it was about thirty centimeters wide, sixty deep, and about two meters long. There was a faint chalk line in the grass going both directions in a large circle around the building. As Sari's eyes followed the line, she glanced back at the building and realized it was an old barn. The last vestiges of red paint were peeling from the broken-down structure. They were camping under what looked like an abandoned barn. *How curious this peace event is turning out to be!*

"Dig like the example here," Curt instructed, pointing at the ditch. "Follow the chalk line. Remember, Larry and I will be watching you."

Sari wondered why he had added that last sentence. She could see Larry over in the garden teaching Kareem and Alex how to pull weeds.

Asmina was watching the boys too. "Hey," she said to Curt, "those boys are much stronger than us, and I'm very good at gardening. You'll get your ditch dug faster if we switch roles."

"I have my orders and you have yours," Curt retorted. "Now shut up and dig." He marched back to the barn.

As each of them started on opposite sides of the ditch, it was clear that neither had ever used a shovel to dig before. They stabbed at the ground and pulled up a few dirt clods. They tried twisting the shovels in the ground. They jumped up and down on the shovels. Nothing they were doing seemed to make an impact.

After about fifteen minutes Curt returned, stunned at how little they'd accomplished. "What's wrong with you? Don't you know how to dig?"

They both grinned sheepishly. "We've never done it before," Sari confessed. "She comes from the desert," she pointed at Asmina, "and I live on a swamp. Can you teach us?"

Curt jerked the shovel out of her hands and angled it toward the grass, pushing it down with his foot. Then he leveraged it up and tossed the dirt to the side. In seven or eight smooth strokes he had cleared out another length of ditch large enough to stand both feet in.

"Ohhhh…" both girls said, giggling. Curt thrust the shovel back in Sari's hands and stomped off. The girls tried again with a bit more success this time, though much slower than their muscular teacher.

When Sari got down to sixty centimeters deep, she stepped into the ditch up to her knees and declared, "I did it!" She and Asmina were both sweating profusely. "I wonder how long we've been digging?"

"Not long enough," Asmina answered. "At this rate, we should make it all the way around the barn by about Idul Fitri." Both girls laughed.

Sari was curious about something. "I love your necklace! Such large beads! Does it have any special religious or personal significance?"

Asmina fingered the brown beads affectionately. "My mother gave this to me when I left home. Each bead represents one member of our family, so that I'll feel close to them no matter how far away I am."

"That's beautiful. I'm so glad I had the chance to come here, but I hate being far from my family too."

"When I was a baby," Asmina continued, "my mother was travelling to Safaha with a group of mostly Dinka Christians. The Baggara Arabs captured the group and made them slaves. Once we discovered this, my uncle was able to convince her captors that my mother was a Nubian Muslim, and he purchased her freedom. After that, she came up with the idea of the necklace, in case she was ever separated from her family again."

"Wow. I'm so glad you got your mother back. Are you two close?"

"Yes, very close."

Sari couldn't help but think back to braiding her mother's hair, cooking with her, laughing with her, dancing for her. Her heart ached for a loss nothing in this life could replace.

It was like Asmina could read her mind. "Are you close to your parents?"

Sari stumbled a bit over how to answer. "I, uh, never met my father. I was very close to my mom. We were the only Christians in our neighborhood, and struggled with so much fear for so many years…it felt like we only had each other. It's just been recently that I learned to love others around me, and let them love me."

"Where's your mother now?"

Sari's throat tightened. "She, uh, she's probably looking down on us right now. I hope she's proud of me."

There was an awkward silence.

"I thought you said you missed your family?" Asmina was still puzzled.

"Oh. I meant my adopted father, and the boys who live with us. They're my family now."

"Huh…"

"Hey, I have an idea," Sari decided she'd prefer a new subject. "Maybe the time would pass faster if we sang. Can you teach me a song from Sudan?"

"I'm not a great singer,"Asmina answered. "I really prefer sketching or painting. How about you sing me a song from Indonesia?"

"Okay. I have a favorite band, their name is 'Gigi.' They do a lot of rock and pop songs, but some of my favorites are almost like prayers. Oh, and they're Muslims. This one is called, 'Saying the name of Allah.'"

Sari began to sing: *Surrender your life or death / Surrender to God alone / Surrender your suffering or joy / So your life will always be at peace.*

Asmina was looking at her with a terrified expression. Sari stopped singing and mouthed the word, "What?"

Then she realized that Asmina was looking past her. She heard pounding footsteps and turned around just in time to see Larry racing toward her, knife in hand.

"Shut up!" he screamed at her, coming fast. Sari reflexively stepped backwards and tumbled into the ditch.

Larry appeared over her, blocking out the sun, still holding the knife and breathing heavy. "No singing! No noise! Work quietly or we'll all be in trouble!"

26

Sari felt that old familiar panic trying to rise up and seize control of her. She fought it down by closing her eyes and whispering to herself, "Jesus, you're with me, I'm not alone."

She heard a grunt, then a cry from Asmina. Sari forced one eye open. Curt had Larry's arm twisted behind him and Larry's knife at Larry's throat.

"You're the one who'll get us in trouble," Curt growled.

Larry's menacing façade crumbled and he whined like a child. "Stop it, Crush! How do you silence the songbird? You cut off its head. She's the songbird, not me." Larry pointed accusingly at Sari.

Curt pushed Larry away from Sari and stuck the knife in his own belt.

Larry begged, "Please, can I have my knife back? Please, Crush, I need my knife. Please?"

"Later. Who's watching your gardeners?"

Larry's eyes popped open and he spun around and sprinted back to the garden, almost as though he expected his workers to have disappeared. Asmina helped Sari climb out of the ditch.

"Larry's right. No singing. No noise. Work quietly or you'll get no lunch." Curt turned back to the barn.

Sari was still shaking, and took a few moments to lean on her shovel and catch her breath.

"I don't like this place," Asmina whispered, leaning close. "These people are scary."

"Especially Larry," Sari agreed. "Scary Larry…" She giggled in spite of her fear. "But let's give them a chance. There may be a method to their madness. We're getting to know each other, aren't we?" She smiled. Asmina smiled back and picked up her shovel.

By the time they heard the whistle for lunch their hands were raw with blisters and they were weak with hunger and thirst. But they were also becoming friends.

Chapter 6

When lunch arrived, Sari was in the bathroom washing her face and hands with water from the tank of the toilet. She dried them on her jeans and opened the bathroom door. Everyone had gathered back in the main room, and Abagail, Yasmin and Lotanna were carefully handing out plastic bowls and spoons from a large tray. Sari waited until everyone else was served, then took one. Abagail left two bottles of water this time, then exited and locked the door.

"What is this stuff?" Jolly asked.

Sari took a closer look at her bowl. The soup was red and watery. She fished around with the spoon and found a couple small chunks of potatoes and carrots, but mostly red kidney beans.

"Vegetable soup," Bol answered, slurping the broth from the edge of the bowl.

"Not bad, eh," Kareem added. "Be thankful there be no pork."

Kareem was right, thought Sari, it wasn't bad, and she was starving. She followed Bol's example and put the bowl to her mouth to get every last drop of broth.

But not everyone was so happy. Yasmin picked out only the potatoes and carrots and left the beans and broth, with a scowl on her face. Danilo noticed, and asked if she wasn't going to eat the rest if he could have it. Yasmin turned her head in disgust and pushed the bowl slightly in his direction.

"You should have finished it," Usman rebuked her. "You'll need the calories to do the chores around here."

"I can count my own calories, thank you!" Yasmin snapped. Sari looked at Yasmin's trim figure, perfect face and long silky hair. Someone had mentioned Yasmin was a model, and Sari believed it.

"It's just not fair," Yasmin continued. "Why wouldn't they give us the beef?"

"What beef?" Alex asked.

Yasmin and Lotanna exchanged glances. "Might as well tell them," Lotanna shrugged.

Now everyone's attention was riveted on Yasmin. "We were in the kitchen with that old hag. While we were peeling potatoes and carrots, she was cooking roast beef in the oven. We saw it. Then she told us to put half the potatoes and carrots and all the beans in the soup, the other half she put in a pan with garlic and butter and slipped it in the oven with the roast beef. The staff eats way better than we do and we're the paying guests! When Jack and Mrs. Aliyah get here, they better straighten this out."

"Or what?" Katja sneered. "You're going to stage a protest? Make an international incident? 'Peace Event Fails Due to Lack of Roast Beef'?"

"Bitch," Yasmin said under her breath, but loud enough for those nearby to hear.

"Whoa," Bol interrupted. "We're not getting what we thought from this event. But if we turn on each other, it only exposes that we're no better than the generations before us. They love to talk about peace, but they don't take time to do the hard work of building genuine relationships. Now there are still several people here I don't know at all. Can we at least get a few more introductions each time we're together?"

Several people started gathering in a smaller circle near Bol, and Sari joined them. Yasmin stomped off to the bathroom. A few, like Katja, looked undecided what to do and stayed where they were.

"Imam," Bol began. "You've been very quiet so far. You're from Jordan, right? Tell us more about yourself."

Imam ran his hand over his mouth and beard. "Do you mean like the video yesterday?"

"You can be more personal than that." Fatimah smiled at him.

Imam tugged at the collar of his charcoal dress shirt. "Uh...there's not much to say. I'm studying International Relations at London School of Economics and Political Science.

I'm most accurately categorized as an introvert. I enjoy reading. I like listening to jazz. That's all."

"Are you a leader of some peace-related organization?" Bol questioned.

"Oh, no, I'm not really the leader type. Public speaking terrifies me."

"Then how come you got picked for this event?" Katja called out from her mat, her voice filled with skepticism.

Again, a long pause. "My father considered it useful."

"Tell us about your family," Sari pressed.

Imam shot a glance at Nadia. Sari noticed his hands rubbing each other, than rubbing his thighs, then back to rubbing each other again. "My parents are…honorable. I have an older brother and an older sister. Thank you for your interest. Maybe somebody else?" Imam opened his hand and motioned to the person next to him to share, Daud.

"Cool," said Bol, taking a swig from one of the water bottles and passing it around. "How about you, Daud?"

"Okay," Daud leaned his elbows on his crossed legs and looked at the floor. "Actually, I'm an introvert too." He smiled shyly and several people laughed.

"Why are all the good-looking guys so shy?" Zoe lightheartedly complained.

Jolly protested, "What are you trying to say, babe, you want me to come out of my shell for you?" He blew her a kiss. She pantomimed catching it, rolling it into a cigarette, smoking it, then putting it under her heel and stamping it out, catching several hoots from the guys and giggles from the girls.

Zoe turned to Daud. "Go ahead, handsome," she purred. Daud blushed amidst more laughter.

"Ah…well, I'm a freshman in the two-year Media Program at Bethlehem Bible College in Palestine. I want to document what's happening in my country through film. I did a film about bringing food relief to victims of the Israeli bombings in Gaza, and luckily it won an award at the Barcelona International Amateur Film Competition." Daud looked down as he shared.

"Well done, bro," Usman gave him a thumbs up. Others murmured their support.

Encouraged, Daud looked up and continued. "You know, if you look all around you, there's so much happening, and it's so complex, it feels overwhelming. Sometimes I just do this..." He held his hands up, thumbs at right angles touching the pointer fingers, forming a box about ten centimeters in front of his face. He slowly panned it around the group looking at each face in turn. "The rest of the world disappears and I can try to see the real you."

As he panned past Zoe, she called, "Wait, go back, do me again," and batted her eyelashes at him. He blushingly ignored her and continued around till he reached Imam, who quietly responded with "Brilliant!" Then Daud looked down again, embarrassed. He turned to the next person in the circle. "Your turn, Nandita."

The thin Indian girl cringed. "If you guys are shy, I'm *really* shy," she began. "I don't know what to say."

"Just chill, girl, and take a stab at it," Jolly offered encouragingly.

Nandita looked at him confused. "A *stab*? What do you mean?"

Jolly laughed. Rebecca interpreted for her. "He means just try to say something."

"Oh," Nandita's nose wrinkled. "I'm not that used to American English. Or boys. I just graduated from St. Luke Convent School in Kashmir. I'm, uh, eighteen. My parents want me to go to university, but I haven't decided where yet. There's nothing, uh, that interesting about me." She twisted her long black hair and looked down.

"That last statement isn't true," Taj rebuked her gently. "In 2011 St. Luke's was burned down by extremists. Nandita here went on national television to say that she forgave them."

The murmurs of approval only caused the girl to withdraw even further into herself. Sari decided to try a different tack to pull her out.

"Can you tell us about that gold stud you have in your nose? It's beautiful. But I heard that it was a sign of marriage, like a wedding ring..."

The Indian girl touched her left nostril self-consciously. "In some parts of my country a *phul* does mean you're married, but in my area it's just for, uh, fashion, I guess." She gave Sari a quick smile then returned to examining her blue jeans. "I'm just really grateful to be here."

Sari completely agreed. She couldn't believe her good fortune to get to meet so many amazing people from different parts of the world. This camp was definitely the coolest thing ever to happen to her.

Ismail was next in the circle. "Hey guys, I'd love to share, but I missed my morning *sholat* and I don't want to miss this one. Who wants to join me?" He and Usman discussed which direction they should face, and Imam joined them explaining what he'd seen outside. They started lining up some mats as prayer rugs, and Kareem joined them, then Fatimah and Asmina also filled in behind the men, Ismail leading the prayers from the front.

Sari looked at the other Muslims and wondered why they didn't join. Yasmin was sitting in a corner running her fingers through her hair. Katja sat on her mat, arms crossed, clearly not in the mood. Jolly was flirting with Zoe, and Taj had his head cocked to one side observing everything. To Sari it seemed like he was always observing.

Danilo got up to visit the toilet and was about to pass in front of those praying when Sari noticed and grabbed his leg. "Hey, Danny, Muslims prefer if you walk behind them when they're praying."

His face didn't seem to care, but he changed course and walked around behind them to reach the toilet. Danilo had told her he was part of Peace Generation in the southern Philippines, the same organization Sari had joined in Indonesia. She thought he would have known better. Was it possible that some of these participants really knew very little about the other religion? She'd grown up the only Christian kid in her neighborhood, and in the minority at school. But maybe that wasn't true for everyone here.

She looked around at the Christian youth and wondered if any of them liked to pray. *Should I ask or not?* She thought back to her public elementary school experience, where religion class was

32

required. All the Christians went to one room, Muslims to another. Since practically all her friends were Muslims, she'd wondered why they weren't allowed to pray together. Even in her Peace Generation club not everyone thought it was a good idea. She'd always believed that someone's spiritual journey was one of the most interesting things about them, and if you couldn't open yourself up to share that together, how well could you really get to know each other?

The door swung open and Curt blew his whistle loudly, scowling at the Muslims praying. Sari knew the *sholat* was almost finished. She walked up to Curt to stall for time for them, showing him her blistered palms.

"Excuse me, but do you think you might have any work gloves that we could use when we dig this afternoon? I think it would help us to be more productive, don't you?" She smiled at him, trying to keep his attention until she heard the final prayer phrase of speaking peace on those praying on the right and left.

"I'll look," he said sharply. The prayers were still going.

"And would you happen to have any aloe vera lotion to help our hands heal faster?" She smiled again.

"I doubt it." He scowled at her and was about to blow his whistle again when she put her hand on his arm to stop him. Behind her she could hear the *Assalamu alaikum warahmatullah, Assalamu alaikum warahmatullah,* and she knew the prayers were over.

"Thank you," Sari said and stepped aside.

"First shift, let's go," Curt commanded. Sari peeked out the door and saw Jeremy, Abagail and Scary Larry waiting. She headed back to her mat to take a rest.

As everyone filed out leaving Curt behind to close and lock the door, Sari remembered what Daud had said and made a box with her hands so she could only see the broad-shouldered white man. If she could strip away everything around and just see him, she wondered who he really was, and what his story was.

A few moments later she was fast asleep.

Chapter 7

"**A**re you sure this is the right road?" Congressman Louis Staunton asked Aliyah Mahmudi. She had just turned the car off of a windy county road onto a pot-hole-filled lane barely wide enough for one vehicle. They were two hours north of Atlanta, and Louis, compulsively time-conscious, was worried they wouldn't make it on time to lead their two o'clock session at the peace camp.

"Yes, sir, I'm sure. Jack and I took this road multiple times in preparing for this event. It's only about twenty minutes more."

Louis looked at his Rolex, a gift from a Muslim businessman in Pakistan where he'd spoken at a peace rally—1:45. Though he was used to traveling the world with people who considered time a fluid concept, it was deeply engrained in him to never keep others waiting.

He shifted his bulky body uncomfortably in the small front seat of Aliyah's rented Nissan Maxima, wishing she'd splurged for a four-wheel-drive with Icon suspension. The chicken fried steak and baked potato he'd just eaten weren't helping things. *Still, it beats the heck out of when I rode that camel in Libya...*

Aliyah was apologetic. "You should have taken a helicopter, sir. I'm sure you have better things to do than bounce around the countryside with me."

"I'm afraid I must disagree. My term is up in January, and you already know I won't be seeking reelection. I hope to do even more of this 'bouncing around' with world changers like you and those amazing young people we get to serve this week."

"At least on paper they are a remarkable group," agreed Aliyah. "Activists, innovators, overcomers of incredible odds, and at such a young age! And of course, there's Imam."

"Yes, his father is an extraordinary man. Imagine a young Arab starting from that place, what he could build in a lifetime—it boggles the mind."

"I hope he's doing well so far. I hope they're all okay. I hope no one's sick."

"This is at least the fifth time you've said that. Relax, they're probably having the time of their lives."

Louis looked out the window at the deepening forest. Towering red cedar trees, sturdy maples and oaks, mixed with a variety of pines and even white hickory. This was hunting territory. The forest was probably full of white-tailed deer, fox, maybe even black bear. He'd never been into hunting—hated guns—but he could feel the call of the wild luring him out of this metal popcorn shaker and into the wide open spaces.

They rounded a corner and came to an abrupt halt. A police car was blocking the narrow road, with a middle-aged white cop leaning back on the hood chewing on a long piece of grass as though he were waiting just for them.

Aliyah put the car in park and waited. At first the policeman just stared at them, then he slowly tossed the grass aside and meandered towards the driver's side of the car. Aliyah rolled down her window.

When the policeman leaned forward and placed his forearms on Aliyah's window, Louis could read his name plate—Deputy Ted Olsen.

Ted spoke first: "Howdy, folks. I'm going to have to ask you to step out of the car and answer a few questions."

Aliyah looked worriedly at Louis, who shrugged and reached for the door handle. He could use a stretch about now anyway.

He strode around the front of the car and held out his hand to the deputy. "Pleased to meet you, Ted, I'm Louis Staunton, and this is Aliyah Mahmudi."

Ted kept his hands on his belt and cocked his head at them, examining them from Louis's bald head and Aliyah's head covering down to their toes. Louis had been in enough situations like these before to not take offense. He put his hand down and smiled warmly. "What kind of questions can we help you with, Officer?"

Ted pursed his lips and spoke in a strong Southern drawl. "Well, I reckon we can start with how come a black man and a Mooslim woman would be driving around the back waters of Georgia?"

"We're on our way to a retreat center which I am told is just a few miles up that road," Louis answered, pointing past the patrol car. "This camp is for Muslims and Christians who want to pursue a life of peace."

"That so?" Ted eyed him skeptically. "And are you sticking with that story, Missy?" he looked at Aliyah.

"Of course, it's the truth," she protested.

"Maybe it is, maybe it isn't," the policeman pursed his lips again. "I ain't never heard of no Mooslim gatherings in this here part of Georgia. But it don't make no difference. Just around that bend," he pointed up the road, "is a washed-out bridge. I'm stationed here to wait for the repair crew and warn travelers to turn back. Guess this just ain't your day."

"Perhaps you'd be so kind as to suggest an alternate route?" Louis tried.

"There's only one retreat center at the end of this road, and this is the only road in or out. You folks are gonna have to turn back."

"But when will the bridge be fixed? It was fine just three days ago!" Aliyah pressed him.

"Repair crew should be here today or tomorrow. Or the next day. These things happen. Now move along."

Louis took a closer look at the patrol car. Printed on the side was the name of the county, which if Louis wasn't mistaken, was closer to Savannah, on the coast.

"One last question, Ted. You're a long ways from your jurisdiction, aren't you?" He wondered if the local cops would at least try to help them find a solution to get to the camp.

Ted's eyes narrowed. He hitched up his belt around his forty-inch waist. "You're pretty observant for a black man. The Catoosa County sheriff's office called me in to help when the bridge went out while the sheriff's on his two-week vacation. There ain't no other law enforcement working these parts today but me. So when I say, 'Move along,' ya'll had best be movin' along." Ted's right hand slid back toward the gun on his belt as though to emphasize their lack of choice.

"All right, Officer, have a good day," Louis smiled, perhaps half-heartedly, but doing his best to follow his motto and see every potential enemy as a potential friend. "Let's go," he told Aliyah, and they climbed in the car, turned it carefully around, and headed back down the road.

"Where to?" she asked.

"Let's get back to I-75 and find a hotel. I need to make a few phone calls and see what options we have."

"We have to call Jack! He'll have to rearrange the schedule to do our sessions later."

"Give me your phone. I'll call Jack while you drive."

Louis scrolled through the contacts and dialed Jack's number. A recorded message said the number was out of service.

"Must be bad reception up in these mountains," Aliyah reasoned, "though we tried it three days ago and were able to get through."

"Yeah, these things are unpredictable. Do you have anyone else you can try?"

Aliyah had Louis call the camp director with the same result. "Could be where they're standing in the camp," Louis guessed. "Well, Jack will call us eventually if he can get a signal."

He noticed Aliyah's worried expression. "Try not to be bothered by what you can't change," he encouraged her. "Unpredictable situations have a way of bringing out the hidden greatness in people. If we're not there, Jack, or even one of the participants, someone will have to step up and lead. This will all work out for the good, believe me."

He looked at Aliyah's unchanged expression and wasn't sure his advice had gotten through.

Chapter 8

Dinner that night was a small piece of dense, grainy yellow cake that only the two Americans recognized. Rebecca told them it was called "cornbread." That was it. No meat, no vegetables, and worst of all no rice. Indonesians joked that they never felt full until they'd eaten rice. Sari definitely didn't feel full tonight.

Fortunately, Curt had switched Asmina's and her assignment with the boys', letting them dig the ditch and the girls feed the animals. She had immediately volunteered to feed the pigs so Asmina could stay in the half of the barn where the goats and chickens were. At this gesture of understanding, Asmina's round face had burst into a huge smile.

After her cornbread and a couple swigs of water, Sari surveyed the group. Everyone looked exhausted, most of them too tired to talk. Danilo was asking Rebecca questions about America, Bol was whispering with Taj in the corner, and Yasmin was visibly upset about something with Lotanna trying to calm her down. The others just sat on their mats, like in a daze.

Jolly came and plopped down beside her, shoving the back of his hand under her nose. "Smell this," he demanded. Sari took a whiff and nearly gagged at the combination of bleach and other cleaning chemicals. "Disgusting, isn't it?"

"Yes," Sari choked out. "I guess you were on the cleaning crew?"

"Yup, me and Daud. We scrubbed toilets, sinks, showers, walls, floors… This facility is a lot larger than it looks. The staff quarters are pretty decent—flowery comforters on the beds, bookcases full of books, mostly religious ones though, looks like they could live here year round. What did you do?"

"Ditch digging and feeding the pigs," she answered, holding out her palms to show the blisters.

"Dang, babe, that looks painful." He noticed the slight discoloration on the edge of her right hand and took it in his, turning it over. "Whoa! Did you get burned today too?"

Sari felt embarrassed, but not nearly as badly as she used to be. "No, this happened when I was a kid." She looked down at the scarred, disfigured back of her hand. "I used to hide it, but a couple years ago I met a guy who could see past it and fell in love with me. He helped me accept it." She shrugged.

"You still on the board with this dude?"

A sharp pain pierced Sari's chest at the memory. "No, he uh…" she blinked rapidly, as though it would stop her from seeing Bali's head in her lap, his blood on the floor, "…he's in a better place."

Jolly seemed to rightly interpret her meaning. "Duuuuuude…" He elongated the word like it was a poetic tribute. "That's heavy. He was right, though. You're a breezy times ten."

"I don't understand." Sari blinked at him in confusion.

"You know, a hottie, a stone-cold fox, not like some of those llamas over there…" he angled his chin toward Yasmin's side of the room, "…who think society could collapse from the lack of a lipstick."

She stifled a laugh. Jolly grinned, happy to have an audience to appreciate his humor.

"Do you think there will be an evening session?" Sari asked.

The words were hardly out of her mouth when the large door swung open, and in walked Henry and George, the latter carting an old radio.

"Attention, everyone!" Henry's booming voice commanded the room. Everyone turned to see what was coming next.

"Your hard work today was appreciated. Tonight you will be rewarded with some entertainment. We will be listening to a radio broadcast, and afterwards we will engage in stimulating discussion. Reverend George?"

George turned on the radio, already preset to a station, and cranked up the sound of what must have been the introduction music to the program.

Over the din of the music, Usman yelled, "Where's Jack?"

Henry held his finger over his mouth, then pointed to the radio. Sari heard the radio announcer begin: *Coming to you live on Christian radio, it's the Raging Patriot, Rick McReynolds.*

Then a new voice echoed off the steel walls of the room, an angry, aggressive voice. She wondered what they would be learning from this exercise.

It's the Raging Patriot, everybody, welcome to another edition of our show. I'm Rick McReynolds. And if you want to survive this so-called New World Order, you know what you have to do... (a chorus of voices joined Rick in repeating the next line) *...STICK WITH RICK!*

Today we're talking about immigration. Yeah, I did it, I said the dirty word. One of the greatest destructive forces of our time, worse than any hurricane, fire, earthquake or flood, immigration is destroying our nation.

Have you heard the statistics released this week by the president? Friends, this comes straight out of the "Black House," coming into these final months of eight horrific years since we had a "White House." The president said, and I quote, "We celebrate the new milestone of welcoming the largest number of immigrants ever, over two million this year." Two million immigrants, folks!

And guess what the Center for Immigration Studies commented: "The primary threat from a group like ISIS to our homeland is through our immigration system."

Listen, friends, forget all the wetbacks and drug mules sneaking across our southern border, forget all the Chinks and Japs buying up all our land on the West Coast, forget about all our jobs being stolen by illegal immigrants, forget about that. The greatest threat to America today is from the Muslims that our president is legally inviting to invade our shores. He's spent two terms working his secret plan to Islamicize America.

Sari was stunned. She could see the others were equally aghast. Most of them were frozen, eyes riveted on the black box spewing hate. Kareem was the only one fidgeting, fists clenched, as if he were about to jump up and smash the radio. *What was going on here?*

The talk show host continued: *You doubt me? First he wants to close Guantanamo and all other interrogation centers that were set up to combat jihad. Then he welcomes the lunatic Iranian president into the Black House. Then he relaxes immigration standards to take in refugees from Syria, Iraq and even Libya—Libya! Millions of Muslims flooding into our country, and how many of them does it take to crash a plane? Bomb a football stadium? Open fire with an AK-47 in an elementary school or church? One, my friends, it only takes one.*

The ideological godfathers of radical Islam are the Wahhabis from Saudi Arabia. Remember Osama bin Laden? Wahhabi. Twenty-three percent of Saudis are Wahhabis. This year the number of Saudis living in the U.S. grew to over 100,000. Just do the math folks, how many Wahhabis have we handed visas to from one country alone? Thousands. Now imagine how many ISIS soldiers have slipped in pretending to be refugees in this year alone, to carry out their rich Saudi backers' diabolical plans against us?

You don't get to be president by being an idiot. He knows what he's doing. He's the doorkeeper. He tries to close Guantanamo's doors and open immigration doors. Something stinks over in the Black House, friends. If you're a white Christian pastor, just try to walk through the front door of the Black House and meet the president. Can't do it. Can't do it. You know why not? He's at the back door welcoming the rich Muslim Arab sheikhs in. I can almost hear the whispers in the Oval Office, and do you know what they're saying? "Kickback," that's what they're saying. "Offshore accounts," that's what they're saying.

The government says there are six to eight million Muslims in America—liars! Independent sources confirm at least twenty million, and we're on course for fifty million in the next ten years.

So what are we gonna do? Call your congressman? Yeah, if he's not taking dirty money under the administration's table. Burn a Koran? Forget it, the media doesn't care. Stick with Rick, I'll tell you what we're gonna do. Number one, get your gun license and get a gun and learn how to use it. When the Muslims take over, our "right to bear arms" is gonna be revealed as the most important phrase in our Constitution. Stock up on drinking water and canned goods. Our website will give you all the information you need to know to survive when white Christians are no longer served at restaurants and grocery stores, because they don't carry the mark of the Muslim "Beast." The New World Dis-Order is coming, friends, but we will not be powerless. We have numbers, we have knowledge, and we walk in the power of the truth. Stick with Rick!

Till next time, this is the Raging Patriot, Rick McReynolds. Live smart, live strong and survive!

Chapter 9

The air was electric. While Henry and George seemed calm, the rest of the room was swimming in anger, confusion, embarrassment, shock, and, Sari was afraid, the first boiling bubbles of rage, best exemplified by Kareem.

The young Nigerian was on his feet waving a fist at the two camp staff. "That be bullshit!" he exploded. "That be bigoted, black-hating Nazi propaganda and you know it! Why you make us listen to this bullshit?"

Henry smiled calmly. "Good, the discussion has begun. Would anyone else like to share their thoughts?"

"I agree," offered Alex. "You don't have to be white or black, Muslim or Christian, to be offended by that slimebag radio moron. That kind of hate doesn't belong in our world."

Sari noticed others nodding or voicing agreement.

"He's a sicko," she heard Lotanna say.

Henry was unperturbed. "I understand your reaction to his, uh, abrasive style. Perhaps he makes some valid points, though, particularly about the dangers of mass immigration. Would anyone like to comment on the content of the broadcast?"

"Dude, unless that jerk is a Native American, his ancestors were immigrants here too," Jolly argued. "Immigrants built this nation to what it is today."

The Reverend George interjected, *"White* immigrants built this nation."

"On the dead carcasses of African slaves," Kareem retorted with a snarl.

Several people began talking at the same time, gesturing with their hands, building the tension in the room to a frenzy. George and Henry waited quietly, eerily, *watching*.

Imam actually raised his hand before speaking above the din. "Excuse me please, may I ask what is the purpose of us being exposed to this objectionable material?"

Everyone quieted down to hear Henry's cryptic answer. "Sometimes you have to offend the mind to reveal the heart."

He motioned for George to pick up the radio. "That's all for today. We will turn out the lights in fifteen minutes. Good night." They exited, and Sari could hear the clang of the latch as the door locked them in once again.

Kareem launched into a tirade in his native tongue directed toward the door. Usman pulled him aside, quietly attempting to calm him down. Sari watched as the others moved toward the bathroom line, or rearranged their sleeping mats to be next to a friend, and still others sat in stunned silence at what had just transpired.

Asmina pulled her mat towards Sari. "Could I sleep next to you?" she asked with a shy smile. "I woke up between two boys this morning."

"Of course! I had Jolly on my right and Fatimah on my left—where do you want to sleep?"

"Like I'd want to be near that playboy surfer!" Asmina said as she squeezed her mat between Fatimah and Sari.

On the far side of the room, Usman, Kareem and Ismail were setting up for *sholat*. "Aren't you going to pray?" she asked Asmina.

"I'm too exhausted." Asmina collapsed on her mat with a sigh. "I'm a designer, not a ditch digger or goatherd. What would my family think?" She fingered her beads.

"You seem to me like someone who has always chosen to make the best out of a difficult situation. Sudan isn't the easiest place to live, I imagine."

Asmina yawned. "I guess you're right. I'm glad to make a friend like you, Sari."

"Me too," Sari smiled. Bol was approaching.

"Sari, after the *sholat*, I'd like to get everyone to talk for a bit. Would you help me?"

She was surprised to be asked. There were so many other leaders in this group. "Sure, I think it's a great idea."

"Thanks." And Bol moved on.

The room went black. The Arabic prayers so familiar to Sari's ears continued in the dark . After the worshippers could be heard crawling back across the room, bumping into people on the way to their mats, Bol spoke up.

"I know it's been a long day, but I suggest we gather in a circle like this morning and talk for a few minutes before we go to sleep."

"Good idea," Sari spoke awkwardly into the darkness. "Grab a hand, everyone." Across the room she heard Yasmin protest, "Leave me alone." *What is her problem?*

Bol ignored Yasmin. "This was a highly unusual, even disturbing day for many of us. But I think we need to keep the big picture in mind. We came here to learn new ways to forge peace in our generation. Are we making any progress in that?"

"It would help if we had some clean clothes," Katja complained. "Did anyone see our suitcases today?" No one answered.

"Yeah, and Alex really needs a shower," Jolly added.

"Shut up, beach bum."

"Make me, guitar hero."

Asmina interrupted them. "Larry nearly killed Sari today."

"What?" several people exclaimed. Bol asked for the story, and Asmina provided it.

"Anyone else experience something weird today?" Bol asked.

"I don't like that the staff gets fed decent food and we get scraps," Katja complained again.

Lotanna chimed in: "That radio broadcast wasn't weird, it was *wrong*."

"The bigger unanswered question for me," Usman cut to the point, "is where are Jack and Mrs. Aliyah? They're the ones who invited us to this event. I thought it was *their* program, didn't you?" Several people grunted in agreement. "This doesn't feel like what we signed up for." More sympathetic sounds. "I think there's something bogus going on here and we should do something about it."

"Do something like what?" Bol queried.

"Make them tell us what's going on. Make them give back our stuff." Sari heard fewer rumbles of agreement.

"And just how do we *make* them do what we want?" Bol asked.

"We refuse to do their work tomorrow."

The circle seemed to be digesting that thought silently. Sari decided to speak up.

"I know the methods they're using are unorthodox. Larry scared my spirit right out of my body! But nothing bad happened. Maybe they're trying to create a difficult, or even a hostile environment, to teach us how to come together when it's hard. Anyone can talk about peace when we're playing team building games. I think this may be a live simulation, where we're tired, we're insulted, we're deprived of comforts, to see what we're really made of."

She continued, "Don't some of you come from war-torn areas, places of violence, how hard it must be to work together under those circumstances! At least, that's what I think."

"That be more white man bullcrap talking," Kareem objected.

"Chill out, dude. Sari's got a point. Come on, we scrub a floor, feed a goat, what's the big deal? Just one day, and we stick it to our leaders with a strike? What kind of wusses are we?" Sari felt relieved to have Jolly support her.

Bol wanted to put it to a vote. "What do you others think? Let's go around the circle and say, 'Revolt,' or 'Stick it out.'" Sari heard him bump someone.

"Ow!" said Daud. "I guess I'll stick it out."

"I will as well," Imam agreed.

"Me, too," added Zoe. "Besides, I think Jeremy's cute." Sari heard several groans.

"Not me," objected Kareem. "We got to do something."

"I'm with Kareem," said Usman.

Rebecca was next. "Sari's probably right. We should trust that they know what they're doing."

46

"Well, I'm not sure they know what they're doing," Katja disagreed, "but I'm not ready for a revolution."

Alex, Taj, Nandita, Fatimah, Nadia, Jolly and Asmina sided with Sari. Ismail said he wouldn't go against the majority. Lotanna was last.

"Revolt is not my way," the Nigerian girl began. "But I don't agree with you, Sari. I'm telling you, something is not right here. I can feel it. These people are hiding more than our suitcases. We need to be vigilant, or something bad could happen."

The lightheartedness some had felt moments earlier dissipated like the puff of smoke when a candle burns out. It was like an unseen shadow in the dark came to rest heavily upon their hearts, reminding their bodies of their physical exhaustion.

No one seemed to have anything else to say, so Bol wrapped it up.

"All right then. Let's get some sleep."

DAY 2

Chapter 10

Sari was dreaming she was sitting on her mother's lap. Her mother was stroking her hair and singing. An indescribable peace filled her. Then a harsh voice interrupted: "Get up!" She and her mother looked around, but no one was there.

"Thirty minutes till work." A door slammed, jarring Sari awake. The lights were back on, and the vision of her mother sadly slipped away.

She tried to sit up, but had to stifle a groan. Her lower back protested loudly, all the way around to her abdomen. When she moved her arms, her shoulders joined the chorus. Last night she hadn't realized what her body had gone through. *I hate ditch digging. Please God let me do something easier today.*

The girls went through their morning ritual of helping fix each other's hair. Bol passed around the new water bottle. Ismail led a quick *sholat*. There was a lot less chatter this morning, limited mainly to a few moans, complaints about the bathroom line, and some gruff retorts. She did her best to smile at each person, but less than half smiled back. A knot formed in Sari's stomach. *At the rate we're going, we may be killing each other by the week's end.*

Much too soon, the camp staff assembled before them and Henry was handing out job assignments. Sari held her breath as he assigned the tasks of ditch digging, animals, gardening and cleaning. Thankfully, she and Rebecca were given the first shift in the kitchen with Abagail.

Abagail handed them green aprons. "You girls wash your hands with that there soap." She pointed them to the sink without looking them in the eye. Sari let the running water soothe the blisters on her palms, sighing contentedly, until she realized Abagail was tapping her foot impatiently.

"Oh, I'm sorry," Sari smiled at her. "My hands were just so raw from digging ditches yesterday, see?" She showed Abagail her palms. "My name is Sari, and this is Rebecca. She probably knows all about American kitchens, but I don't, and I'm really excited to learn something new from you."

Abagail seemed unsure how to respond. "Well, I can learn ya a thing or two, I reckon."

"Can you teach me how to make that dinner we had last night…what was it called, Rebecca?"

"Cornbread."

"Yes, cornbread. I've never eaten anything like it." She smiled warmly at Abagail and got the briefest flash of a smile in return.

"All right. The cornmeal's running low as it is. You ever grind corn?" Sari shook her head. Abagail led the girls to a back storeroom behind the kitchen where a large pile of old, dried ears of corn were piled up in a corner on newspapers. Next to them was an odd-looking black iron contraption shaped like an enclosed wheel in the center, with a cylindrical opening on the top and an elongated *S*-shaped curved appendage coming out the side with a wooden handle to grip at its end.

Abagail grabbed an ear of the already-shucked corn. "This here corn is old and dry. Ya cain't grind it fresh. See, ya drop the ear in here," she pushed it into the cylinder, "while turning the crank." Sari heard the crank squeak and the wheels whir, and sure enough, the dried kernels dropped into a metal tub while the cobs were spit out of another hole onto the floor.

"Ooooooh," Sari cooed, "look at that!"

"Be careful putting in them ears or you'll lose a finger," warned Abagail. "Why don't you two take turns and shell me about forty of them ears."

"Then what?" Sari pressed excitedly. "Then can we make the cornbread?"

"Not with these here kernels. We'll cover them with a cheese cloth for a few more days before we grind 'em. But I done got enough cornmeal left for a few days. I reckon we can bake up a new batch." Once again, there was an almost-smile on Abagail's face before she disappeared back into the kitchen.

Sari was giddy. "You've probably done this before, huh?"

Rebecca laughed. "Nope. I'm a city girl. I've never seen one of these machines before."

"Really? Oh, are we going to have fun!" Sari giggled and started to stuff an ear of corn into the machine while turning the crank. At first it was awkward doing both, so Rebecca offered to handle the ears while Sari used two hands on the crank. Within a few minutes they found a rhythm and both were grinning.

"You know, all I know about you is that you're American and have the most beautiful red hair I've ever seen," Sari began as she turned the crank. "Can you tell me more about how you got here?"

Rebecca touched her shoulder-length hair self-consciously. "Sure, I'm a student in the Dental Assistant program at Everest Institute in Dearborn, Michigan. Do you know where that is?"

Sari shook her head.

"Well, it's in the north-central part of America. And Dearborn is famous as having one of the highest Muslim populations in the country. My school has a lot of Muslim students, so I got involved trying to understand their needs. Out of that, I ended up starting a free after-school program to help immigrant kids learn to speak, read and write English, called "iDream.""

"How cool!"

"My program got featured on *The Today Show*. You know what that is?" Sari shook her head. "It's a morning news show on TV. I imagine that's how I got invited to this event. How about you?"

Sari shared briefly about when ISIS invaded her city in Indonesia, and how her adopted father Abdullah had risked his life to try and stop them non-violently, and how since then she and Abdullah had been speaking to groups of young people about peace.

A cloud passed over Rebecca's face. "But you're a Christian, aren't you?"

"Yes," Sari replied.

"I guess your adopted father *used to be* a Muslim? Isn't Abdullah a Muslim name?"

"Oh, he's still a Muslim," Sari explained. "He's so wonderful, and the only real family I have since my mom died."

"But…" Rebecca seemed stumped about something, but Sari had no idea what. The American girl tried again. "Why would you have a Muslim father? Aren't there any Christians where you live?"

Sari was beginning to understand Rebecca's confusion. "Christians are a minority in my city. But there was this time when my mom was trapped in a burning church and Pak Abdullah nearly died saving her life. I knew then that he was more like Jesus than most of the Christians I knew."

Behind her freckles, Rebecca's face muscles tightened. "But Christians are our *true* family. Muslims…I just don't know how you can really trust them. They're so deceived. They don't know the truth like we do."

The words were Rebecca's, but the voice of Sari's pastor echoed through her memory saying much the same thing. Maybe it was time to take a different approach.

"Would you like a turn with the crank?" Sari smiled, and moved to Rebecca's position stuffing the corn ears into the machine. Rebecca frowned and started cranking.

"Have you gotten to know any of the Muslims here yet?" Sari probed gently.

"Not really. Some of them scare me."

"Really, who?"

"Kareem, Usman, Ismail…they all seem so angry." Rebecca's head was down, hair covering her eyes, cranking much faster than Sari had been. She had to hurry to keep stuffing the corn in.

"And then there's Imam," Rebecca continued. "He's hiding something. I can feel it. You don't think terrorists would try to infiltrate an event like this and blow us up, do you?"

Sari wanted to laugh, but realized her American friend was serious. "I'm sure nothing like that will happen," she assured Rebecca empathetically. "What about any of the girls? Have you gotten to know them?"

54

"Just the Christian ones. Lotanna is nice, and Nandita. I feel safe with them."

Sari reached for another ear of corn and realized they'd finished the forty ears laid out for them.

"Oh! We're done. I should tell Abagail," Rebecca said, hurrying off.

This is why we need an event like this. Because even the best of us have a long way to go.

Abagail entered and pointed at Sari. "You, put them there cobs into that sack over there for the pigs later."

"Sure thing, Abagail," Sari responded cheerfully. "And you can call me Sari."

For that day's soup, Abagail assigned Rebecca to chop onions, squash, and okra, a slimy green vegetable Sari had never seen before. Meanwhile, Abagail taught Sari how to mix the ingredients for the cornbread. Sari decided to give Rebecca a break and chatted with Abagail. At first it was hard to get much out of the older woman, but little by little Sari began to win her over, and Abagail shared about her childhood in Georgia, about meeting Henry, raising their boy, and about a few of the places they'd lived.

As they were putting the chopped up vegetables into the stew pot, Rebecca spoke to Abagail for the first time.

"Are you and your husband Christians?"

"Of course, dearie. Been a Christian all my life. My daddy was a minister."

"Doesn't it make you a little nervous being cooped up here with all these Muslims?" Rebecca asked.

Abagail shuffled over to the sink and washed her hands, mumbling, "My husband always knows what's best." Head down, face hidden by her straggly brown hair, Abagail bustled past them back into the storeroom. Sari glared at Rebecca, who looked away.

A whistle blew in the distance. Abagail reappeared, her face expressionless, and motioned for them to lay their aprons on the counter. Then she silently walked them back to the common room.

Sari hoped she would get another chance with Abagail. She would love to know what the woman truly thought.

As they passed the staircase, Curt and his workers were descending and filed in behind them. Approaching the door to the common room, Sari heard someone yelling angrily inside.

Chapter 11

"**S**top laughing!" Jeremy screamed. He was examining his clothes, wiping his face and checking his hands, going crazy because he couldn't figure out why people were pointing at him and laughing.

Sari saw it instantly and had to choke back a giggle. There was a bright green stripe straight down the middle of Jeremy's blond head.

He grabbed Larry's collar, demanding through clenched teeth, "Tell me why they're laughing!"

Larry looked at Jeremy's hair again and cackled with glee. "Kid, your hair is a glorious green!"

Letting go of Larry, Jeremy put his hand on top of his head, then held it out—his hand was green, all right. He glared at Usman. "You!" he shouted. "I'll get you for this!"

Curt pushed his way past Sari and Rebecca. "What's going on?" he demanded menacingly. Then he saw Jeremy's head, and the boy snarling at Usman.

Usman turned and walked away, still grinning. Curt looked to Larry to explain.

"Your kid brother just got punked!" Larry was still laughing hysterically. He looked at Jeremy, teasing him with a baby-voice: "Someone wants to teach this little puppy dog some new tricks!" He cackled again, holding his ribs.

"Shut up!" Jeremy yelled, the veins in his face about to pop. Behind Curt, the last one to enter the room was Zoe, who innocently asked, "What's up?" When Jeremy heard her he spun around in horror, tried hopelessly to hide his green hair with his hands, and with a face like a tomato, raced past her out of the room.

"Looks like the walking traffic light has turned red," Usman said with a straight face eliciting more laughs and a loud howl from Larry. Curt glared at Usman and at Larry, then grabbed Larry by the ear and pulled him out into the hall, slamming the door. Sari realized that Abagail hadn't entered either, and it was just them.

Jolly burst into song: "It's not that easy, being green..." All he got were quizzical expressions. "You know—Kermit the Frog?" No response. "My talents are wasted here." He shook his head.

Zoe asked again, "How did that happen?" Usman just shrugged, so Daud explained that while they were painting, Usman had told Jeremy there was a caterpillar on his head, to hold still and he'd flick it off. After three flicks with a paint brush, the imaginary caterpillar was gone and they went back to work. Jeremy had no idea his hair was now green, and when he'd entered the room and they'd all laughed, he couldn't figure out why.

Once Zoe found out her compatriot from France was the guilty party, she slapped him hard on the arm. "Usman, you jerk! He's just a kid." Then she seemed to be ripping the tall young man to shreds in French, but he kept on grinning.

When she had finished, he defended himself. "The kid deserved it. He acts like we're his slaves. He needed to be taken down a notch."

The door reopened, and Curt stepped inside. He called names and sent them into the hall for the next work shift, announcing that there would be a brief respite for the cleaning crew. Before he left, he pointed across the room at Usman.

"You just moved yourself up on the list," he growled ominously, then turned and slammed the door.

Usman mocked him: "The list of who is taking you down."

The knot was tightening in Sari's stomach. It seemed like Usman wasn't happy with their plan to give these camp staff another chance—he wanted a revolt and he was ready to provoke it with or without their approval. She found herself wishing Bol hadn't been sent out to work. He would know what to do.

At lunch, she ate her bowl of squash, onion and okra soup next to Bol, and told him what Usman had said after Bol had left.

58

"I've dealt with guys like him before. It only takes one hothead to jeopardize all the bridge-building we try to do." He shook his head in frustration. "'I'll try talking to him."

"Thanks. I'm starting to worry that not everyone here is really as committed to peace as we thought." She told him about her conversation with Rebecca in the kitchen.

"Oh, you're on kitchen duty? If you go back there this afternoon, see if you can beg, borrow or steal some candles and matches for the night."

"Sure, I can ask Abagail. She seems like a sweet person."

Bol changed the subject. "You know, I'm really glad you're here. I've been watching how you make friends so easily with people from all different backgrounds. And I think people respond to your leadership."

Sari felt herself blushing. "Bol," she protested, "*you're* the leader! Not me! How do you, you know, get everyone to work together so well?"

Bol shrugged. "I'm just being myself. In Sudan, I've seen so many people respond to difficulties with anger or withdrawal. I just always try to respond with some practical, positive step forward. Don't look back. Learn something new every day. Keep putting one foot in front of the other." He shrugged again and smiled.

Keep putting one foot in front of the other... Yes, that was a lesson she was learning too.

Sari nodded. "I feel like I have so much to learn—from you, from the staff, from everyone here—I'm so lucky to be here."

"That's another thing I like about you, Sari. You see the good in everyone." Bol smiled at her.

Sari's face felt hot again. She looked down at her soup.

Perhaps he noticed her blushing, because he immediately stood up. "Hey, I need to check in with Taj about something. Catch you later." And Bol moved on.

Sari returned her bowl and spoon to the tray by the door, took a swig of water, and was about to lie down for a nap, when she remembered something Rebecca had said. Imam and Nadia were sitting in a corner of the room, but it didn't look like they were talking very intensely. Sari decided she should find out if Rebecca was just imagining that Imam was hiding something. She strolled over and plopped down next to Nadia.

"Hi! You guys are from Jordan, right? I haven't really got to hear your stories yet. Can you tell me about yourself and how you got here?" She looked at Nadia first and smiled.

Nadia returned the smile, adjusted her black-rimmed glasses on her elegant Arab nose, and pulled her straight, sandy-blond hair out of her face, turning her body toward Sari.

"Hey, Sari. Yeah, sure. My family is in the textile business. I help at the branch my older brother runs in Amman. For the past few years I've often joined events of the Youth for Coexistence Program at the Jordanian Interfaith Coexistence Research Center in Amman, and I started volunteering with JICRC's internship program for international students. I've met a lot of great people that way. I guess that's how I got recommended for this event."

"Sounds amazing!" enthused Sari. "What kind of hobbies do you have?"

Nadia giggled. "I'm like any girl, I guess. I like shopping, singing in my church choir, and karaoke with my friends."

"Is there a special guy in your life?" Sari dropped her voice conspiratorially.

Nadia blushed. She grabbed her long hair in her fingers and put it between her teeth. "Uh, not really. I mean, yeah, there is, but he doesn't...I mean...it probably could never happen, but..." She took to biting her hair again, her face showing this was a question too complex for her to answer to a stranger.

Sari touched her knee. "Don't worry. I'm sure it will work out."

She turned to Imam. "And how about you? A smart, good-looking guy like you probably has a girlfriend waiting for him back in, where did you say, London?"

"No, no girlfriend," Imam answered.

"What do you do for fun?"

Imam paused, thinking. Sari didn't consider this such a hard question. "Any hobbies?"

"I believe I already mentioned them—reading and listening to jazz."

"So you did." She tried a new tack. "What do you hope to do with what you learn here?"

"That would depend on what I learn," Imam answered with a serious face.

She turned to Nadia. "Is he always this serious?" she asked jokingly.

Nadia didn't seem to find it funny. "Oh, he's…very dedicated, and determined, and thoughtful…" Sari was beginning to get a glimmer of who Nadia's "special guy" might be. She wondered if cross-religion relationships were as problematic in Jordan as they were in Indonesia. A familiar, bottled-up pain leaked out of her heart, remembering the Muslim boy who had loved her, and suddenly she didn't feel like talking any more.

She thanked them for the chat and lay down on her mat, closed her eyes, and imagined she was with Bali sitting on the roof of the Sudimampir market looking at the stars and dreaming about a future together that they would never have.

Chapter 12

It was a disappointing afternoon shift in the kitchen for Sari. Rebecca was giving her a cold shoulder and she didn't know why. No matter how hard she tried to get Abagail to talk, the woman had decided to clam up completely. Sari tried to make the best of it by memorizing the recipe for the cornbread they were baking for dinner. She asked for some candles, too, but Abagail refused to respond. By late afternoon the silence started to get to her. It made her recognize how tired she was, and how desperately she wanted a bath.

The only real interaction came when Henry popped into the kitchen.

"What's cooking, girls?" he asked jovially.

"I learned to make cornbread today," Sari boasted. "I hope Abagail will teach me more American food!"

Henry smiled. "That's the spirit! Your willingness to learn new things is precisely what we're looking for at this camp." He turned to Rebecca. "And how are you, my daughter?"

The red-head managed a tight smile. "Ready for anything."

Henry looked at Abagail. "See that? These Christian youth are just as I told you. And we will lead them to the promised land of peace." Henry met Sari's and Rebecca's eyes. "When the going gets tough, and when some choose to take offense, remember, you must help us lead the others to the light. I'll be counting on you two."

"Yes, sir," Rebecca's shoulders straightened. Sari nodded.

When Sari's cornbread showed up for their dinner again, she heard a chorus of groans. None of them were used to this diet, and the heavy work was taking a toll on them.

Ismail found out she had worked in the kitchen and quizzed her relentlessly about whether any of the pans or cooking utensils had touched pork, making the whole meal unclean. She assured him that no pork had come near the cornbread, though Abagail had been cooking some unknown meat in a frying pan for the staff. Ismail looked torn between risking contaminated food passing his lips, or starving. In the end, he ate the cornbread.

Just like the previous night, after dinner Henry and George appeared with the radio. Another groan went up, but Henry responded with a smile.

"Good evening. Once again I thank you for your hard work today. It will take all of us playing our parts to make the world a better place, don't you think?"

"Where's Jack?" Usman interrupted. "And where's Kareem?"

Sari looked around. Sure enough, Kareem was not in the room. How had she been so oblivious?

"After the radio broadcast I'll answer all your questions. Reverend George?"

George turned on the radio.

"Answer me now!" Usman challenged. George responded by turning the volume up to near deafening levels as the same intro music they'd heard last night throbbed through the room.

The announcer began: *Coming to you live on Christian radio, it's the Raging Patriot, Rick McReynolds.*

(Rick's voice) *It's the Raging Patriot, everybody, welcome to another edition of our show. I'm Rick McReynolds. And if you want to survive this so-called New World Order, you know what you have to do… (in chorus) …STICK WITH RICK!*

Today we're talking about tolerance and diversity—two words that sound as friendly and fluffy as a cottontail until you discover exactly what it is the liberal politicians and media expect you to tolerate. If you think people shouldn't kill their unborn babies, guess what? You're intolerant! If you think marriage should be between a man and a woman, guess what? You're intolerant. If you even hint that a man who gets a sex-change operation and breast implants might possibly be confused, guess what? You're intolerant.

63

In other words, if you have the same moral compass as the founding fathers of our nation, you're intolerant.

But check this out—if you publically announce that Christians who reject the Big Bang theory and billions of years of evolution that formed us without any God in the equation, are, and I quote, "backwards, religious fanatics, and idiots," as one well-known television science-show host recently said, were his remarks considered intolerant? Of course not. Because tolerance is just another word for liberalism in this country.

Let's say you work in the military, perhaps at the Naval Nuclear Powered Training Command, and you tell someone that you think being gay, lesbian, bisexual, transgender, and all other sexually deviant things are cool. You are tolerant. Line up for a promotion. But if you share your personal religious belief that any of those things are wrong, like the Navy Chaplain Lt. Cmdr. Wesley Modder did, you're fired. Apparently Navy Chaplains are no longer allowed to have the religious freedom guaranteed in our constitution. They have to preach a godless, liberal pro-gay sermon if they want to get a paycheck from our federal government.

Friends, new studies are coming out all the time that link all sorts of diseases including AIDS, STDs, cancer, and several blood diseases directly to the twin issues of homosexuality and racially-mixed sexual partnerships. If you're a white man out there listening to me today, and you want to live a long and healthy life, you're going to need to protect your bloodline. You find yourself a nice, pretty white woman. There are plenty of them out there, and my sister is waiting for your call! (Laugh)

Diversity is great when you're conducting an orchestra. Each instrument adds a beautiful quality to the overall group. But friends, if they ain't playing the same song, it's a train wreck. What have the Muslim immigrants contributed to America's song? I'll tell you what—female genital mutilation, arranged marriages, honor killings, and thousands dead from acts of terrorism. Not only aren't they playing the same song, they're crashing planes into our orchestra pit!

The Cubans have taken over Miami, the Mexicans are pushing the whites out of Los Angeles, and Dearborn, Michigan is officially a Muslim city, folks. Each one is playing their own kind of music, and it don't sound like anything we ever heard. Are we intolerant for wanting our good White Christian music that dreamed this country into being to be heard above the devilish noise?

Tolerance is a train wreck, my friends. Diversity is the road to destruction. Our liberal baby-killing, gay-parading, Muslim-pandering government is sending our country to hell in a handbasket. It's up to us, the true patriots of America, to keep our guns loaded and our ammo dry. Stick with Rick!

Till next time, this is the Raging Patriot, Rick McReynolds. Live smart, live strong and survive!

Once again, Sari's ears were burning, as she figured all the others' were too.

"So, what response do you have to Rick's points about tolerance and diversity?" Henry asked.

"How about you tell us what's really going on here," Usman pressed. "Where's Kareem?"

"Your friend Kareem made it clear to me that he would rather not continue in this program. So we honored his wishes by sending him home with Jack, who had just arrived. He wanted to speak with you, but Kareem was so angry, Jack recognized the urgency of a swift resolution for the young man. Hopefully Jack will be able to join us tomorrow."

"When can we get some clean clothes? And a bath?" Katja asked.

"Ah, tomorrow morning there will be an announcement to that effect. Now back to the topic of this evening. I am curious what the Muslims among us believe about homosexuality. Are any of you gay, or supportive of a gay lifestyle?"

Sari had never anticipated a Muslim-Christian event diving into this issue. But the more she thought about it, the more she realized that prejudice was prejudice, no matter what group she was stereotyping or avoiding or pre-judging without getting to know them as individuals. Now she understood what Henry meant

65

about some taking offense. Maybe he was going to help them see that their group wasn't as open-minded as they thought they were.

It was several moments before anyone answered, but since Henry didn't seem to want to leave without a discussion, finally Asmina spoke up.

"Where I live in the South Sudan, many young men have been killed in the war, or have become killers. For those women lucky enough to have a man in the home, our government reports that seventy percent of women in my country are the victims of domestic violence. Seventy percent! So when I work with young women, I automatically assume that many of them are dealing with this issue.

"In such conditions, is it any surprise that some are looking for affection from other women? Abused or widowed young women don't automatically lose their sex drives. Even though the *ustad* at the mosque preaches against homosexuality, I think there are more important issues these girls need first, such as safety, respect, education, and the care of a society that values them."

Some murmured agreement. Henry countered, "So you're saying a troubled situation makes being homosexual less wrong?"

"I'm saying let's not—what is your idiom—not put the wagon in front of the horse?"

"The cart," Rebecca corrected quietly.

"Do we have any other gay activists here?" Henry joked, looking around.

Jolly spoke up. "Dude, I'm chill with everybody—flamers and femmes, wastoids and weed whackers. But I'm also whatcha might call a 'food activist.' Is it just me, or is the food here seriously bunk?" Several people agreed.

George's gravelly voice was heard for the first time: "Whose end is destruction, whose God is their belly, and whose glory is in their shame, who mind earthly things."

"Amen, Reverend," Henry intoned solemnly. "Tomorrow we will also address this request. Believe me, though you cannot see it, the wheels are in motion for something truly extraordinary, of which each of you will play a part. Good night."

Henry abruptly turned and left, George and the radio following in his shadow.

When the door had slammed shut, Taj caught the attention of everyone in the room by announcing, "He's lying about Kareem."

Chapter 13

The room went immediately silent, every eye on the youngest member of the group, the slight Indian boy with his hair uncombed and his thick glasses. In his typical high-pitched tone he continued.

"Kareem and I were working in the garden this afternoon. He told me he regretted his angry words of yesterday and was planning to apologize to Henry in front of all of us tonight. He said he realized he still had some prejudice against Whites in his heart, and he needed to change."

Like everyone else, Sari was surprised to hear this. If Kareem was willing to give this camp and its strange methods a chance, hopefully some of the others would now too.

"So what happened?" Bol asked. "Where is he?"

"When it was quitting time," Taj continued, "Curt told Larry to walk me in with his workers, while Curt took Kareem somewhere else, I don't know where."

"Does anyone believe Jack actually showed up, and then left again? Did anyone see or hear any evidence of a car arriving?"

No one answered.

"We can look for evidence of tire tracks tomorrow morning," Taj suggested.

"Good idea, Taj. Anyone else feel like Henry isn't telling us the whole truth?" Several murmured agreement. Sari wanted to give Henry the benefit of the doubt, and hoped finding the tire tracks tomorrow would put everyone at ease.

"Guys, it's time to face the facts," Lotanna jumped in. "We're not guests here, we're prisoners."

"Oh, come on!" Danilo protested. "This is America! This isn't some war-torn place like the southern Philippines, or wherever you come from. This is the land of freedom, tolerance, Mickey Mouse and the NBA!"

Jolly laughed. "I guarantee these white dudes aren't here to teach us basketball."

Sari was worried that fear was rearing its ugly head again. "Americans are also known for innovation, so if their camp is different than what we're used to, that doesn't mean it won't be effective."

"They took our cell phones—no contact with the outside world. They took our clothes and won't let us bathe—a power move to show their dominance and keep us dependent on them," Lotanna countered.

Sari didn't back down. "Having no cell phones means we can focus fully on each other. Perhaps no clean clothes or bathing is helping us to get beyond trying to impress each other with our appearance, and share our more real, vulnerable selves."

"Crappy food, slave labor, and those ridiculous radio broadcasts?" Katja complained. "Come on, Sari, wake up and smell the b.o. I'm with Lotanna. This feels more like an internment camp."

A rare comment from Yasmin: "This is the single most horrible experience of my life."

"That's why we need to take control," Usman said. "Everyone be on the lookout for intel that could help us in our struggle against the oppressors." Bol rolled his eyes.

"What do you think, Imam?" Sari saw a chance to put the mystery man on the spot.

Everyone looked at the bearded Jordanian, who took his time answering. "Certain aspects of this experience are troubling, it is true, but we all have a basic trust in those who invited us, and a responsibility to those who sent us." He paused, then continued, "Perhaps more information would be expedient."

Bol nodded. "Imam's right. Since we do have a seed of doubt regarding Henry's story about Kareem, I agree that we should keep our eyes and ears open and learn as much about this place and these camp staff as we can, just in—."

He was interrupted by Ismail. "Sorry, we need to *sholat* before the lights go out." He started arranging the mats as prayer rugs in the corner. Usman, Imam, Fatimah and Asmina joined him.

Bol finished his thought for those left behind: "—just in case. But let's not jump to conclusions yet, there may be a reasonable explanation for everything."

He turned to Sari and asked quietly, "Did you get what I asked for?"

She felt embarrassed. "Sorry. I asked, but Abagail wouldn't let me have any."

"Don't worry about it." He smiled at her, but she knew she'd let him down.

As they all got ready for bed, Sari approached Lotanna and asked if she could bring her mat alongside for the night. "I guess so," was the less-than-enthusiastic reply.

She waited until the lights were out to whisper with Lotanna. "I just wanted to say that I felt bad about arguing with you in front of everyone. But you can't be right about us being prisoners. I don't want fear to take over our group and cause us to miss out on all the good that can happen."

"How can you be so naïve?" Lotanna hissed back. "If everyone follows your flawed fantasies, we won't be prepared for what's coming. If we are truly prisoners, believe me, it's not so they can have help with their cooking and gardening. There's some evil purpose behind it."

Lying in the pitch darkness, Sari pictured Lotanna's beautiful face just inches away from her—her large brown eyes with those long eyelashes, flawless skin, full red lips and long wavy hair. She pictured Lotanna scowling at her, and wondered if she were blushing in the dark. *Am I naïve, or is she paranoid?*

Sari thought back to her few interactions with the Nigerian girl so far. More often than not she'd seen a hardness—or was it a sadness—etched in that face and wondered why. Then it dawned on her.

"You've been a prisoner before, haven't you?"

She heard Lotanna take a deep breath before answering. "Have you heard of the Boko Haram kidnappings?"

70

Sari couldn't help raising a hand to her mouth. "Don't tell me you…that was you?"

"Yes. My friends and I were kidnapped from a boarding school in Chibok. We were kept as slaves for our Muslim captors to do with as they wished. I didn't mind the hard work. But to keep us subdued, they would constantly come up with new ways to humiliate us. We were imprisoned in the Sambisa forest for a year before the military found us."

"How horrible!"

"The reason they invited me to this camp is because I became an activist, speaking out on behalf of the girls who were raped, forcibly married, and even worse, the ones who were brainwashed into extremism at the camp—my friends, cute little schoolgirls, who would be handed guns and execute other girls to please their captors…

"I know what kidnappers act like, how they think. And I know what it takes to survive. If I'm right, and we're in worse trouble than you think, I'm going to need your strength with me to help the others get through this."

Sari didn't know what to say, so she fumbled in the darkness till she found Lotanna's hand and grasped it tight. The Nigerian girl's palm felt hard and calloused, so different from the smooth skin of her face. Sari wondered what kind of work Boko Haram made her do, and after the work…

She managed to squeak out, "Were you… you know…?"

"What they did to me could not break me. They couldn't take who I choose to be away from me. And after a few weeks in captivity, I made a decision, that I would not be afraid."

Sari realized that Lotanna had been speaking out of concern for the group, and not from fear. Could she have been wrong, and Lotanna right? Were they in danger?

And if so, will I be strong like Lotanna?

Chapter 14

The sun was high overhead when Louis Staunton and Aliyah Mahmudi made it back to the turn in the road where the deputy had halted their progress the previous day. After failing to get through to Jack or anyone at the camp by phone, they didn't know what else to do except give the road another try and hope the bridge had been repaired.

Today there was no police cruiser blocking the road. In its place was a large beech tree, as big around as Louis's forty-inch girth. They parked the car and got out to examine it.

"You've got to be kidding me," Louis grumbled. "What are the chances?"

He followed the line of the tree back to its stump and looked at the clean break, bark and wood shavings scattered around. "Chainsaw. Someone cut this tree down on purpose." He surveyed around them. "No other stumps, just this one."

He frowned at Aliyah. "Looks to me like someone wanted to block this road."

"But why?" she asked. "The only thing up this road is the retreat center."

Louis had an idea. "How far away is the bridge from here, the one that is supposedly washed out?"

"I'm not sure, but I don't think it's that far away."

"You feel like walking?"

They left the car and circumnavigated the road block, then continued walking down the road. With no real breeze to take the edge off the heat, Louis was sweating inside his blue-gray Brioni suit within minutes. He loosened his tie and collar.

Aliyah looked beside herself with worry. "Something is wrong, sir, I can feel it. I even called Jack's workplace and his parents and he hasn't checked in with any of us. When we didn't show up yesterday, I'm sure he would have tried to contact us. Now this tree! Why would someone want to keep us from getting to the camp?"

"This may have nothing to do with us or the camp," Louis tried to calm her. "Possibly putting a tree over the road was to protect drivers from going off the broken bridge ahead, rather than waste a policeman's day sitting out here in the middle of nowhere."

He tried to distract her imagination from running wild. "What activities did you have planned for the second day?"

"Today they were supposed to go on an obstacle-story-hike in the morning, then do group survival simulations in the afternoon."

"Obstacle-story-hike?" Louis wondered if he'd heard correctly. "What is that?"

"Along one of the hiking trails through the woods, Jack and the camp staff were going to set up several obstacles. Each time the group came to an obstacle, they'd pause to listen to one of the participants share about the biggest obstacle he or she has faced in pursuing peace. They the group would find a solution together to get past the physical obstacle before them and continue the hike."

Louis couldn't help but see the irony. "Now just look at us. Wanting to do our bit for peace but we can't even get to the party." He laughed dryly. Aliyah's smile still looked forced.

She stumbled, and he caught her by the arm. "You okay?"

"I wasn't planning on joining the hike." She looked down below her ankle-length brown pleated skirt at her high heels. "Picked the wrong shoes for this."

"We'll take it slow." Louis slowed the pace his long legs naturally wanted to take.

It wasn't long until they came to the bridge. Louis examined it carefully from every angle and could see nothing wrong with it, and with the chipped wood on the railings and beams, it looked about as new as his father's Oldsmobile Jetstar.

"Let's head back. That cop was lying. We need a faster way to get to that camp and we need it now."

Even in heels, Aliyah managed to walk at a near sprint back to the car.

While Aliyah drove, Louis worked the phone. He started to call "911," then hesitated. Based on yesterday, the local cops might find more ways to hinder him than help him. So he dialed a D.C. number and shared his suspicions with a friend at the FBI, who directed him to drive back to Atlanta, promising that by the time he got there a chopper would be ready.

They had no sooner entered the FBI's Century Parkway office when they were stopped at the front door by two men. "Congressman Staunton, Ms. Mahmudi?" They nodded. "Come with us."

They were whisked out a side door and into a black SUV. As their tires squealed out of the parking lot, the man in the front passenger seat turned around to introduce himself.

"Sorry about the rush. We got a call from D.C. that informed us getting you airborne ASAP was a priority. I'm Special Agent Casey Durak," he held out his hand to each of them, "and your Daytona 500 driver is our Special Agent in Charge Todd Pritz." The driver grunted and took the next corner on two wheels.

Louis sized up these agents: Pritz was balding with a five-o'clock shadow, while Durak had a darker complexion and Roman nose with short, black hair gelled to give it some spike. Both men were as tall as Louis but much more fit. Both wore open-collar dress shirts with no ties.

On the next corner Aliyah gripped his arm tightly, terror written all over her face. "Thank you for your prompt assistance, but there is no bomb counting down the seconds, so let's make sure we get to the chopper in one piece."

Pritz grunted again and slowed to about sixty miles per hour for the next corner, then skidded to a stop. There, in a private location, stood a helicopter with four blades already rotating and a pilot in the cockpit.

Durak jumped in first, offering his hand to Aliyah and then to Louis, Pritz leaping in last. They strapped on seatbelts and headphones, and within seconds they were lifting off.

Durak taught them how to talk into the voice-activated microphones and asked if they were okay. Aliyah's face looked a bit green, but they both nodded.

Louis had been in choppers before. "What model is this?" he shouted.

Durak smiled and responded into the mike in normal voice. "A Bell 407GT. The larger glass windows will make it easier to spot your target location in the forest. This baby is locked and loaded as well if we meet any resistance."

"Loaded with what?"

"Machine guns, rockets, anti-armor missiles…better safe than sorry."

Louis hoped there'd be no need for a firepower demonstration.

Pritz produced both a map marking every road from the highway to dirt country lanes, and a topographical map, and soon they had made a mark on each where they thought the camp should be. Pritz handed the maps to the pilot, who informed them that the roughly one hundred twenty miles before them should take about forty-five minutes.

Once they spotted the county road leading toward the camp, the chopper dropped lower, and Louis pointed out the tree in the road, the alleged washed-out bridge, and then just over a hill, they came upon the camp. Everything looked quiet. There were no vehicles anywhere, no people visible. The pilot circled slowly from several hundred feet in the air while Pritz scanned for gun muzzles in windows, Durak explained. But from the best they could ascertain, the camp looked empty.

Pritz pointed to a grassy spot about a half-mile from the camp protected by a tree line, and the pilot set the whirlybird down. Louis could tell Aliyah desperately wanted out, so he got permission to take her into the trees away from camp, while Pritz and Durak, guns in hand, advanced on the retreat center.

After Aliyah threw up in some bushes, she felt better.

"I'm amazed you held it in that long," Louis grinned. "That's some will power!"

"I was too afraid to breathe," she confessed. She sat on the grass and leaned her back against a tree. "Solid ground never felt so good."

But her anxiety over the peace participants quickly returned. "Why did they take guns? Do you think something terrible has happened?"

"As Special Agent Durak said earlier, 'Better safe than sorry.' If something is wrong, they'll know what to do. All we can do is wait."

He sat down on a log near Aliyah and pulled out his cell phone. "Three bars." He didn't need to explain for her the implication. Aliyah's face went even paler than when she'd wobbled out of the chopper. She put her head in her hands, a perfect picture of what Louis felt inside. The sun was about to set over the lush green forest to the west, but the orange-gold sky held no pleasure for him tonight. The faces of Jack and those twenty kids paraded through his mind.

There was nothing they could do now but pray.

One of the longest hours of Louis's life passed by, and the sun had already set, when the pilot whistled to them to return to the chopper. Louis helped Aliyah stand and steadied her arm as they walked back. They could see Durak in the rear seat of the chopper giving his attention to something.

As they climbed inside, they managed to sneak a peek.

It was Jack.

He was unconscious. Aliyah stifled a cry. Pritz motioned for them to strap in and put on headsets, and they took off.

Once Jack was stabilized, Durak explained, "The camp was empty. No signs of anyone having cooked or eaten food there—I'd say it's been empty for a while."

"That's not possible!" Aliyah exclaimed. "Jack and I were here not even a week ago and the camp staff had everything prepared for us to spend two weeks."

"No food supplies left, ma'am. Place was cleaned out. We were about to head back to the chopper when we noticed a tool shed in the trees. This poor fellow was inside, tied and gagged. I don't know how long he's been there, but he's very dehydrated.

We'll take him straight to the hospital and then drop you two back at your car."

"This is Jack Porter," Louis explained, "one of our colleagues, who delivered the international participants to this camp just forty-eight hours ago. And please, just drop us at the hospital with him."

"As you wish. Hopefully by tomorrow morning Jack will revive and can tell us what happened. While we wait for him, there's something I'll need you two to do for me."

"Of course, we'll help in any way possible," Louis assured him.

"By nine a.m. tomorrow, I'll need a list of every participant, every camp staff, every detail you two know about everyone involved."

"You'll have it."

"Don't worry, sir, wherever they are, we'll find them."

DAY 3

Jim Baton

Chapter 15

The now familiar scraping sound of the door opening wakened Sari. She yawned and blinked, expecting to see the lights on, but all was still dark. Across the room she thought she caught the flash of a small light, on, then off, then on a short distance away, like flashing Christmas lights. She rubbed her eyes and wondered what it meant when suddenly the light shone much brighter, about knee-high above the floor, on the twisted face of Scary Larry.

"Boo!" Larry shouted. A horrifying shriek pierced the night, and Sari nearly joined in. Then Larry let out a maniacal laugh and jumped over the stirring sleepers and out the door, slamming it shut behind him.

They were once again in total darkness, but Sari followed the incessant screaming, trying to crawl toward Yasmin.

There were murmured questions about what had happened, and a rude, "Shut up!" but Sari ignored them. By the time she reached Yasmin, she could hear Lotanna's soothing voice there too.

"It's okay. You're safe now."

"Yasmin," Sari spoke her name softly, reaching out her arm to embrace the hysterical girl. She could feel Yasmin's body shaking.

The Filipina girl brushed her arm away roughly. "Get away from me!"

Lotanna spoke again. "We'll stay with you."

"No! Leave me alone! I hate you! I hate this place! Go away!"

Sari heard the sound of a slap, but wasn't sure who had slapped whom. Then she felt a hand on her arm and a whisper in her ear. It was Lotanna.

"Sari, right?"

"Yes."

"Help me keep an eye on her today, so she doesn't do anything destructive?"

"Sure."

Lotanna spoke more loudly to address the mumbled questions in the dark. "She's fine. Everyone go back to sleep." Yasmin blubbered incoherently and would not be comforted, so Sari and Lotanna made their way back to their mats.

Before Sari could get back to sleep, the lights came on and Yasmin was gone.

Sari found her locked in the bathroom and begged her to come out to no avail.

"Leave her in there," Katja touched Sari's arm as she was about to knock once again on the bathroom door. "She's a pain in the neck."

Katja kicked Danilo's leg. "Hey, Danny, how did your evil twin get invited here anyway?"

The Filipino boy shot her a dirty look. "Yasmin's cool, give her a break. She's a researcher. She wrote some thesis like on the dialogues between the government and the Muslim extremists and stuff. She has like a million followers on Instagram. But she spends all her time in libraries and modelling shoots, not digging ditches and feeding pigs."

Bol joined them and convinced Danilo to try using Tagalog to coax her out. He sighed and slowly clambered to his feet and approached the door.

Whatever he said worked. Yasmin emerged without a word. Her long, black hair hung over her face, and instead of returning to her mat, she slumped into a corner, oblivious to the world. Sari started to go to her, but both Katja and Danilo pulled her back.

Dejectedly, Sari returned to her mat and drank her morning ration of water. She had lost the urge to fix her hair and try to look presentable. Her clothes were wrinkled and smelled of body odor. She could feel the dirt from the ditch clogging her pores. She was exhausted, not from the kitchen work yesterday, but mentally, emotionally…and the hard floor wasn't making it easy to rest.

She needed help if she were going to make it through this day. She prayed under her breath. *God, if you don't help me, I could end up like Yasmin.*

Ismail and the others were just finishing morning *sholat* when the camp staff filed in. Right away Sari noticed the smirk on Larry's face. Then she noticed Jeremy's beautiful blond (and green) hair was gone, shaved right off like Curt's. Jeremy's defiant look matched Curt's hard glare as well. Only Abagail refused to make eye contact with the young people—the men all seemed to be looking right through them, challenging them with their eyes.

"Good morning," Henry began as usual. "I trust you all slept well."

Larry snorted.

"In a moment we'll divide up today's work teams. However, I first want to address your requests from last night. I have decided that some of you will be given the chance to bathe, put on a fresh set of clothes, eat some better food, and even have a break from your chores. Tomorrow morning I will announce to you what you must do to be among the chosen few that receive these privileges. Today I'd like you to think about what you would be willing to do in order to gain these pleasures.

"Curt, please read the assignments for today."

"Excuse me," Lotanna interrupted. "One of our members is not well. I respectfully ask that you consider letting her rest from chores today."

"And who is that?"

Lotanna pointed to Yasmin slouched in the corner, face still covered with hair.

"I see. Well, Miss, I guess you'll have to work double shifts today to take your friend's place."

Lotanna nodded her acquiescence.

"Curt?"

Sari noticed Bol whisper something in Usman's ear, but it looked like Usman blew him off. *Probably telling him not to make trouble. Everyone's tense enough as it is.*

Curt had paired Sari up with Katja today for the first shift in the garden. When she and Katja approached Larry, he smirked and licked his lips. Sari shuddered inside, trying not to let him see.

As Sari followed Larry up the stairs and outside into a muggy, overcast morning, conflicting emotions wrestled inside her. Part of her was scared of what Larry might do to her. Part of her was angry at him for giving Yasmin a heart attack. And part of her, from somewhere deep inside, was curious to understand what made Larry act like this.

He showed the girls two shovels and six bags of manure collected from the animals. "We're fertilizing a new patch of ground today," he pointed to a plot of unseeded ground about ten meters squared at the far end of the vegetable garden. "We're going to try planting lima beans and snap beans for the fall harvest. But not yet. First we need to spread this manure."

He dumped the contents of one bag into a corner of the plot, took a shovel, and showed them how to scoop and toss it across that quadrant.

"Think the little songbird can handle it?" he grinned crookedly at Sari.

She felt courage well up inside her. "I can handle it. But can you handle answering questions from a little songbird?" she challenged.

He cocked his head at her warily, "What kind of questions do birds ask?"

"Why did you scare Yasmin this morning?"

"She deserved it. She called me stupid. I'm not stupid. Now who's sitting in a corner sucking their thumb?"

"You're right," Sari agreed. "You're not stupid. Let's try another question: Where do you come from?"

Larry's brow wrinkled. "Why are you asking me that? I can't answer that. Are you trying to make me feel stupid?"

Sari was surprised—she'd thought it an easy question. "No, I'm not. I'll change the question. Where is your family?"

"Stop doing this to me!" Larry was getting agitated, the opposite of what Sari wanted. "He won't like it! He won't like it one bit." Larry was almost hopping from one foot to the other.

She knew she should back off, but she couldn't help herself. "Who's 'he'?"

"Unnnnhhhh!" Larry looked like he was trying to hold a volcano inside. He thrust a shovel in her hand. "Scoop the poop! Now! Scoop the poop!"

His eyes looked like they might pop out of his head, and Sari realized her eyes were mirroring his. She broke eye contact, looked down at the smelly feces, and started spreading it over the plowed up dirt. Katja mumbled, "Freaky," and joined the labor.

"Scoop the poop! Scoop the poop!" Larry chanted. She glanced behind her and saw he was still hopping foot to foot. Once he saw they were busy working, he wandered off into the woods, talking to himself.

When he was out of earshot, Katja commented, "Someone forgot to put the baking powder in that guy's *kljukusa*, if you know what I mean."

Sari didn't have a clue, and giggled. "What he did was horrible, but I just wondered, you know, where that came from."

"And your answer is, 'Scoop the poop!'" Katja joked.

"I feel really bad for Yasmin. I hope she's okay."

Katja laughed through her nose. "She's a diva. Find the right person to give her attention and she'll be back to her bitchy self."

Sari remembered Henry's morning announcement. "So what do you think Henry meant by thinking about what we're willing to do to get our clothes, etcetera back?"

Katja froze, and whispered out of the side of her mouth, "Look over there."

Sari immediately assumed it was Larry, but when she followed Katja's gaze, there in the grass at the far edge of their garden plot sat a fluffy gray bunny.

"Ohhh," Sari cooed softly. The bunny's ears twitched and it looked straight at them. Then it nonchalantly turned and hopped back into the trees.

Sari was thrilled. "A bunny in the wild! Like Thumper!"

Katja smirked. "I was thinking Donnie Darko—girl, you and I do not watch the same movies." They both laughed.

Sari still wanted an answer. "What would you do for the privileges he said?"

"Oh, right. Well, I wouldn't prostitute myself if that's what you're thinking. Or listen to twenty hours of that perverse "Rick the Prick" radio talk show. But I'd be willing to put an anaconda choke on Larry. You think Henry would like to see that?"

"You think tomorrow will be like a survival of the fittest contest?" Sari asked. "If it is, I'll definitely come in last."

"Not if you can get Yasmin to break a nail, or if Taj has to run into a light breeze." Both girls laughed.

They had finished one bag of manure, so each took the corner of the second bag and dragged it down the garden plot, then dumped it out and started shoveling again.

"What do you miss about home?" Sari asked.

Katja looked up at the sky. "I miss the food, my friends in college, my mom, my boyfriend, the usual." She went back to shoveling.

"You have a boyfriend? Tell me about him."

"His name's Mijo. I met him in the Peace and Conflict Studies summer program. He's tall, blond, muscular, and really cute, with gorgeous eyes. He wants to be an ambassador."

"He sounds perfect."

"Oh, he'll be a lot closer to perfect when I get done with him," Katja quipped. "But maybe the most interesting thing about him is that he's a Serbian Christian."

Sari was shocked. "But you're a Muslim, right?"

"Check this out—my mother, a Bosnian Muslim, was raped by a Serbian soldier during the war, and I was born. Can you imagine what my mother said when I told her about Mijo?"

"Did she freak out?"

"I thought she would. But she said, 'No better way to make peace than through marriage.' I was stunned. But I thought about it, and I could see the potential healing there. Who are our kids supposed to hate?"

Sari had never thought about it like that. "There was a Muslim guy in Indonesia who wanted to marry me, but I refused. I didn't want a home divided over issues of faith."

"Yeah, I'm lucky Mijo supports my faith, and I support his, and we're both committed to not letting religion rob us of that commitment to each other."

Time flew by working with Katja. The smell of the manure and the horrors of the night had been replaced by the beauty of nature and yet another chance at friendship with a truly extraordinary person. Yesterday she had thought of Katja only as a complainer. Once again, taking the time to get to know someone revealed the judgments in Sari's heart that shackled her from living out true unconditional love.

It wasn't until the whistle blew that she realized she'd spent the whole time chatting with Katja and had forgotten to do what Bol had asked of them last night, to gather more information to help them understand what was really going on.

Chapter 16

Washing her hands and face with the water in the toilet tank didn't get out the smell of manure, but what else could Sari do? She went to check on Yasmin, who was still sitting in the same position as when Sari had left her.

"Yasmin? Are you feeling better?"

No answer.

She wondered if the girl had had anything to drink, but when she tried bringing the water bottle to Yasmin's lips, she pushed it away.

"You're poisoning me," she slurred. "Get away!"

Sari wished Lotanna was there, but her friend had the double work shift. She looked around for help.

Fatimah came over. "Let me try."

After talking in Yasmin's ear, and praying over the water in Arabic, at last Yasmin was willing to take a drink. Sari felt so helpless, but thankful for Fatimah's compassion. She lay down next to Katja and tried to rest.

Lunch was the same soup as on the first day. Perhaps Henry was trying to sweeten the offer of better food by making them bored with what they had.

Bol convened their normal lunch meeting. "What did each of you learn?"

Taj went first. "We were right about the generator. It's the only source of electricity. And I found where it is."

Usman nearly jumped up. "Take out their power source and we have control!"

Taj continued, "It's behind a locked fence in the forest south-southwest of us. I told Larry I had to pee and did a whole circle of the barn. The ditch is about half done, and it's not for electricity or sewage, so what is it for?"

"Let's try to find out. Great work, Taj. Anyone else?"

"I got the candles and matches," Asmina shared.

"Excellent! Better hide them." She tucked them under the closest pillow.

Nandita spoke timidly, "I might have learned something."

"Come on, spill the beans," coaxed Jolly.

Nandita looked down at her empty soup bowl. "I ate all the beans."

"That's priceless," Jolly chuckled. "I mean, out with it, tell us what's up."

Nandita still looked confused. "Well, I went with Abagail to serve the lunch to the staff in their meeting room. They had fried chicken and mashed potatoes with green beans and eggplant cooked in a garlic—"

"You're killing us, girl," Katja chided. "Skip to what you learned about them already."

"Oh, yeah. Well, it may not be important..." she paused, uncertain.

Sari gently prodded her. "We'd love to hear it."

"Well, Henry and George were arguing about the internet not working right, something about bouncing, and tracing, and tunnels—do you think there are tunnels down here?"

"Taj?" Bol turned to the young Indian IT expert, who pushed his glasses up.

"They're either hacking, or uploading something they don't want traced back to them, or both."

"But what?" Alex asked.

Everyone stared at each other. Ismail stood up, signaling the time for *sholat*.

Sari had been thinking. "Hey," she began with those still sitting, "the Christians don't have any time that we pray together. Don't you think we should learn from our Muslim friends and be praying too?"

"Good idea," Lotanna agreed. "I'm in. Anyone else?" She raised her hand. Up went the hands of Daud, Rebecca, Danilo, and Nandita. Sari noticed Nadia looked at Imam bowing in his *sholat* before starting to raise her hand, then she put it back down and looked away.

"Or even better," continued Sari. "After *sholat*, what if we all prayed not formal prayers, but heart-prayers, together as a group, both Muslim and Christian?" She looked around to gauge the response.

There was an uncomfortable silence. She remembered the first time her Muslim friend Hafiz had heard her pray, and disparaged it. She had hoped this group would be more open-minded.

"Personally, I would love that," Fatimah said. She hadn't joined the *sholat* this time. Sari figured she might be having her period. Fatimah smiled at her.

"Me too," Lotanna agreed. "How about the rest of you?"

"You mean, we can do it together?" Nadia asked. "But how would that work?"

"You know, each person can pray in their own style whatever is in their heart," Sari explained. "The rest of us can say 'Amen' if we want, or just silently support our friends. Keep it simple."

Nadia glanced at Imam again. "I'd be willing to try," she said.

Rebecca's freckled face looked flush. "But it isn't the same God."

Danilo angled his chin toward those at *sholat*. "They're different than us, Sari, you can't mix religion."

Everyone started talking at once, some very animated. Sari realized she'd launched into something they weren't ready for and wondered how best to take it back. Fortunately, Alex rescued her.

"Guys, hold on!" the punk rocker practically yelled. "In my country this issue is being debated as well. And last year there was an impressive speech that rocked our youth delivered by none other than our own Katja." He turned to his Muslim compatriot. "Why don't you tell them what you shared at the peace conference?"

Everyone looked at the red-faced Bosnian girl. "Alex, I'll get you for this!" she hissed.

Bol added his support. "Yeah, Katja, we'd love to hear it."

"Please?" Sari joined in.

Katja looked around the circle and rolled her eyes. "It wasn't anything really. I just talked about how we're all different, but we're all the same. When we look at our differences—our ethnicity, culture, religion, etcetera—we feel connected to those like us and distant from those unlike us. But except for ethnicity, all those differences we can change, and we can even get plastic surgery to change our ethnic features if we want.

"But at the deepest level, there are unchangeable things common to us all, that which makes us human—like the need to love and be loved; to understand and be understood; to be accepted and belong; to be appreciated and enjoyed; to be safe; to have a purpose in life bigger than ourselves. At this level is our most basic human connection." She shrugged as if to say that was enough.

"Well said," Bol praised her. "I majored in psychology but never heard human relations expressed so beautifully."

"I need to write this down for my kids in Palestine," Fatimah echoed. A few others murmured agreement.

Alex beamed proudly at Katja, who flashed an ugly face back at him, seemingly embarrassed that she had been forced to reveal her intellectual side.

Sari's life story completely confirmed what Katja had said, but she realized some of the others might lack that experience. She saw Rebecca and Danilo especially looking uncomfortable, and wanted to reduce the tension in the air.

"I'm sorry I spoke too soon about the prayer idea. We don't have to do anything together if that's a problem. Maybe if anyone feels you'd like to pray, you can come find me, or go find someone else you feel comfortable praying with, and we can pray in smaller groups of two or three for now. The important thing is that we support each other, I think."

Bol looked at her with disappointment in his eyes. She wasn't sure why. Maybe because she had sent everyone off on a useless rabbit trail keeping Bol from collecting his precious information? Well, prayer was important too. If he thought his brain, or Taj's, was all they needed in here, he was delusional.

If Yasmin's condition was any indication, if Lotanna's premonitions were right, they were going to need all the help they could get.

Chapter 17

Louis Staunton was regretting his decision to spend the night with Jack in the hospital. Between trying to calm down the hysterical Aliyah and a gang war on the Atlanta streets that resulted in a ward full of angry, wounded young men and their homies yelling about how they were going to get revenge, the "peacemaker" found no peace.

Agents Pritz and Durak appeared looming over him at precisely nine o'clock. He was sitting sideways in a hard plastic lobby chair, his long legs humped over the armrest with his feet in the chair next to him, shoes scattered below on the floor, chin on his chest trying his best to grab a few minutes sleep.

"Morning, Congressman," Durak greeted him. Louis opened his eyes in time to see Pritz nod. He nodded back and tried to swivel upright. Pain shot through his lower back and he winced. If the two agents noticed, they didn't show it.

"Have you had any breakfast, sir?" Casey Durak asked. Louis wondered if the agent was planning to offer him a sip from the greenish-brown drink in his hand. He shook his head. Casey pulled a power bar out of his London Fog jacket pocket and handed it to Louis, who took it gratefully.

"Where's your partner?" Todd Pritz demanded gruffly.

Louis looked around. Aliyah had disappeared. Maybe she'd had the good sense to go back to the hotel while he was snoozing in these red and orange chairs like a fool. He shrugged, then started tying his shoes.

"You trust her?" Pritz asked Louis.

He was taken aback by the question. "Of course I trust her! She's worked tirelessly with me for over a year to set up this event. She helped me hand-pick each participant. And I know she cares about every one of them."

"What country is she from?" Pritz continued, unconvinced.

Louis spluttered, "What country? She's American, born and raised in Virginia, a Georgetown graduate. I know her parents well. What are you implying, that she could have had something to do with this?"

"She's Muslim," Pritz grouched.

Durak stepped between them. "Sir, our job is to collect information, on everyone and everything, to sift through that information and make connections. We are prejudicial against no one, and suspicious of everyone."

"Of course. Go right ahead, ask away," Louis relented.

Pritz covered his hand with his mouth and said something to Durak, who nodded and walked away. Then he turned back to Louis.

"Sir, you may as well hear this from me. Special Agent Durak and I are also assigned to the Joint Terrorism Task Force connecting the FBI to local, regional and national agencies in the case of a potential terrorist threat. Since Muslim individuals from various nations known both in the past and present to be harborers of terrorists are missing, we consider this a matter of national security. As we speak, Homeland Security and other law enforcement agencies are being notified of this potential terrorist threat, and no doubt their agents will be joining us here in Atlanta soon."

"Terrorist threat? These are missing kids!" Louis protested.

"As I understand it, these 'missing kids' are from nations such as Indonesia, India, South Sudan, Jordan, and Palestine. Am I correct, sir?"

"That's correct."

Pritz responded gruffly. "The majority of terrorist recruits and suicide bombers from those nations fall in the age range targeted by this event. The fact that ten of them are loose somewhere in America doing God knows what is of great concern to us."

"There are twenty missing young people, Agent Pritz, and our world's best hope for the end of terrorism and a lasting peace rests with people like them. I think you should be putting your resources towards solving a kidnapping, not stopping a terrorist attack."

94

"We'll put our resources to all of the above," Agent Pritz assured Louis soberly. They stared at each other for a moment, interrupted by the sound of Aliyah Mahmudi entering the room.

Pritz turned to her and asked bluntly, "Where have you been?"

"Oh, hi Agent…uh…"

"Pritz," Louis provided.

"Hi Agent Pritz. I had to run to an internet café so my assistant could email me all my files on the group participants and I could print out these copies for you." She handed him a stack of papers.

He wrote something on a piece of paper and handed it back to her. "Call your assistant and have her email all these files to this address as well."

"Okay," she said, and dialed her cell phone to pass on the message. While she was on the phone, Durak came back with a doctor.

"Jack's awake."

Pritz turned to follow him, as did Louis. "Wait here," Pritz barked, and Louis sat down again in the hard plastic chair.

Eventually, Aliyah slumped down beside him. "Where did they go?" she asked.

"To see Jack. He's awake."

"*Alhamdulillah!*" She touched her hands to her face, then looked to the heavens. "Let's go see him!"

"Apparently the FBI wants to question him first."

Her face was downcast for a moment, but brightened. "At least he's awake. Surely he'll be okay."

"I'm sure he will." Louis weighed carefully what he was about to say, and decided she should know.

"Aliyah, the FBI thinks it could be a terrorist plot against America."

"What?" she was clearly disbelieving. "I don't understand. Terrorists kidnapped or killed our youth peacemakers?"

"They don't know anything yet, they're just guessing. But you should be warned, their first line of questioning will be related to all things Muslim. Including you."

Aliyah opened her mouth to reply, then clamped it shut. Tears formed in her eyes. Louis's heart went out to her. He knew her story, of everything she'd had to put up with all her life for being an American Muslim. Now this.

"I really hoped that we were getting past all that," she mused softly. "I really hoped that we were making a difference." She shook her head sadly, then turned her glistening brown eyes up to his. "Are we? Are we actually making a difference?"

Louis swallowed hard. As a public figure, he had to be careful about situations like this, but whether it was the injustice torturing the soul of the young woman beside him, or the exhaustion that caused him to no longer care what the paparazzi did, he extended his long arm around Aliyah's shoulders and pulled her head onto his neck.

Pritz and Durak found them that way. "Let's go."

Aliyah jumped up. "Can we see Jack now?"

"Doctor said he can't take any more questions," Durak replied.

"I promise I won't ask him anything, I just want to make sure he's all right."

Durak looked at Pritz, who growled something unintelligible and started walking away. Durak gave in. "Okay, one quick peek in the door."

And that was literally all they got. Jack's eyes were closed, but the color was returning to his face. Louis noticed the IV connected to his hand. "Did the doctor say how long he'd be here?"

"Two, three days at the most. He's healing fine. Mostly just dehydrated."

Louis and Aliyah both breathed sighs of relief. "Let's go back to the hotel and get some food and sleep," he suggested.

"Sorry, sir, you both need to return to our office for a few more questions. I promise it won't take long."

"You have the files, what else can we add?" Louis asked as they exited the hospital toward Pritz and the waiting SUV.

"We want to know more about the deputy who blocked the road, the camp staff, the bus driver, the extra security detail Jack

96

told us he hired, and what Muslim groups were aware of this event, to start."

Louis figured his sense of "won't take long" and Durak's was probably miles apart.

"Jack told you he hired extra security?" Aliyah looked puzzled. "He never mentioned that to me." She turned to Louis sheepishly. "I'm afraid I told him we didn't need security guards at a peace camp. I thought keeping it secret from the media was protection enough. This is all my fault." She looked as though she were about to cry.

"That's not all he said," Durak disclosed as they climbed into the SUV and peeled out of the parking lot. "According to Jack, while the youth participants were unloading the bus, the head of security took Jack to look at what he called 'a jimmied lock' at the back of the building. While he was bending down to inspect it, two large men dressed in Arab robes and turbans, at least one carrying a sword, knocked down the security guard, then beat Jack until he blacked out and woke up trussed up in the tool shed."

Aliyah and Louis were speechless.

Pritz's explosive response left a spray of saliva all over the dash: "Terrorists."

Chapter 18

That afternoon Sari talked Katja into helping her find out as much about Larry as possible. He had moved them over to the back of the larger vegetable garden, where a trellis separated the garden from the forest. The trellis had posts as tall as Sari about three meters apart, with three strands of wire stretched across them. The bushes interweaved among the wire strands were full of berries.

Larry handed them each a bucket. "Only pick the bigger berries that look ripe. When your bucket is full, bring it to me."

"What kind of berries are these?" Sari asked, trying to be friendly.

"These are Dormanred raspberries. Those down there are blackberries. Don't mix them in the same bucket. Use different buckets."

Sari reached for one of the bright red berries. "Ow!" She jerked her hand back, her finger pricked by a thorn. Larry laughed, a high-pitch cackle, while Sari sucked on her finger.

"Does it taste good?" he asked, eyes freakishly wide.

"What?" Sari was confused.

He tilted his head down and sideways getting closer to her face. "Licking your own blood."

Sari jerked the finger from her mouth and turned away, hoping he didn't see her shudder.

Katja reached in carefully and picked a raspberry, popping it in her mouth. "A bit tart, but not bad," she commented, hoping to draw Larry's attention.

It worked. "Don't eat them!" he yelled at her. "They're not for you!"

Katja picked another berry. Sari was sure she was going to eat it just to challenge Larry, and shot her a warning look. Katja dramatically dropped the berry into the bucket.

Larry seemed to relax a little, and Sari realized she'd been holding her breath. The unpredictable nature of the man still scared her. Lotanna's words echoed through her mind: "I made a decision, that I would not be afraid." *God give me courage.*

She started picking berries with Katja, more cautiously this time. Larry wandered off to inspect what looked to her like pumpkin leaves. She wracked her brain for what kind of questions would help them to understand Larry, without setting him off.

After a few minutes, she took a stab at it, calling out to him. "Larry, you know a lot about gardens. Where did you learn so much?"

"He taught me."

"Who? Henry?"

Larry found her question funny for some reason. He snorted. "He thinks he's so great. He doesn't know me. He doesn't know what I can do."

This isn't getting anywhere. "I'd like to get to know you," Sari said, getting a concerned glance from Katja. "Tell me what you can do."

Larry looked at her suspiciously. "Stay away from me." He took a step back from Sari.

"I just want to be your friend," Sari explained. "Don't you have any friends who are girls?"

Larry looked horrified. "No! You can't be friends with girls. You can't trust them." He had stepped even further away and it looked as though his body were trembling.

Katja broke the tension. "Hey, look! There's that rabbit again." The same gray bunny was hopping into the far corner of the vegetable garden.

Larry spun around. "Thief! Robber!" he shouted. Then he gave Sari a terrible look. "You want to see what I can do?" And off he galloped through the garden chasing the bunny, who hopped nimbly into the forest. Larry disappeared after him.

"Sari, be careful," Katja warned. "Don't get too close to him. That guy's a psycho."

She sighed. "I just wanted some information to take back to Bol. Besides, there's something intriguing about him."

"Why do the squeaky clean girls always go for the bad boys?" Katja moaned.

Sari rolled her eyes. "I'm not 'going for' him. My mom always said to look for the hidden treasure in people. Sometimes the dirt hides a diamond."

"Or sometimes the dirt hides a bear trap," Katja objected.

They were both sweating profusely under the hot summer sun by the time their buckets were full. As long as Larry was gone, they decided it wouldn't hurt to sit down and try a few of the berries for themselves. As Katja had declared, the raspberries were a bit tart, but Sari found the blackberries sweet. They tasted so good after the monotone meals they'd had recently.

Sari was about to pop another berry in her mouth when she caught Katja's warning look, and quickly dropped it in the bucket. Slowly she turned around expecting to see Larry's return.

What she saw caused her to scream.

Larry had quietly crept up behind her, and when she turned she was staring straight into the eyeball of a dead bunny, run completely through with Larry's knife, its blood dripping down, covering Larry's hand.

At her scream, Larry's eyes went wide. "Shut up, Songbird!" he warned. Sari clamped her hand over her mouth to muffle the sound.

Larry grinned mischievously at Sari and licked some of the blood on his hand.

"This is what I can do," he bragged.

Except for Rebecca and Asmina on the kitchen crew, everyone else was given the second shift of the day off. Yasmin and a few others took the chance for a nap, while most gathered in smaller groups to chat. It felt strange to Sari to watch this group of her peers with no cell phones, laptops, books or magazines, make up, cigarettes, not even a deck of cards to entertain themselves. All they had were *people*—people who were from different cultures and religions, people who weren't exactly at their best either. This was the truest crucible of relationship Sari could imagine. *Whoever planned this peace event may be evil geniuses, but they are certainly geniuses.*

Lotanna and Fatimah came over and asked Sari if she was serious about praying together. She nodded and explained again that each person was free to pray their own way, but to try and use words which the others could understand.

"So you believe God will hear all of us, even if we're different religions?" Lotanna asked.

"Of course," Sari answered. "Don't you remember that Bible verse, 'those who seek Him will find Him'? That's all we're doing, just seeking God together."

Both were enthusiastic to try, but wanted Sari to go first and model for them.

Sari closed her eyes and began to praise God for His goodness. She thanked Him for the friendships and new perspectives she had gained. She confessed her continual need for cleansing from prejudicial thoughts, and asked God to fill her with love for all mankind, including the camp staff. She prayed for Yasmin, for Jack and Kareem, for wisdom for their leaders and grace to face each challenge. Both Lotanna and Fatimah said, "Amen."

Sari looked up at Fatimah. "Your turn." Fatimah began with some Arabic phrases. Sari recognized the first one as being "In the name of God, Most Compassionate, Most Merciful." Fatimah prayed for protection for them all and blessings on their parents and families, and that they would make their families proud. The Christian girls echoed her "Amen."

Lotanna was choking up, and whispered that she would pray in her heart. The other two waited respectfully in silence, and when Lotanna spoke out her "Amen," they added their own.

Afterwards, Sari asked the others how they felt.

"Usually I don't speak such things out loud," shared Fatimah. "I just keep them in my heart. It felt good to say them out loud."

"Maybe next time I can do it too," Lotanna said. "It's just that, well, when you were praying, Sari, I felt like it's been so long since I talked to God, since I trusted Him. I think I'm ready to let Him back into my life."

Jolly came over to interrupt them. "What you chicks up to? Planning a strategy for tomorrow's reality show? If you're making an alliance, I want in."

Lotanna smiled at him. "How about this alliance—if any of us gets picked for the shower, that person has to smuggle back enough shampoo and soap for all four of us to bathe either with the toilet water or a bucket from the well outside."

Jolly felt his long brown hair, now matted and nasty. "I'm in. This is worse than after a week of surfing, dude."

A commotion across the room grabbed their attention. Usman was jumping up off his mat to square off with Alex, who said something Sari couldn't hear. Usman pushed him and Alex came back swinging his fist at Usman's head. Usman sidestepped and smacked his fist into Alex's stomach, knocking the wind out of him.

Bol and Daud grabbed ahold of Usman and pulled him away. Imam grabbed Alex's shoulders and tried to help him stand, but Alex brushed him off and cursed at Usman before returning to his mat.

"Dude, what's eating them?" Jolly wondered.

Lotanna turned to Sari and quietly said, "This is what I was talking about. The captors try to turn the victims against each other, so they can swoop in and attract some of the victims to join them."

Sari watched Bol firmly holding Usman against the wall, trying to calm him down. Alex snapped at anyone who came near him. When Rebecca finally brought the tray of cornbread, it was a welcome break in the tension. But then Alex threw his piece at the bolted door, yelling, "I'm sick of this crap! Bring us some real food!"

Rebecca had passed out all the cornbread except one piece. "Did anyone not get one?" No one answered. Sari checked to make sure Yasmin had a piece, and there it was on the floor in front of her, untouched.

"Is someone missing?" she asked. Everyone looked around until Nandita figured it out. "Where's Asmina?"

The bathroom door was open. She clearly wasn't in the room. "Wasn't she on kitchen duty with you?" Bol asked Rebecca.

"Yes," the red-head replied. "But after a few minutes, Curt came and took her for some other job. I thought she'd be back by dinner."

Lotanna put down her half-eaten cornbread. "I think I'm going to be sick," she whispered to Sari. Lotanna moved quickly off to the toilet. Sari felt the war begin again in the pit of her stomach. *I made a decision, that I would not be afraid.*

Everyone started talking at once. Sari heard fearful cries from some of the girls, Usman's loud voice demanding that they do something, and Bol's voice trying to get everyone to calm down. But if Bol had been successful at uniting them before, he was losing his influence now. Sari wished she knew what to do, but felt utterly helpless. She reached out for Fatimah's hand and just held it, surveying the chaos before her.

When Henry and George entered with the radio, the group was clearly not in the mood.

"Good evening," Henry began. "I would—"

Usman interrupted him. "Where's Asmina? And where's Kareem? And where's Jack? What are you hiding from us, old man?"

"I will not tolerate such outbursts. After the radio broadca—"

"Forget the frickin' radio broadcast," Usman continued loudly. "We're not interested. We want the truth." Several murmured their agreement.

George turned on the radio at top volume. Sari covered her ears. But Usman marched straight towards the radio, jerked it out of George's hand, and smashed it on the floor.

George glared at the much taller Frenchman with fire in his eyes. "He takes revenge on all who oppose him and furiously destroys his enemies!" his gravelly voice ominously intoned.

"If you two are peace camp directors, I'm Napoleon Bonaparte," Usman challenged. "Tell us what you're really up to or you'll have another French revolution on your hands, and it will be your necks in the guillotine." He pointed directly at the two white men.

"Now, now," Henry held out his hands palms down, trying to calm the boy.

"Your blood will be poured out into the dust, and your bodies will lie there rotting on the ground," George grated, eyes boring holes in Usman.

"Your friend Asmina fainted during her work shift today, so we let her lie down and rest on the couch in the staff room. Remember the room where we filmed the first day? She's sleeping now, but hopefully will rejoin us soon. Now for tonight—"

"Liar!" Usman wouldn't back down. "We don't believe a word you say. Kareem, now Asmina, we have a right to know what's going on."

Sari heard Katja and a few others give vocal support.

Henry pursed his lips. "I'm sorry you feel that way, young man. Would it allay your fears if you saw Asmina for yourself, and could report to the others that she is, in fact, resting on the couch as I said?"

Usman tilted up his chin in defiance. "Let's go."

Henry looked down at the shattered radio and shook his head sadly. Then he said to the group, "I apologize for the derailing of our evening's activities. I am a man of purpose and order, and I resent being forced to change my plans.

"However, it seems prudent to help this troubled young man gain some perspective. If you'll all excuse us..." He gave a slight bow, then pointed for George to lead the way and Usman to follow, and the three of them left the room.

It was silent for a few moments, then Jolly spoke: "Hey, Taj, you any good at fixing broken radios? I'm feeling like a dance party tonight."

The joke fell flat in the silent room. No one was in the mood. They all sat quietly, waiting for their hot-headed friend with the Afro to come back and tell them Asmina was okay.

Several minutes went by. Sari could see her fellow participants were getting restless. Lotanna was shaking her head and muttering to herself. Nadia was biting her hair. Taj was blinking rapidly behind his glasses. Imam's eye seemed to be twitching. It looked like he was about to explode and was doing everything in his power to keep in control.

Several more minutes passed. "I hate waiting," Sari muttered to herself. She heard a faint humming and turned to see Rebecca with eyes closed, quietly humming a song to herself. She looked at Bol for encouragement, but their *de facto* leader was staring up at the ceiling, lost in thought.

How long had it been? Twenty, thirty minutes? Without a watch Sari had no idea. But waiting for Usman to come back seemed like an eternity.

The lights abruptly went out.

And with them was extinguished Sari's hope that all would be happily explained in the end.

DAY 4

Jim Baton

Chapter 19

After a mostly sleepless night of tossing and turning battling her fearful thoughts, Sari was startled by the scraping sound of the door opening. She heard a thump in the pitch dark and was instantly   wide   awake.

She called out, "Larry, if that's you, don't do it! Larry?" The door closed.

Her words woke a few others. "What's going on?" someone said.

"Shh! Listen!" It sounded like Alex, who slept nearest the door.

Sari strained to hear it, but Alex was right, there was something making noise near the door. A sound like a baby rattle.

"What the −" Alex exclaimed. Then he was yelling. "Everyone get up! Now! Move away from the door! There's a snake in here!"

Bedlam reigned as people were screaming and scrambling, banging into each other in the dark, trying to get as far away from the door as possible. Someone fell on top of Sari. She heard his exclamation and guessed it was Jolly.

"Guys, that's a rattlesnake," Jolly declared, "common in my part of America and very poisonous. Stay as far away from that rattle sound as possible."

Sari heard Yasmin getting more and more hysterical, but couldn't figure out how to get through the mass of bodies in the dark to comfort her. She heard a loud slap, and Fatimah's voice saying, "Get ahold of yourself... Ow!" Yasmin must be fighting back.

"Shut up!" yelled Jolly. "Listen for the rattle." Everyone quieted down and Yasmin's screams were being muffled by something or someone. Faintly they could hear the rattle, still near the door. They breathed a collective sigh of relief.

Bol was thinking the clearest. "The candles! We were so stunned last night we forgot them. Who has the candles?"

"Asmina hid them under a pillow, but now she's gone," Zoe said.

"Who slept next to Asmina?" Bol asked.

"I did," Sari answered.

"Well, what are you waiting for, go find her pillow and get those candles and matches."

Sari swallowed hard. *God help me* she prayed silently. She got down on all fours and crawled in the general direction of where she had slept, ears focused on the sound of the rattle. Each mat she came across along the way she checked under the pillow just in case, but after three pillows, she hadn't found the candles.

"Hurry up, Sari," Rebecca urged.

"Shh!" several voices said.

Sari got to where she thought her mat should be and turned left to Asmina's. But there were no candles under her pillow.

And the rattle sound seemed to be getting much louder.

"They're not here," Sari said in a panicked voice.

"Wait," interjected Zoe. "She didn't put them under her own pillow, but under one near where she was sitting."

"You're right," Bol agreed. "I remember now. It was nearer to Danilo's mat. Danny, you feel any candles under your pillow?"

"No. Kareem's was next to mine, maybe they're under his."

"Well, go find them."

"Sari's already out there," Danilo objected. "Sari, you know where I sleep, near the bathroom, go that way."

"I'll help her," Lotanna offered, making crawling sounds from the group's location toward the toilet. Sari was grateful for her friend, and scooted over there as quickly as she could, putting some distance between her and the rattle sound.

Lotanna found them first. She struck a match and light blazed into the darkness. Everyone's eyes scanned the doorway for the snake, but it was gone.

Sari clung onto Lotanna, but Lotanna peeled her hand off and put a candle in it, then lit the candle. Sari stood up, holding the candle high and turned toward the middle of the room.

A shadowy figure was weaving between the mats on the floor coming towards her.

She jumped back screaming and tripped over Lotanna, dropping the candle. Fortunately, her friend scooped it up before the light went out. Sari heard Yasmin's scream over her own. She scrambled behind Lotanna, who held the candle out toward the snake like a sword to keep it at bay.

The snake's narrow green head came within a hand's distance of the candle and stopped, eyeing the flame.

From out of nowhere someone pounced on the snake's head with a pillowcase, startling both Lotanna and Sari, who screamed again, while Lotanna this time fell backwards on top of her.

Once they untangled themselves and held up the candle again, they saw Jolly's triumphant face holding the top of the wriggling pillowcase.

"Chill out, dudes. I got this poser."

"Jolly, you could have been killed!" Sari exclaimed.

"Not by this pretender," the surfer explained. "Rattlesnakes are brown. When I saw this dude's face next to the light, I realized he was a harmless green garter snake."

"But the rattle sound?" Lotanna questioned.

"We'll check him in the light," Jolly said, "but I expect we'll find something attached to his tail to make noise when he moved. This little guy was meant to freak us out, not hurt us."

Little by little people started to breathe again, move back to their mats, and lie down. Yasmin stayed in the corner farthest from the door, babbling incoherently through strong tears. Lotanna lit a second candle, but when everyone was settled, Bol told her to blow them out and hide them before the lights came on, so she did.

The absolute blackness returned. Sari could feel the fear, the despair hanging over the group. For some, this exciting adventure they had dreamed about had become their nightmare.

Two weeks. And this was only the fourth day. What had Henry said on the first day about "those of you who survive?" She had thought he was joking at the time. *What if he wasn't?*

Chapter 20

Henry stood before them, flanked by his compassionless comrades, but he was smiling broadly.

"Good morning! In spite of unforeseen obstacles, I'm pleased to report that we are actually ahead of schedule. And you'll be happy to know that Asmina is doing fine."

"Where are they, sir?" Lotanna asked politely.

"Last night when your friend Usman checked on Asmina, he was concerned that she may need a doctor, and insisted we take her to the hospital. So we had Jack come out late last night, and Usman chose to go with her to make sure she was well-treated.

"I called Jack at the hospital this morning, and each of them recorded a message for you." He held up a cell phone and pushed some buttons. The voices were crackly, but clearly Asmina's and Usman's:

"Hi, Asmina. I'm trying to recover from my pain. I hope to join together soon."

"Muhammad Usman here. Everything is peaceful. I believe in leadership. Persevere, march on."

Sari found the phrases more than a little bizarre, but maybe Asmina was drugged at the hospital and Usman was lacking sleep. Maybe they were okay, and she had worried all night for nothing.

Henry had strange methods, but reminded her of her Economics teacher—once he'd requested they all bring money for a field trip. Then in the classroom he recreated the stock market and required them to buy and sell shares. At the end of class, the top three traders got all the money to cover their airfare to the real stock market in the capital. At first she'd felt deceived; later she realized she had learned a valuable lesson that day about the dangers of investing her money without really learning about the process first. Her teacher could have saved her from a much bigger mistake down the road. Perhaps Henry was just such a "life-lessons" teacher whose methods required hindsight to fully appreciate.

And Larry—Larry was a harmless practical joker. She had let her imagination run away from her. All things looked different in the light of day. *Everything is going to be fine.*

Jolly held up the pillowcase. "Dude, we haven't eaten any meat all week. Could you barbeque this up for us?" He tossed it at Abagail's feet. The little green head poked out of the bag looking to escape, but Larry quickly grabbed it and held it aloft. Sari could see a small aluminum cylinder duct taped to its tail, probably with a few beans inside.

Henry scowled, "How did that snake get in here?" No one answered. He glared at Larry. At first Larry glared back, but slowly he wilted under Henry's gaze.

"It was just a joke," he whined.

George had a strange smirk on his face. "And the serpent seduced the woman," his gravelly voice intoned, "producing the cursed line of Cain, son of the devil, driven out of the garden, a restless wanderer on the earth, a godless line from generation to generation."

When Sari looked back at Larry, she noticed the smile on his face was a perfect copy of George's.

Henry pointed to the door. Larry scowled, but took the snake out, returning a few moments later empty-handed.

"Now I haven't forgotten my promise, that today some of you would have the opportunity to bathe, dress in clean clothes, eat better food and have a break from chores. Does that sound good to any of you?" He smiled warmly.

Sari nodded, and noticed others nodding too. She could almost feel the warm water running over her hair and skin, smell the perfumed shampoo, brush the tangles from her long black hair, silky and shiny once again.

"Here's how we're going to do this. First, let's split into two groups, Muslims on this side," he pointed to his left, "and Christians on this side." He pointed to his right. Everyone but

Yasmin moved. She continued to sit against the back wall, oblivious to the world.

Henry frowned. "What's wrong with her?"

Lotanna answered. "Please, sir, she hasn't felt well and has eaten very little. I would like to request that she be released from her chores again, and that one of us be assigned to watch over her, to keep her eating and drinking at least a little so she doesn't end up in the hospital like Asmina."

Henry seemed to be considering the request. He looked at George, who raised his eyebrows but said nothing.

"Well, your concern for her is commendable. You may be her nurse for today, and if she's not improved by the evening, we'll certainly be happy to ask Jack to take her to the hospital as well."

Lotanna made a slight bow and dissolved once again into the Christian group. Sari noticed their group was larger than the Muslims, with Kareem, Asmina, Usman and Yasmin not involved.

"Are you ready? Do you want to know what you have to do to receive all these good things?" Henry tried to get everyone refocused on his game-show pitch. Sari wondered what crazy tasks they might be assigned now.

"You may be surprised at how easy obtaining all these benefits is. All you have to do is be a Christian."

He let that sink in for a moment. Everyone looked confused.

"Say what?" Jolly asked.

Henry looked pleased with the impact of his surprise. "It is exactly as I said. All of you Christians are welcome to come with me to get your food, baths, clothes, etc., and the Muslims will do all the chores for us today."

Sari looked over at her Muslim friends. Katja was steaming mad, and none of the others looked any happier.

Imam stepped forward. "I feel I have no alternative but to protest!" he stated in his British accent, with a passion Sari hadn't seen from him before. "We are guests in your nation, and this is the very epitome of discrimination. We have endured much hardship, but found companionship in facing it together. Now you want to take that away from us too? Reprehensible leadership, that is what I say."

Henry countered, "What, you have no minorities in your nation? How do you treat them—exactly the same as the majority, or not?"

A light dawned for Sari. She reflected on how the Indonesian government policies consistently favored the Muslim majority and made life difficult for the Christians and other minorities. Maybe this was what Henry was trying to do. Perhaps Henry was hoping to help those from Muslim nations identify with their persecuted minorities.

Imam seemed to want to continue, but closed his mouth, stared at Henry for a moment, then retreated to the back of his group.

"No other questions? Good. Now if you Christians would like to follow George to the staff quarters." Henry motioned toward the door. George opened it and exited. Danilo, Rebecca, Daud, Bol and Nandita stepped forward. The first three followed George into the hallway. Bol looked from them to the Muslims across the room and paused in front of them all. Nandita was behind him and waited for Bol to move.

Henry's eyebrows rose. "Can't decide?" he questioned Bol. "What about the rest of you?" he asked the remaining Christians. "This offer will only be extended once." He searched their faces.

Henry's gaze paused on Sari, sensing her hesitation, and he arched his eyebrows as though inviting her to reconsider.

Before the doubts had a chance to sway her decision, Bol effectively decided for her. The natural leader of the youth pointedly turned away from the door and walked to the Muslim side of the room and stood next to Imam while answering. "When you are ready to offer the same treatment to both groups, we will gratefully accept." Nandita followed Bol's lead. Then Sari and the other Christians moved to join the Muslims and there was only one group once again.

Henry scowled at their protest. "If the Reverend were here, he'd remind you to not 'cast your pearls before swine.' But I will honor your decision. Curt, divide these remaining for the work crews." He turned to go.

"Wait!" Katja called to him. Henry paused at the door. "What if one of us Muslims would choose to become a Christian, could we then join you?"

"But of course!" Henry's smile grew even wider than before. "Is that your desire?"

"My boyfriend is already a Christian, I guess it couldn't hurt." Sari was shocked, but not as shocked as the look on the other Muslims' faces.

"Then in front of these witnesses, repeat after me: I turn my back on the false religion of Islam that deceived my parents and people. I pledge my life to follow Jesus and the Christian religion forever."

Sari knew there was no way Katja would say those words. But she did.

When she finished, Henry motioned for her to follow him. But after just one step Ismail blocked her way.

"You have betrayed us, and sealed your fate in hell, *murtad*!" He spit in her face.

Katja wiped her face with her sleeve, sidestepped him and exited the room.

Chapter 21

With the reduced workforce, and Lotanna nursing Yasmin, Sari knew she'd have to do double work shifts. At least she got Zoe as a partner on the cleaning crew with Jeremy. Zoe seemed like a fun girl and Sari was looking forward to getting to know her.

Jeremy led them through the small room where they had filmed their introductions, past an office, then down a long hallway to a door at the end. Sari was astounded at how far-reaching this underground facility was. Surely someone had put a lot of thought and effort into designing this place.

Jeremy unlocked the door to a large storeroom, comparable in size to where they slept. It had steel walls, like the hallway and their common room, but most of the walls were hidden by cardboard boxes stacked haphazardly everywhere.

"Today, we, uh, have to clean out this room." It seemed to Sari that Jeremy was trying a bit too hard to act confident.

She tried to put him at ease. "That sounds fun!" She smiled at Jeremy and held out her hand. "We haven't really been introduced yet. I'm Sari," he nervously shook her hand. "And this is my friend Zoe from France." Zoe held out her hand, and when Jeremy took it, he blushed.

He abruptly let go. "Some of these boxes are empty. They need to be folded and stacked in the hallway to be burned later. Any boxes with stuff in them we're supposed to pile up against that back wall."

"Will you be helping us too?" Zoe asked Jeremy in her cute accent.

"Uh, yeah, I guess so," he stammered.

Sari reached for the first box, with SONY printed on it. It was empty, so she folded it up and took it out to the hallway. She wondered if it was for the video equipment.

Some of the brand names on the boxes she recognized, but others she didn't, so she decided to engage Jeremy and try to get to know him.

"Do you know what PINE-SOL is?"

"Oh, that's a cleaning supplies company."

"What about this one?" She pointed to a box marked EVIAN.

"It's a bottled water company. We have a well, but ol' Henry is so paranoid he won't drink from it."

Sari folded another box. "What's this one?" She pointed to a long box labeled REMINGTON.

"That's a...that's nothing. Why do you talk so much?" He looked both nervous and irritated.

"I'm sorry," Sari said gently. "You know us girls. We like to talk a lot. And we like it when guys talk back."

She nudged Zoe and whispered, "You ask him something."

Zoe shot her a dirty look, but rose to the occasion: "Hey, Jeremy, the other day Larry said that you were Curt's brother—is that true?"

Jeremy looked at his shuffling feet. "Yeah, he's my brother."

"Are you guys close?"

"Not really."

"Did you grow up together?"

"Nah, he was away at the war in Iraq. I missed him a lot. But when he got back, he was...different."

"Is this camp helping you to, what do you say, reconnect?"

"He thinks this camp will make me a man," Jeremy blurted out, then tried to pull the words back in. "Not that I'm not, I mean, a man, it's just he wants me to be tough, but I am, you know, tough." He clenched his jaw and stuck out his chest.

"Excuse me," he said and bolted out of the room.

Sari and Zoe looked at each other. "That boy really has a crush on you, Zoe," Sari giggled.

"That's ridiculous, look at me!" Zoe protested. Sari looked at her friend's cute blond pixie-cut hair now matted with dirt, her tight white t-shirt smudged in various shades of gray and brown, her wrinkled black-and-white patterned miniskirt and her black leggings with a hole in the knee. Zoe looked down at her shirt and leggings. "Between the garden and the ditch, my outfit is completely ruined."

"But it can't hide that you're beautiful," Sari smiled. "And believe me, Jeremy can see it too. So use it! You know Bol is always pushing us to learn more about the staff."

"I don't like to use people," Zoe frowned.

"That's not what I meant. Use your attractiveness to get to know him. He may be a really sweet guy."

Zoe looked doubtful.

"I know you're going to flirt with him anyway," Sari teased.

Zoe punched her in the arm. "You're terrible!" They both laughed.

"I've noticed you don't flirt with the boys," Zoe glanced sideways at Sari with a teasing smile "Is there someone waiting for you in Indonesia?"

"No," Sari shrugged. "I was never good at flirting anyway. I lived a pretty sheltered life. I didn't have my first crush till senior year in high school. It, uh, didn't work out."

"There's always Jolly," Zoe arched her perfectly manicured eyebrows. Sari rolled her eyes.

"Zoe, Zoe, Zoe...we should get back to work."

They found some boxes marked PARK SEED that were still full, so they pushed together to get them to the far wall. Sari could feel the sweat forming under her hair, though the room was air-conditioned. She commented, "Don't you wish we were bathing right now?"

Zoe sighed. "I think in my whole life that was the hardest decision I've ever had to make. I literally heard my makeup bag talking to me—my lipstick, my eyeliner, my blush—so many voices!"

Sari laughed. From the first day seeing her at the Atlanta airport, Sari imagined Zoe as a *fashionista*. She was right. But Zoe was also so much more.

"How did you get here, to this event?" Sari asked. "Probably everyone is asking the same thing, but I really want to know."

"Actually, I'm surprised how few people have asked me that," Zoe responded. "Let's see, Fatimah, and Jolly, but I think he was just hitting on me." They giggled.

Zoe began, "Well, in Paris I joined the Movement for a Non-Violent Alternative youth camp as well as their training for civil peace intervention. It was there I decided I wanted to become an advocate of immigrants' rights. I actually met Usman once at a rally. He is a, what do you say, rabbly-rouser? But his passion gets people to listen."

Sari didn't know what a "rabbly-rouser" was, but she guessed it was like the Indonesian word *provakator*. "Has this event helped you so far?" she asked.

Zoe ran her fingers through her tangled hair. "It hasn't helped my image," she joked. "But in a way I think I'm learning to look beyond people's appearances. Some of the Muslims still, what do you say, they bug me? Kareem, Katja, Ismail—they seem so angry. The only Muslim I've been able to get close to is Fatimah."

"At first I thought Katja had a bad attitude, but after gardening with her, we actually became friends," Sari countered. "Though what she did today shocked me. I still can't believe it."

"What do you think is really going on here, Sari?" Zoe stopped working and seemed desperate for an answer.

Sari didn't know what to say, but she was saved by the arrival of Jeremy. She winked at Zoe. "Why don't you ask him?"

"Ask me what?" Jeremy scowled at them.

Zoe batted her eyelashes at him. "It's nothing really. You probably don't even know the answer. But I would be interested to hear what you think about it."

"Go ahead, ask me," Jeremy stated more confidently.

Zoe smiled. "Jeremy, you know we all came here from many nations to learn about peace, right?"

He nodded his head.

"But something deep inside here," she placed her hand on her stomach, "feels, what do you say, like the butterflies? When that man Henry speaks with us, I feel like he's hiding something. Do you feel the same as me?" She fixed her gaze on his blue eyes.

"Yeah, I know what you mean. They're hiding something from me too."

"Really? Go on," Zoe urged.

"Like, they make me clean all day long, but at five o'clock when you guys have dinner, they always make me stay inside while they go outside and do stuff, and they won't tell me what they're doing."

"What do you think they're doing?" Zoe asked.

"I don't know. Sometimes they make Larry stay with me too. We just play cards till they come in for dinner."

"Have you ever asked your brother about it?"

"What's the point? If he wanted to talk to me, he would, right? He's changed, and I hate it."

Jeremy seemed to be getting emotional. Sari motioned to Zoe to put her arm around him and got a glare in return, but she did put her hand on his shoulder.

"Am I right that you love your brother?"

Jeremy trembled at her touch. Then his jaw clenched again. "I don't want to talk about it." He pulled away. "We should be working or I'll get in trouble."

Sari quickly grabbed a box and started folding it. "Don't worry, we won't do anything to get you in trouble," she promised. "You're just like us, a great young man trying to do his best in a difficult situation."

They worked quietly for a while, but eventually Zoe got him to talk more about growing up in rural Mississippi, his father losing a leg in the first war with Iraq, and his brother's enlisting for the second war with Iraq. *Will he ever be able to find peace for his heart in a family entangled in so much war?*

By lunchtime the room was more than half-way cleared. Sari was tired, but had enjoyed this job more than the previous ones. She reflected that Jeremy was the camp staff who had opened up the most. And if they could build a friendship with him, it gave her hope to keep trying with the others.

Lunch felt different than previously without seven of their group present. Fatimah and Nandita served them bean and okra soup. It tasted really bland for Sari, who was used to adding spicy

122

chili paste to practically everything she ate in Indonesia. But hunger drove her to finish every last drop.

Fatimah and Nandita were peppered with questions about what the others might be eating for lunch. At first they didn't want to say, but eventually they admitted they had roasted three chickens, cooked a big pot of rice, and stir fried onions, bell peppers, and canned pineapple into a sweet and sour sauce.

All the Asians responded in unison—"Rice!" But Sari didn't hear anyone wishing they'd made a different choice.

One thing she did notice was that some of the Muslims who had tended to keep to their own group before, like Taj and Imam, were sitting with Christians at lunch and laughing. She overheard Taj trying to explain something about a portal he created for youth organizations from different religions to connect, while Jolly and Alex teased him good-naturedly for being such a computer geek. Only Ismail was still keeping his distance.

After eating, Sari went to check on Lotanna and Yasmin. "How's she doing?"

Lotanna sighed. "When she's cognizant, she just yells at me and refuses to drink. When she slips into a semi-conscious state, I manage to get spoonfulls of water into her, but she's really dehydrated. As much as I hate it, because I don't trust Henry, I think I have to tell him to take her to the hospital."

"Yes, I think he should too. Poor thing."

"The problem is, I don't trust Henry."

"But he sent Asmina to the hospital and she's doing better."

Lotanna lowered her voice. "How can we be sure? Did you hear those bogus messages? What if he cut those together from the video interviews?"

Sari was taken aback. "Surely not," she protested. But every time she got with Lotanna, doubts assailed her. Was her friend so traumatized from her past that she couldn't see the sunlight for all the shadows? Or was Sari the one deceived?

Chapter 22

"My darling, this must be horrible for you!" Selena Staunton kissed her husband and held him tightly. Having her near gave new strength to him, and he hoped she'd bring comfort for Aliyah. He introduced Selena to his Muslim co-planner of the youth peace event.

"And for you, too! I can't imagine how you're feeling, my dear," the effervescent African-American woman hugged her new friend warmly though here at the Atlanta airport was the first time they'd ever met.

"Thank you for coming, ma'am," Aliyah said.

"Just call me Selena. Now what's the latest from the FBI?"

"We're headed there now. Do you want to join us, or rest at the hotel?" Louis asked, though he already knew the answer.

"Join you, of course," Selena answered. After many years of resisting his peacemaking work with Muslims, something had transformed his wife into a passionate activist who always wanted to be at his side. More importantly to him, his wife had found a new capability to truly love Muslims. Louis watched her take Aliyah's arm affectionately as they walked to the rental car.

Thirty minutes later, they were parked on Century Parkway and hustled into a second-floor office filled with people. Special Agent Casey Durak emerged from the crowd to introduce himself to Selena and find them some rolling desk chairs.

"This room," he waved his arm, "is entirely devoted to finding your missing youth. A few minutes ago we had representatives from the Georgia state police here for a briefing, and that gentleman over there," he pointed to a tall beanpole of a man wearing a suit vest and John Lennon glasses talking on a cell phone, "is our liaison with Homeland Security. They want to know everything we know in real time."

Louis paused him to explain to Selena, "Agent Durak and his partner, the bald guy over there," he pointed to the approaching agent, "Agent Pritz, were the ones who flew us to the camp and discovered Aliyah's colleague Jack tied up in a tool shed."

"I certainly hope you find whoever did this and rescue those poor kids!" Selena said.

"Don't worry, Mrs. Staunton, we will. Pritz here holds the record for cases solved in the Atlanta office." Pritz joined them, cup of coffee in hand, and greeted them with a grunt and a nod. "Not only that, he's especially hyped up about this case."

"Terrorists," Pritz spat. "When I find them..."

Durak shook his head. "Only three things Pritz hates worse than terrorists…"

"What's that?" Selena asked.

"His three ex-wives," Durak said straight-faced. Pritz grunted.

"Can you give us an update?" Louis asked the agents. Durak motioned for Pritz to speak, but he took a swig of coffee and walked back into the crowd of agents, yelling something.

Durak pulled out his notebook. "Here are some of the things we've followed up on so far.

"Number one: the deputy Ted Olsen who stopped you on the road—he's disappeared, but we'll find him.

"Number two: you said that the deputy told you the Catoosa County sheriff's office called him in while the sheriff was on vacation. The sheriff's office informed us that the sheriff was not on vacation, but had to attend to an act of vandalism at his elderly mother's home in Savannah and was gone for two days. The office did not call in help from anywhere else. We now have an APB out looking for your suspicious deputy.

"Number three: we've discovered that the number of Muslim organizations in and around the south-east region of the United States is in the hundreds. Thirty-seven of those were holding special events of some type over the past few days. Thirty-one of those had invited Muslims from other parts of the U.S. to attend, numbering roughly four hundred Muslims travelling into airports within a day's drive of your retreat center. Six of those events included Muslims travelling in from overseas, with an expected number of twenty-six foreign Muslim guests. Those are the ones getting the greatest scrutiny at the moment. But that's not to say they couldn't have flown into an airport farther away, say Dulles or JFK, and driven two days down here. What I'm trying to say is, it is going to take some time to sift through the data.

"The biggest break we've had is number four: Georgia State Patrol discovered a group of people bound and gagged in a boathouse over in Savannah. The nine people identified themselves as the staff of your retreat center, led by a Bill Houghton—"

Aliyah interrupted, "Yes! Bill is our camp director. I don't understand..."

"Bill and the others were questioned separately and their stories were consistent, that one by one they were knocked out by physical force, most from behind, but a couple caught glimpses of their attackers as wearing Arab clothes and turbans, exactly what Jack testified. When they woke up, they were in the boathouse unable to call for help. They are all being treated at a Savannah hospital but I'm happy to report they will be fine."

"My goodness!" Selena exclaimed. "Thank God none of them were killed."

"An excellent point, ma'am, they were not killed, which leads us to believe your young people may not be in imminent danger. Whatever group is behind this has planned out this disappearance carefully, but their goals may not include violence to the kids. Pritz's theory is that the whole group disappearing is merely a cover so that one or more of these young Muslim participants can embark upon a *jihad* mission. We foil their mission, we find the kids."

Louis wasn't so sure Pritz's theory was correct. "As we told you before, Agent Durak, we vetted those kids thoroughly. I think you need to consider kidnapping as the motivation, especially since one of those kids comes from the family that he does. Did you read the bios we gave you?"

"Yes, sir, we did, and we are considering that possibility. But kidnappers contact someone asking for a ransom. Have you or any of the families been contacted yet?"

"Not that we know of. We were discussing last night if we should call the families or not to tell them what's going on."

"No less than the White House has ordered us to keep this out of the press if possible, but make the calls. If any of the families has received a ransom call, we'll put all our assets on kidnapping instead of a terrorist plot. Although jihadists also frequently use kidnappings to raise funds for *jihad*, and we can't rule out a combination of the two."

"I understand." Louis looked at Aliyah, whose face was ashen. "We'll call the families today."

Selena jumped back in. "Excuse me, you said the retreat staff were found at a boathouse, correct?"

"That's right."

"What if the young people were put on a boat and taken out of the country already?"

Durak flashed her an appreciative smile. "Congressman, does your wife have any background in intelligence?"

"No matter where I am, she always seems to find me," Louis joked. Selena smiled at him.

"That's excellent analysis, ma'am. It's, uh, number eight on my list. In the past four days there have been approximately one hundred and twenty ocean-going vessels that have departed the port. We're having a devil of a time tracking them all, and will need help from several foreign governments to search the vessels when they arrive at their destinations. But I assure you, we are on top of it, and wherever those kids are, we will find them."

Agent Durak stood up. "I need to get back to work. Why don't you head back to the hotel and make those calls. Let us know what you find out, and we'll keep in touch with what we find out."

Louis thanked him and escorted the two women out to the car and back to the hotel. Aliyah headed to her room to make a master list of the peace participants' families, phone numbers and time zones so they could meet after lunch to make the phone calls.

Louis sat with his wife on their hotel bed and held Selena's hand. "Honey, I don't want to make those calls."

"I know, baby, I can't imagine if I were the parent, hearing news like this…" She shook her head sadly.

"Especially that one—you know the one I mean."

Selena nodded.

"That family put their trust in us," Louis said. "And how they respond could send shock waves around the world. In fact, it could put me out of the peacemaking business forever."

"No, baby, no matter what the newspapers say about you, that peacemaking radiates out of here," she placed her hand on his chest, "and nothing, not even this, can stop you from making a difference."

Chapter 23

The whistle blew, catching Sari, Zoe and Jeremy in mid-laugh about Americans bumbling through France. The afternoon had flown by. The storeroom was cleaned out and Jeremy had cracked open an EVIAN box and nicked bottles for each of the girls. They were sitting on some boxes swapping stories as though they were hanging out at the mall food court.

Jeremy looked at his watch. "They're early," he scowled. "It's only three."

Sari and Zoe stood up to head back to the common room. But before Jeremy could open the door, Zoe put her hand on his arm.

"Jeremy, tonight after lights out, we'll light some candles and sit around and talk. Why don't you join us?"

Sari could sense the struggle inside the American boy. "I...I'd get in trouble for sure."

"Think about it," Zoe said, running her fingertips lightly down his arm. "Maybe it would be nice for you to have some friends to, what do you say, chill with? I'd love to introduce you to the others."

Jeremy turned and marched back to the common room. Sari was surprised to see Henry, George and Larry there too. The four privileged youth weren't back yet; they must be with Abagail or Curt, she thought.

As usual, Henry took charge. "Thank you for your hard work today. We'll give you an extra rest period. It's come to my attention that we have a young woman who needs medical help, so we are going to make her our top priority this afternoon. Please bring her here," he instructed Lotanna.

Lotanna helped Yasmin stand. The Filipina girl immediately grabbed her head and swayed. Lotanna waited for the dizziness to pass, then slowly helped her walk forward.

As they neared the front, Lotanna bravely petitioned the camp leader. "Please, sir, allow me to accompany her to the hospital, as you allowed Usman to accompany Asmina."

Henry smiled, "You have a sweet Christian spirit, my daughter. But Usman is already there able to help take care of her. I don't want you to miss out on anything here. We'll take her from here."

He turned to find his lieutenant, but Curt wasn't there. His eyes fell on Larry. "Larry, you take over and help the young woman walk up to the surface."

Larry jumped back shaking his head violently. "No, no, no, not me!" He pointed at Jeremy. "Make him do it!"

Henry grunted. "Jeremy..." He gazed firmly at the young man.

Jeremy rolled his eyes, took a quick apologetic glance at Zoe, then came on Yasmin's other side and wrapped her arm around his shoulders, put his arm around her waist awkwardly, and slowly led her out the door. Larry started shaking his hands like he was flicking water off of them. Sari noticed George flash a creepy smile.

When they were gone, Lotanna collapsed in tears. Sari rushed to her friend and threw her arms around her. "She'll be all right," she said comfortingly.

Lotanna rudely brushed her off. "No she won't! You just don't get it, do you? She's not coming back and it's my fault!" Lotanna was sobbing violently now. Fatimah and Nandita came over to offer assistance. All Sari's cheerfulness from the storeroom evaporated.

She stayed with the girls while she watched Bol across the room moving from person to person having short conversations. As always, the Sudanese young man was obsessed with collecting information. *When this is over, he'll probably write a book about it.*

When Bol reached Imam, the conversation went longer than with the others, and began to get louder as well. She heard Bol demand, "Tell me what you're hiding!" Imam just turned away.

Bol grabbed the bearded Jordanian's arm to spin him around, but Imam's foot caught on something and he stumbled to the ground. Out of nowhere Ismail flew in between them taking the Indonesian martial arts *silat* stance.

"Jangan, Ismail!" Sari yelled at him in her native tongue.

"Keep your *kafir* hands off my Muslim brother!" Ismail hissed.

Jolly tried to get between him and the shocked face of Bol. "Whoa, chill out, dude!" But when Jolly raised his hands in protest, Ismail chopped at his arm knocking it away.

"Ow! Not cool, dude!" Jolly backed off a step, then abruptly launched himself at Ismail's waist like an American football tackle. Ismail was caught off guard and the two tumbled to the floor intent on inflicting pain on each other.

Bol shook his head with regret. He looked at Imam. "Hey, I'm sorry. I take it back." Then he jerked his head at the two wrestling men and Imam nodded. Each of them grabbed one and tried to separate them. Alex had to help restrain Jolly, who was really upset and kept yelling at Ismail.

"You idiotard kook! No one needs your Jackie Chan crap. We're supposed to be kickin' it, dufusmonkey. You make me wanna—"

Zoe got in Jolly's face while Bol and Alex held his arms. She grabbed his jaw, pinching his cheeks together. "That's enough, big guy. But come talk to me later and I'll teach you how to cuss him out in French." She smiled. When he met her gaze, she let go of his cheeks.

He grinned at her. "You smell good, like roses buried under lots and lots of dirt."

"You disgust me," she turned up her nose and pirouetted away from him. The boys let go of his arms. He pointed to his own eyes, then to Ismail, but grinned. Imam released Ismail who retreated silently to his mat.

After giving him a couple minutes to cool off, Sari cautiously approached Ismail and sat down an arm's length away. He ignored her. She decided to try talking to him in their national Indonesian language.

"Older brother, why did you do that?" she asked gently. Ismail glowered at the wall. She prodded, "You came here to be a peacemaker, not a fighter, isn't that right?"

"Tell that to Bol," he snapped.

"Why are you so angry? You seem angry most of the time. Are you angry like this back in your home town in Aceh?"

"I'm not angry," Ismail protested. "I just don't stand by and let my brothers get taken advantage of or bullied, that's all."

"Does that happen a lot in Aceh?" Sari hoped her compatriot would open up and share.

Ismail frowned at her. "Don't you know anything about Aceh? Since the tsunami in 2004, we've been flooded with Christian 'relief organizations' trying to buy or bully our people into converting to their religion. So here I am in America and we Muslims still get no respect. If I could leave this camp today I would. But just like in Aceh, I'm stuck in a world where rich Christians hold all the power, and I'm supposed to 'be at peace' with that? I don't think so."

Sari opened her mouth and then closed it again. She knew Christians who had volunteered to help when the tsunami struck. She always imagined how grateful the Muslim Acehnese must be, and felt proud of her religion serving others. Ismail seemed to see it differently.

"I don't expect you to understand," Ismail added. "But for the true Muslims, we have a sacred duty to defend our brothers. So do me a favor—leave me alone and save your little pep talks for the Christians."

He turned his back on her completely and faced the wall. Sari was too stunned to know what to do, so she retreated to her mat utterly discouraged.

The atmosphere remained tense, but they managed to make it through until dinner without any more drama. Katja and Rebecca entered with the traditional tray of cornbread, Daud and Danilo on their heels.

Alex groaned. "I'm really starting to hate this stuff." He noticed the four who had just entered didn't receive their usual piece. "Don't tell me you guys already ate!" Danilo and Rebecca looked away and moved to the corner farthest from the group. Daud looked down.

Katja, however, boasted loudly, "Darn right we already ate! Roast chicken for lunch, and steak for dinner, with apple pie for dessert! Rebecca here is getting to be quite the cook, aren't you Rebecca." The American girl ignored her.

"And don't we look great," Katja continued, showing off her clean outfit of a gray tank top covered by an open blue and white vertically striped shirt with clean blue jeans. Sari noticed her previously loose long brown hair was now parted in the center and wrapped in circles around her ears. She scanned the others: Rebecca's shoulder-length red hair practically glimmered; Daud was wearing clean khakis and a green button-down shirt; Danilo had an Atlanta Hawks basketball jersey over a black t-shirt and was wearing an Atlanta Hawks hat with the tag still dangling from the back. Part of her was jealous, but another part felt how little those things meant to her anymore.

Alex and Ismail seemed to agree on one thing—they were both glaring holes through Katja. She marched straight over to Bol. Sari couldn't hear what she said, but Bol nodded.

It didn't take long for them to finish off the cornbread and pass around the water bottles. When they had finished, Bol called them all to discussion time before Henry and George showed up. Most of them gathered in a circle, except for Rebecca and Danilo in one corner, and Ismail by himself in another.

Bol began. "Katja here has something to say to everyone." He called Ismail to come over. "You might want to hear this too." But Ismail pointedly turned his face away and stayed put.

Bol shrugged. "Go ahead, Katja."

The Bosnian girl pressed her palms together in apology. "Just so everyone is clear, I'm just as much a Muslim today as I ever was. My faith is deeply rooted in my heart, in my family, in my culture—it can't be undone with two sentences. I figured Henry was lying to us, why should we feel compelled to treat him differently?

"The reason I wanted in had nothing to do with clothes or food. We needed someone on the inside, and we can't trust those two," she motioned with her eyes towards Danilo and Rebecca, "to bring us any decent intel."

"Why didn't you tell us?" Fatimah asked.

"No time, plus I had to sell it. Ismail's reaction was priceless." She grinned.

"Now that I'm on the inside, hopefully I can figure out what they're up to."

Bol put his hand on her shoulder and smiled. "Well done."

Daud raised his hand and Bol nodded. "I also want to apologize. I left because I thought we had no choice and that you all were behind me. When I got outside and saw only three of us, I immediately felt guilty. I haven't enjoyed a minute of this day. The whole time I was wishing I were here with you all. Tomorrow if they offer this again, I'm staying here with my Christian and Muslim brothers and sisters."

"Daud, we appreciate that, and don't worry, no one here thinks less of you," Bol assured him. "But if you get another chance to go, you go, we need you on the inside to help Katja, okay?"

Daud nodded his willingness.

Bol looked at them both. "So, tell us what you learned today."

Katja started, "First of all, Daud and I both brought you something." They emptied their pockets. Katja held up two zip-lock bags. "This one is soap, this one shampoo." A cry of sheer joy rose up from the girls. "But I suggest we hide it till lights out so Henry doesn't walk in on one of us with wet hair." She put the bags back in her pockets.

Daud passed around some chocolate Katja had sneaked out of the kitchen to fill his pockets. The boys greedily stuffed the candy in their mouths and exclaimed over its deliciousness.

"Listen, this facility is way bigger than I ever imagined," Katja resumed her debrief. "This morning we were allowed to take one outfit from our bags and shower. The bags are all kept in a closet, but none of us found our cell phones or watches anywhere. They must be hiding them somewhere else."

Alex interrupted anxiously, "Was my guitar there?"

Katja looked at Daud, who immediately nodded. Alex breathed a sigh of relief.

"After that, we had a session with George talking about the Christian religion. I didn't understand much of it. How about you, Daud?"

The Palestinian Christian boy took over. "Honestly, I didn't understand much either. Most of it was rehashing the book of Genesis about the fall of mankind into sin, Cain and Abel, Noah and his sons—mostly focused on various curses."

"Then we had lunch with the staff," Katja continued. "During lunch, Henry tried to pretend they're all one big happy family. But they're not. Curt is tense about something, Jeremy clearly hates being here, and Abagail is treated like a slave. Some serious dysfunction going on.

"After lunch we had a short rest time in the room where we did the filming. I tried to look around, pretending I was looking for the toilet, and discovered the office where Henry and George work on a laptop. But they were in there the whole afternoon working on something and I couldn't see what it was."

Bol interrupted. "Tomorrow, that's top priority for you two—find a way to get a look at that computer!"

They both nodded. "The last thing was they took us to a room like this one with boxes against one wall, and Curt led us in an hour of basic hand-to-hand combat training. Then we were allowed to wash up before coming back here."

"Combat training?" Lotanna asked. "Did they say why?"

Daud answered. "Curt said the Reverend George wants us to be ready when the time comes. That's all."

"They're going to try to turn you against us," Lotanna concluded. "Be careful. I've seen brainwashing turn innocent teens into killers."

"Don't worry about us," Katja assured her. "It's those two I would worry about." She pointed to Rebecca and Danilo with her eyes once again.

Sari couldn't help herself. "But did you guys actually find out anything that points to them doing something, you know, evil?" She shot a glance at Lotanna.

Katja was about to answer when the door scraped open bringing Henry and George into the room. Everyone quickly shoved the candy wrappers under mats as they turned to face the two white men.

"Good evening," Henry began as usual. "You'll be pleased to hear that Yasmin is receiving excellent care in the hospital, attended to by her friends.

"Unfortunately, we haven't been successful in procuring a new radio yet, but I promise we'll have one by tomorrow. So tonight I thought we'd hear some comments from those who enjoyed extra time with the staff today. Is there anything you'd like to say?"

Henry looked at the four youth, but no one spoke up.

"If you want to come join us again tomorrow, I'm afraid I insist that each of you share something of your experience. Let's begin with you, Rebecca."

Rebecca looked defiantly at the rest of the group across the room. "I, for one, am grateful for what I received today. One thing I noticed is that even though the camp staff have very different personalities, they stick together. I think that's what Christians should do, they should stick together." It looked like Rebecca had more to say, but she closed her mouth abruptly.

"Daud?"

Daud looked uncomfortable. "I am also grateful. I was amazed at the facility that has been prepared here for us. It's so well-designed, must have been a genius who came up with it." He paused. "I just hope I can see more of it. I know I'll be telling my father, who studied architecture, all about it when I get home."

Henry looked pleased. "Danilo?"

The Filipino boy hadn't said much the whole week, but he was on the spot now. "Well, it's always been my dream to come to America and meet some real Americans. Having meals with the staff today was really cool. I love the food. This is really a great country."

Henry smiled even wider. "And now the newest member of our faith-family, Katja?"

The Bosnian girl took a deep breath. Sari could almost see Katja's dramatic spirit possess her body.

"Words can't describe how great it felt to bathe today—it's like I felt clean inside and out!" she said confidently. "American ways are sometimes confusing to me, but once I trusted myself to the process, I feel I'm changing, like a new life is forming inside of me. I can't wait to see what I can learn and experience and how I can grow tomorrow."

"Lovely, my daughter," Henry positively glowed. "Now after hearing these testimonies, if any of the rest of you would like to join us tomorrow, be ready to convince me in the morning of your worthiness."

George offered one of his predictably enigmatic comments: "We have come to open their eyes, and to turn them from darkness to light, and from the power of Satan unto God."

"Rest well." And Henry and George were gone.

Zoe grabbed the soap and shampoo from Katja and practically sprinted past a frowning Rebecca into the bathroom. Imam joined Ismail in *sholat* prayers.

Sari made a beeline for Katja and grabbed her by the arm. She needed an answer. "Well, did you find anything that proves they're up to something really wrong? I mean, did you find any *proof*?"

Katja shook her head. "Not yet. But I will." Her eyes narrowed in determination.

Sari looked over at Lotanna, who sadly turned her face away.

Chapter 24

After the lights went out, Lotanna lit both candles—one for the main room, and one for the girls washing their hair in the bathroom. They put the one for the main room in the center, held upright by first dripping wax on the inside of the ceramic top of the toilet tank to create a base.

Bol wanted to continue the afternoon's discussions, but Fatimah protested. "We've discussed enough. We need some time to just relax and remember there's a big wonderful world outside this door." Some of the girls expressed their support, and Bol backed off.

Fatimah began. "Anybody got a happy story? Or a funny story?"

Jolly broke the silence. "Check this out: Buddha, Jesus and Muhammad walk into a bar…" Groans broke out around the room. "Come on, give it a try," Jolly prodded. "Buddha, Jesus and Muhammad walk into a bar. They sit at the counter, and Jesus says, 'Drinks are on me.' Muhammad says, 'Alcohol is forbidden in my religion. I'll just have water.' Buddha says, 'The key to enlightenment is denial of the flesh. Give me water too.' Jesus says, 'That's cool, that's cool. I'll have a glass of wine.' The bartender brings their drinks. Jesus says, 'Now before we drink, we should pray.' Each of them bows their heads. While the other two are praying, Jesus turns their water into wine. And after that the three religious leaders get along like best friends for the entire evening. World peace in a bottle."

More groans mixed with laughter. "You made that up right now, admit it!" Alex said.

"No, dude, my Christian surfer bro told me that one. Late one night when we were at a bar."

Jolly got more laughs this time. Just then Nandita came back from the bathroom and offered the tiny portion of soap and shampoo left to Sari. "I think you're the last one," the Indian girl said.

Sari hated to miss out, but was dying to wash her hair. She held the shampoo bag up to the bathroom candle and saw that there wasn't nearly enough for her long black hair. But it would have to do. Then she remembered there was one more person who really needed it, and sighed, resigned to using just half of the precious contraband.

She wet her hair with the water in the toilet tank, scrubbed the shampoo through it vigorously, and tried to rinse it the same way. It took a long time, but in the end, her hair felt so much better, and so did her spirits. She used the soap to rinse off her body, and left the bathroom feeling like a new person. *Katja's act wasn't so far from the truth—I almost feel brand new inside and out.*

She gave the last spoonful of soap and shampoo to Jolly, who looked up surprised. His brown hair was as long as Rebecca's, and she knew he took pride in it. He gleefully left the circle, saying to Sari, "When I'm clean, I'll be giving you a hug, babe."

Rejoining the others, Sari found the atmosphere had completely changed. People were talking about happy times, about falling in love—though Danilo was already asleep, Sari noticed Rebecca and Ismail were listening intently from their respective corners.

Sari imagined if she had met these people around a campfire at the beach—they would probably all become great friends. Suffering together had bonded her with some of the girls, but laughing together was needed too. It was the laughing together with Asmina, Katja and Zoe that made her want to come back for more.

She took a seat next to Zoe. "So Jeremy didn't show up while I was gone?"

"No," Zoe answered. "You told me to flirt with him to learn more about him, remember? Well, the more I got to know him, the more I actually did grow to like him. These American boys are, what do you say, so macho?"

Sari giggled. "Well, let's try to invite him again tomorrow night."

Imam interjected a rare question. "Brother Daud, I'm curious about something. You are a filmmaker, correct? If you were filming us this week, what would the storyline be?"

Other conversations died down as everyone wanted to hear Daud's response. He hesitated, so Nadia urged him on: "Oh, I love movies! Would it be like the struggle for justice, or a freaky horror flick, or, I don't know, a tragic comedy?"

Daud scratched his head. "I have been thinking about this," he admitted timidly. "Did you guess that?" he asked Imam, who gave an encouraging smile.

"I think I would take my camera and just follow one person, day and night, experience everything through their eyes. And every time they had a thought, about anything, I'd try to capture those thoughts on film. If they felt fear, I'd want to know why. If they felt prejudice, how did they feel knowing that prejudice was a part of them? If they did anything noble, how did they reach that decision?

"And if I had enough cameras and crew, I'd do that with every one of you. Because to me, the story isn't a camp, or a program, or a common human struggle. The story is you."

"But if you could only choose one of us, who would it be?" Zoe asked, tossing her hair. "Because everyone tells me I have star potential."

"Believe me, I've thought about that too," Daud shared. He lifted his hands before his face, forming his familiar rectangle with thumbs and pointer fingers just large enough to see one person at a time. Slowly he worked his way around the circle, making eye contact with each one. "And I know exactly who I'd pick," he said. When he got to Sari, was it just her imagination, or did he linger longer upon her than the others?

"Tell us already!" Nadia said hopefully.

Daud finished the circle and let his hands drop to his lap with a smile. "You'll have to wait till my movie hits the theaters."

As Sari lay down to sleep that night, she reflected on Daud's words. What if he made his movie about her? How would she want to be portrayed? Could she live like that person she wanted to be?

Through all that she'd been through, there had always been someone there to be strong for her when she was weak. Now it was her turn to ease the burdens of others. She determined in her heart once again, that the story of her life would have one overarching theme, triumphant over all others. *My life will be a story of hope.*

Chapter 25

A ringing sound.

Louis felt disoriented. Where was that ringing coming from?

Finally he realized the sound came from a telephone somewhere on his right. He removed his hand from his wife's shoulder on his left, and fumbled in the dark to find the source of the ringing.

"Hello," he croaked. "Who's this?"

"It's William, sir. I tried your cell phone but couldn't get through."

"Battery must be dead," Louis answered his congressional aide. "What time is it?"

"Just after midnight, sir. I'm so sorry to disturb you. But there's something you really, really need to see."

"To see? I'm not flying back to D.C. tonight, William, can't it wait till the morning?"

"Uh, sir, remember how you have a standing order for your staff to let you know when any event happens in America that has potential to seriously damage Muslim-Christian or Muslim-American relations?"

"Go on," Louis yawned. Selena rolled over with a questioning look. He held his finger up for her to wait a moment.

"Well, one of our contacts sent us a link to something online yesterday, but it wasn't until we took another look at it tonight that we realized its significance."

"Spit it out, William," Louis grouched.

"Sir, it's better if you see it for yourself. I've already sent the link to your cell phone. Please look at it right away, sir."

"Fine, William, I'll look at it. Good night." Louis hung up, and turned on the reading light.

"What is it, dear?" Selena asked.

"Hopefully nothing. One of my staff wants me to look at something online that could spell the end of the world as we know it."

He moved from the bed to kneeling on the floor, searching through his suitcase for his phone charger. Once he had plugged it in, he turned on the phone and waited for it to be internet ready.

"This better be good," he grumbled to himself. His stomach was still cramped from the buttered lobster he'd eaten with Selena last night. He'd likely have a hard time getting back to sleep.

Finally he clicked on the link, which took him to a YouTube video. He watched it silently. When it finished, all he could say was, "My God. My God."

Selena looked up at him again, concerned. "Is it the end of the world?" she asked anxiously.

He couldn't take his eyes off the screen. "Honey, please go next door and get Aliyah. Right now."

Selena's eyes popped wide awake now. She threw on a robe over her pajamas and some slippers and banged loudly on Aliyah's door. After several tries, no one answered.

She came back in. "Just call her, dear."

Louis hadn't shifted an inch from staring at his cell phone. Selena sighed, picked up the hotel phone and dialed Aliyah's room number. Eventually the poor woman woke up and promised to come right over.

When she was seated on the bed next to Selena, Louis started the video again for them, turning the sound all the way up this time.

By the end, the women were equally undone. "Sweet baby Jesus!" Selena exclaimed, hand over her mouth.

Aliyah started shaking from head to toe. Selena noticed and grabbed her arm just as she passed out and crumpled onto the floor.

While Selena picked up the unconscious woman and laid her on the bed, Louis closed the website and scrolled through his contacts for Special Agent Casey Durak.

The married couple put their arms around each other. Selena began to weep.

While he waited for Durak to pick up the phone, all Louis could say was, "My God."

DAY 5

Jim Baton

Chapter 26

Mercifully, Larry didn't appear before dawn, allowing Sari and her friends to get an undisturbed rest. *Maybe he was just after Yasmin, and now she's gone.*

Before Henry showed up with whatever twist he had planned, Bol called the core group together. Ismail reluctantly joined, with only Rebecca and Danilo whispering their own plans for the day.

"Listen, there are a lot of us. They can't watch us all and watch the laptop too. Daud will be indoors most likely. Try to find a way to get him access to the computer. If Taj is indoors, someone get him freed to check it out too.

"For those outside, the garden is on the north. We need to explore the forest to the east, west, and especially south.

"But indoors or outdoors, take every chance to make a distraction, trade places with someone, just move around until the staff doesn't know who is supposed to be where and one or two of us can maybe discover something useful. Got it?"

Everyone nodded. "Let's make like a circus, dudes," Jolly encouraged them.

"One more thing—have you noticed that everyone who supposedly goes to the hospital is a Muslim? I want to try something. Any of you Christians here volunteer to be sick today, and see if you can't get taken to where the others are?" He looked around.

Nandita timidly put up her hand. "Honestly, I'm not feeling that well anyway." Sari peered at her carefully and wondered if the Indian girl had lost weight.

"Have you been eating regularly?" Sari asked.

Nandita blushed. "I can't eat when I'm stressed," she confessed.

Lotanna went straight to her and held her hand. "I'll ask if I can stay with you today. But you need to eat. I'm not sending you out of here in Yasmin's condition." Nandita nodded guiltily.

Bol looked across at Imam and Ismail. "Are you two up for this?" he challenged.

Imam answered heartily, "Yes, I think your plan is brilliant." Ismail just shrugged.

It wasn't long before the camp staff paraded through the door. Sari focused on Jeremy, watched him catch Zoe's eye, then blush. She smiled.

"Good morning. Would our four exemplary Christians please step forward?" Rebecca, Daud, Danilo and Katja joined them in the front. "For you, we have an exciting day planned."

He surveyed the rest of the group. "And as I promised, I will offer this same privilege to only one of you, whichever proves himself or herself most worthy." He waited.

Jolly answered, "Are you still accepting only Christians?"

"Of course," Henry smiled. "Would any of you Christians like to join your brothers and sisters up here with us?"

Nobody moved, or said anything. Henry looked disappointed. "Very well, your loss."

"You have not because you ask not," George's gravelly voice added.

"Pardon me, sir," Lotanna spoke up. "Our sister Nandita here is having stomach issues. Perhaps the lack of iron in her diet combined with her monthly period has made her very weak. I humbly request permission for her to rest today from the chores."

"She may need to go to the hospital…" Bol added.

"For a stomach ache?" Henry waved his hand dismissively. "For today, she can rest here alone. The rest of you have a heavy day of labor ahead. Meanwhile," he smiled at the favored four, "I have a special treat for you. When Jack arrives with the car, he will be taking you four to visit your friends in the hospital, then eating pizza for lunch at the mall."

Sari was stunned. Lotanna *was* imagining things. Tonight her friends would come back with the proof that everything was just as Henry said it was. She had been right to trust that though the

Americans' ways were strange, everything they'd been through was planned out for their good.

Sari got matched up with Fatimah to take care of the animals under Curt's supervision. Before she left, Bol pressed something into her hand. "Start a fire," he whispered in her ear.

She slipped the matchbox into her pocket. "How?" she asked.

"The hay. Just don't burn the barn down." And he was gone.

She followed Fatimah up the stairs to the barn. Curt handed them a basket and told them to collect eggs while he got the three guys assigned to him started digging outside.

The box of matches was burning a hole in her pocket. Sari was terrified of doing what Bol asked. And in light of the morning announcement, it hardly seemed necessary. She needed time to think.

"You're quiet today," Fatimah observed. "Aren't you the one always asking people questions?"

Sari smiled. "Sorry, just thinking about something." She changed the subject. "I'm glad I finally got matched up with you. You're such a beautiful, interesting person. I've been wanting to get to know you."

Fatimah returned the smile. She was beautiful, Sari thought, with her olive skin and black wavy hair blowing from the breeze coming in the open barn door. Her double-hoop gold earrings looked so elegant, in contrast to Fatimah's beige top and black stone-washed jeans which were filthy, like Sari's clothes, but she hardly noticed her friends' clothes anymore. She shooed away some chickens at her feet and moved into the coop where the eggs awaited them.

"I like praying with you," Fatimah began abruptly. "In Palestine we have three religions all claiming to come from the Prophet Ibrahim, I mean, Abraham, but I've never imagined that I could sit with someone from the Christian religion and pray together."

Sari laughed. "In Indonesia, lots of my friends both Muslim and Christian think I'm crazy, so I'm glad you don't."

"Oh, there are plenty of truly crazy people in Palestine," Fatimah said. "In my internship with the Defense for Children

International Palestine in Ramallah, I try to help both Muslim and Christian children facing conflict or being detained by the harsh Israeli authorities. So many of our kids see things that no human being should ever have to see. I do a lot of counselling, problem-solving, and hugging, but I never thought about praying with the kids."

"Palestine is in our newspapers all the time," Sari sympathized. "Our Muslim youth try to volunteer to go there and help fight the Zionists, but I think it's just for show. I doubt they could get a visa."

They worked their way around to the eggs in the back of the chicken coop. An uncooperative hen pecked at Sari's hand. She snapped in its face and the hen retreated.

"You know, some things about this place remind me of home," Fatimah mused.

"You're kidding!" Sari couldn't believe it. "What, do you raise chickens?"

Fatimah laughed, a musical sound that made Sari wonder if her friend could sing.

"No, not that. It's Henry and George and that radio bigot. It makes me feel like I'm at my uncle's house. I hate to say his name, because you may have heard of him. He's a leader in Hamas, and has killed many people. But the way he talks, some of the phrases he uses, they sound almost exactly the same as these Americans."

"Really? Like what?"

"You know, like one race is superior or pure—in my uncle's eyes that's the Arabs—and other races are cursed by God. That one religion should separate itself from anyone from a different religion. I don't know how many times my uncle quoted the Qur'anic verse to me that Allah hates the unbelievers. Remember how that radio guy said the American president was taking money from the Saudis to Islamicize America? My uncle says the American president is taking money from the Jews to Zionize America—it's the same thing. And my uncle agrees with the radio guy that the answer is to get a gun and fight back."

Sari was stunned. "But I thought these Americans were just making us listen to the radio broadcast to help us see the ugliness of hatred and prejudice so we would strive to overcome it."

Fatimah looked skeptical. "Maybe. Maybe not. I'm just saying, those two remind me of my uncle an awful lot. Honestly, the reason I got into peacemaking was because of him. I felt like someone needed to redeem the family name."

Sari thought back to her adopted father's journey out of *jihad* to become a peacemaker. She knew his answer to her next question, but wondered how Fatimah would answer it.

"Your uncle and many others claim the Qur'an supports violence, especially against non-Muslims," Sari began. "I'm just curious how you explain to your family your commitment to peace."

The Palestinian girl gently piled the last of the eggs into the basket. "Did you know that every chapter of the Qur'an except one begins with the phrase *Bismillah ir-Rahman ir-Rahim,* meaning 'in the name of God, Most Compassionate, Most Merciful'? I've argued with my family that if every verse of the Qur'an we read in the context of God's perfect compassion and mercy on mankind, we'd never interpret it to justify such horrible deeds."

"Wow! I've never heard that," Sari responded excitedly. "It reminds me of how if Christians just followed the maxim, 'what would Jesus do?' we'd also always choose love and mercy."

The girls were interrupted by the barn door opening.

They took the basket of eggs to Curt, who traded them buckets of food for the goats and pigs. Sari thought she better grab the chance to ask the muscular man a question.

"Excuse me, but Larry called you 'Crush.' Did you get that name in the war?"

Curt's eyes narrowed. "None of your business," he retorted.

Sari thought she'd stick her neck out one more time. "Your brother is a great guy, but I think he wants your care more than your discipline. You guys could be close again, you know."

"You stinkin' busybody," Curt snarled. "Stay out of my way." He stomped off.

"You really know how to stir the pot, Sari," her Muslim friend observed admiringly.

Sari was disappointed. "I just want to get to know these people and find the good in them, but I feel like I'm failing."

"Yeah, I know what you mean. I've often tried with my uncle, but if there is any humanity left within him, it's buried so deep I doubt I'll ever find it. Killing people can do that to you."

Sari took the pigs' food while Fatimah fed the goats. Her mind wasn't on the animals, though, it was on the box of matches in her pocket. *Start a fire?* That sounded pretty drastic. But she didn't want to let Bol down again.

She looked around for the best place to start a fire. Along both walls in the center were piles of hay bales. They should start on fire easily, but would they burn down the whole barn? What if the roof fell on top of the trap door and they were stuck underground forever?

She was so distracted she almost forgot to save out some of the scraps for the smaller pigs. Curt had told her to feed them separately or the big ones would take all the food. She poured the rest of the bucket into their smaller feeding trough and watched them greedily snort and jostle.

Fatimah was giving the goats some hay with their scraps. Maybe she could start a fire with that. But she didn't want the goats or chickens to be burned. It wasn't their fault. *Think, Sari, think!*

After pouring several buckets of water for the pigs to drink, Sari was still stumped. She decided to ask Fatimah for help in carrying out Bol's crazy plan. Fatimah's brown eyes widened with excitement.

"I get it! While everyone is focused on the flames, our boys can go look around. Genius!" Sari wished she felt as enthusiastic as Fatimah.

Her friend surveyed the barn. "How about if we start the fire at the base of this hay bale here," she pointed, "and I'll climb up on top of the hay bales and scream for help. They'll have to come running to rescue me."

"That's insane," Sari protested. "You could be burned alive!"

152

"I'm sure they'll get the fire put out before that. But even if they don't, I could jump out of that high window up there."

"Wait," Sari grabbed her friend's arm. "What if they don't come to rescue you because you're a Muslim? I'm a Christian, they'll be more eager to help me. I'll climb up there, and you light the fire."

Fatimah looked supremely confident. "Good idea. You scamper up there. I was a theater minor in college. Just watch this act!" She grinned and took the box of matches from Sari.

Oh God, I hope this ends well. She climbed her way up four hay bales that were nearly as tall as she was. By the time she was at the top, Fatimah had a small fire going at the base.

She called up to Sari, "When I reach the door, start screaming."

Fatimah grabbed the four buckets they'd been using for feeding and watering the animals and spread them around the barn. The fire was getting larger now. Then she took her time meandering toward the door. When she was almost there, she looked back at the flames now taller than the girls, took a deep breath, and ran the last two steps outside yelling, "Fire!"

Sari screamed for all she was worth.

Chapter 27

Out of the high window, Sari could see Bol and Alex look up from the garden, alarmed. She gave them a brave smile and a thumbs up, then screamed again at the top of her lungs. Bol glanced at Alex, then disappeared into the forest.

Fatimah and Curt appeared in the barn doorway. "What the—" Curt exclaimed.

Fatimah grabbed his arm and began crying hysterically. "Save her! She's my Christian friend! Please, you have to save her!"

Curt knocked her aside and called out the doorway, "Larry! You boys! Here, now!" Then he raced around the barn picking up the scattered buckets, and as Jolly, Imam and Ismail showed up, he threw the buckets at them. "Get water from the faucet," he pointed to Jolly, "from the well," he pointed to Imam, "from the pigs' trough," he pointed to Ismail, who didn't budge. "Larry, go down and get us help." Larry opened the trapdoor and started yelling, "Fire!"

Sari screamed again. Curt had a pitchfork and was trying to drag the burning hay into the middle of the barn away from the piled hay bales. "Climb down, idiot!" he yelled.

Sari didn't have to act afraid—she was terrified. The fire was now licking at the second layer of hay bales and was really, really hot. She flashed back to her mother trapped in the burning church. Panic began to rob her of breath, began to overwhelm her ability to think. She looked down and discovered her whole body was shaking and she had no way to control it.

She was barely aware of the entire staff emerging from underground, with Fatimah running circles around them all demanding that they rescue Sari. Larry grabbed the bucket dropped by Ismail, who was nowhere to be seen, and Henry grabbed the fourth bucket. Sari noticed Abagail was wringing her hands, her lips moving perhaps in a prayer. George stood silently observing it all.

About half the burning hay was now in the center of the barn, but it looked too late to Sari, as the third level of hay bales was starting to burn. Her skin felt so hot. She wondered if her hair or her clothes would be the first to catch on fire.

Henry was yelling something about the roof, while Curt was cursing at her telling her to climb down, but it was useless, her legs had turned to jelly.

She saw Jeremy frozen in indecision and locked onto his eyes. "Help me!" she mouthed.

The young American exploded up the side of the pile of hay, passing within an arms-breadth of the flames, and in a moment he was there next to her at the top. He grabbed her arms and pulled her to the edge of the first bale, turned her to face him, grabbed on to her wrists, then with his chest he bumped her off the edge.

Panic filled Sari again as she fell, but her feet hit the next hay bale standing upright as Jeremy balanced her with his hands from above. He slid down next to her. She could see the red and gold flames just over his shoulder now. She closed her eyes and he repeated the process down to the next level.

For some reason she felt better with her eyes closed, so she stayed that way, yielding to his grabbing and pushing and dropping like a rag doll. But the third time, strong arms caught her around the waist and Jeremy let go of her hands. Her feet felt solid ground, and when she opened her eyes, there was Jolly's face on her shoulder, holding her from behind.

"No sweat, babe." He half-carried her out the doorway and set her down on the grass, then went back to help with the fire.

In a moment Fatimah was there, stroking her hair and whispering in her ear. "You were wonderful! You're so brave. Don't worry, everything worked perfectly. I'm so proud of you."

With eyes closed, Sari flashed back again to her mother stroking her hair just like that. *Why am I thinking of my mother so much today? Am I just missing her, or maybe am I becoming just like her?*

The animals were making a huge racket, as was the crackling of the flames, but above it all Sari could hear Henry angrily yelling at Curt and Curt yelling back. Finally Imam came out of the barn and dropped his bucket and sat beside her.

"Are you okay?" he asked, genuinely concerned.

Sari couldn't find the strength to speak yet. "She's fine," Fatimah answered for her. "I guess the fire is out?"

Imam nodded. A moment later, Jolly joined them, joking, "I already told you that you were hot. You didn't need to set yourself on fire to prove it."

"Not now, Jolly! This is no time for kidding around," Fatimah objected. "Look how scared she is!"

"Sorry," Jolly mumbled. "It's just how I deal with stuff." He shrugged apologetically, then touched Sari gently on the shoulder. "You okay, Sari?"

She nodded feebly. Sari looked at her hands, with a sudden fear that the left might be scarred from the burning as her right hand was, but the skin was fine. She realized both hands were trembling and forced them back into her lap.

Curt came stomping out of the barn in their direction. He stopped, hands on his hips, towering over the two girls.

"How did this happen?" he demanded.

"How should we know?" Fatimah replied. "This poor girl nearly died. Look how traumatized she is." Fatimah turned away from Curt and started stroking Sari's hair again.

Imam stood up and faced Curt. "I want to express my gratefulness for your excellent leadership in crisis. You saved this girl's life, and we are all eternally indebted to you."

Jolly stood beside him. "He's so right, bro, you were gnarly in there! Like that *Rescue 911* show. You were *born* to save lives. You da man!"

Curt was speechless.

Henry poked his head out of the doorway. "Round 'em up!" he instructed Curt, then disappeared.

"Back to the common room," Curt ordered and went off to look for the others.

Jolly and Fatimah helped Sari's wobbly legs navigate the stairs back underground. She could still smell the smoke, and realized it was her hair that smelled. *Hopefully Katja will manage to steal some more shampoo today.*

Back in the common room, it took a while before everyone was completely assembled. All five staff were there in front, the four privileged youth stood apart near the door, while the remaining twelve of them sat facing the giant white man with a very angry red face.

"Someone here has endangered all of us," Henry began, glaring holes in all of them. "One of you started a fire and when I find out who did it, be assured you will regret that foolish decision forever."

He began to pace back and forth in front of them, in an effort to look more closely in people's eyes. Sari was afraid to look at him, but more afraid to appear guilty by looking away. When Henry reached her, she swallowed hard and tried to look vulnerable as she met his gaze.

"My daughter," he said gently, "are you okay?"

She nodded. He stared at her for a moment, then continued his pacing.

"The question I'm faced with, is who would want to kill this poor Christian girl? Or who would want to burn down this old Christian barn? It can't be too difficult to narrow down the perpetrator. Without doubt it is one of our *Muslims*!" Henry said the last word with such viciousness Sari was taken aback.

"Whose father is the devil," George mumbled, "for whom the eternal fires of hell are prepared, for the devil and his messengers."

"As to how, why that is no mystery, for I've been informed that one of you stole a box of matches from our kitchen." Henry glared at his wife who looked down in shame.

Next Henry motioned with his arm toward the four privileged ones. "Your foolishness has caused the suffering of the innocent. Because of you, I am cancelling their trip to the hospital, that you might gain understanding of how the deeds of the wicked affect the well-being of the righteous." He turned toward the four. "And that you four may learn how important it is to root out and burn the tares sown by the evil one among us."

"If your eye is unholy, pluck it out," George mumbled. "If your hand does evil, cut it off."

"When one suffers, we all suffer. For the rest of the day, none of you will receive food or water. And I will choose one of you as the sacrificial goat to carry the crimes of the guilty. That one will be taken outside the camp and beaten. When the shame of this dastardly deed is past, in twenty-four hours, he or she may rejoin us, praying for forgiveness and a chance at redemption."

Sari looked over at the five remaining Muslims. One of them would be beaten? Would it be Fatimah? Had they guessed she was the arsonist? Sari wanted to protest, but had no strength left.

Henry's eyes narrowed as he gazed intently at the small group of Muslims. In the end, his eyes locked on Ismail and Imam. He looked back and forth between them a few times, undecided.

George's voice in the background helped him make up his mind. "Sons of Ishmael, the race of Arabs, wild donkeys of men, their hands against everyone and everyone's hands against them, living in hostility toward all their brothers."

Henry's gaze settled on Imam.

"You, bearded one, step forward." Sari heard Nadia behind her stifle a cry as Imam started to rise, but to Sari's left she felt someone stumble to his feet and rush past her.

"You want a son of Ishmael?" Daud cried out. "Take me! I am from Palestine, the land that crucified Jesus."

"Sit down," Henry warned.

But Daud got right up in his face. "I'm the one you want! We Palestinians are the greatest terrorists in the world. We blow ourselves up at bus stops and malls. We start fires not caring if we die in them. This fire was my idea and I have many more where that came from. Just try to beat those ideas out of me if you can!" he challenged Henry defiantly.

Henry sneered at him. "To think I exalted you to a place of trust and privilege. And you have betrayed me."

"The spirit of Judas, the betrayer of our Lord," George nodded.

158

"Very well, you shall pay the blood price to remove the sins of this obstinate people. Curt?"

Curt's large hand locked an iron grip on Daud's shoulder.

"Tomorrow at this time we shall meet again," Henry pronounced over the group in benediction.

Abagail, Jeremy and Larry filed out. Curt had Daud at the doorway when suddenly the wiry youth twisted out of his grasp and turned back to the room. He raised his hands in his filmmaking rectangle, as though taking a mental snapshot of the group to remember while he was gone. Sari caught just the glimpse of his smile before Curt jerked him roughly.

The door slammed shut and Daud was gone.

Chapter 28

This is a message for all the enemies of America—ISIS, Al Qaeda, and all Muslim terrorists everywhere—listen up!

The YouTube video was playing on a forty-inch flat-screen television in an FBI conference room. Louis and his wife Selena, Aliyah, Pritz and Durak were accompanied by a growing force of roughly thirty people all dedicated to finding the young peacemakers that had gone missing five days before.

Durak had seen the video last night in his home. He'd immediately called Pritz and dragged him out of bed. It was now eight o'clock in the morning and they'd had very little sleep. But this video had forced them to rethink everything and come up with a new plan of attack.

Most of the other agents were seeing it for the first time. Louis did not envy them. He had nearly vomited the first time he saw it and his stomach hadn't felt the same since.

The voice in the video was off camera. It was a strong, commanding voice with a clearly American accent.

The picture on the screen was of a man in Arab clothes and a turban kneeling on the ground, while behind him stood another man in U.S. Army fatigues with a white mask over his head reminiscent of the Klu Klux Klan.

Louis listened to the hate in the narrator's voice, dreading what was coming.

You spread your devilish religion by enslaving, raping and killing. It's bad enough that you do it to your fellow Arabs. But when you attack the white Christians from the West, do not think you will go unpunished.

The American government may huff and puff, without the resolve to respond to bloodshed with bloodshed. But the white American patriots of this land will rise up and destroy you.

Let me introduce you to the first victim of your murderous ways.

The screen changed, and there was a close up of someone Louis and Aliyah knew quite well. He smiled for the camera. His speech, however, jumped from one facial expression to another as though cut together.

My name is Yabani Kareem. I am…Muslim…Hausa, from Nigeria…In my experience…Christians…are… wild animals…Death…to America.

The screen returned to Kareem's face now in Arab garb kneeling before what had to be his executioner. The off-camera voice continued.

This is for our brothers: the American journalists James Foley and Steven Sotloff, the aid worker Peter Kassig, the British aid workers Alan Henning and David Haines, and for the twenty-one Egyptian Christians that you beheaded. America will be silent no more.

From behind his back the white-hooded man drew a long, curved blade. He raised it above his head. Then in a swinging motion it swept around and down and sliced perfectly through Kareem's neck, severing his head from his body. Blood spurted everywhere as the voice concluded.

We call upon the righteous, the chosen, the white Christians of America to cleanse our land of the Islamic plague. We are ANTSA—Act Now To Save America.

Durak turned off the screen. Pritz took charge. "Scrap the terrorist angle. Scrap the ocean vessel searches. We're looking for white supremacists. Tech, analyze every pixel of that video, and track their uploading IP address. And call in more people—I want monitoring of every white supremacist website, blog and Facebook page in the country. Somebody find me that deputy and the missing security team! And you, go check Jack Porter out of the hospital and bring him here now, I don't care what the doctor says."

People started rushing about. Louis overheard the Homeland Security agent as he walked past speak into his cell phone: "Patch me through to the White House."

161

When the buzz had died down a bit, Durak escorted them back into the larger office and found them some seats.

"Have you called all the families?" he asked.

Louis answered. "Yes, though we've been unable to get through yet to a few of them. No one has been contacted about ransom money."

"We'll have to call Kareem's family again," Aliyah said dejectedly. Louis nodded.

"So now you're looking for white supremacists?" Selena asked.

"Yes," Durak pulled out his notebook. "And if we thought keeping tabs on every Muslim in a five-hundred-mile radius was hard, this will be infinitely harder."

"Why is that?"

"I got back to the office here at one this morning, and here's what my research has turned up so far: There are over seven hundred extremist groups in the U.S., mostly white supremacist groups. It might surprise you that the KKK is alive and well with over five thousand members, and there are hundreds of thousands of people who identify with one of these groups—everything from the more idealistic Christian Identity groups to the more violent neo-Nazis. Although most of these groups are not organized enough to, say, try to overthrow a state government, the vast majority of them own guns and are highly susceptible to the suggestion that using that weapon can be considered a patriotic act of defending the nation.

"What I'm trying to say is, this video is clearly trying to incite these people all across America into random acts of violence against Muslims."

Selena covered her mouth. "Lord, have mercy! We have to warn them!"

"The president is being updated constantly, and he'll be holding a press conference soon. Meanwhile, if you have access to wider Muslim networks, please warn them—we just don't have the resources to do that and focus on the perpetrators at the same time."

"I'll get right on it," Louis promised.

Aliyah was shaking. "Do you really think American Muslims are in danger?"

Durak looked apologetic. "Let me put it this way. I read a recent study from West Point that analyzed hate crimes across the U.S. We have an average of less than one hate crime per month committed by a Muslim. But we have an average of one hate crime *every single day* committed by white supremacists against minorities. If you're an Asian, Latino, Black, Jew, homosexual, or even like me, half-Turkish, you're far less likely to get killed by a Muslim terrorist than you are by the white, Protestant, gun-carrying guy on your street who visits neo-Nazi websites like *Stormfront* or listens to survivalists on talk radio.

"And right now, that's a potential army of hundreds of thousands out there just waiting for a general to mobilize them in a war that could destroy America."

Chapter 29

Everyone was stunned to silence by Daud's volunteering for a beating. Sari wondered how the thin boy could survive.

Bol took the lead as always. "Guys, we need to talk."

Sari sat down next to him and Zoe sat next to her. She noticed Rebecca, Danilo and Ismail turning away.

"Everyone!" Bol called to them. "First Sari was nearly burned alive for us, now Daud is taking a beating for us—we need to respect their sacrifices and stick together to get through this." He glared at Ismail, who shrugged and returned to the circle. Then he motioned with his hand for Rebecca and Danilo to come, and reluctantly they did.

When everyone was seated in the circle, Bol began. "First of all, great job by Sari and Fatimah getting us some time. I know Alex and I both discovered items of interest, so let's go around and share what we each learned. Alex, you want to start?"

"Sure," the Bosnian with the punk hairstyle nodded. "When Sari screamed, Bol went one way into the forest and I went the other. East of the barn, I found an area covered by trees with large tire tracks in the soft ground and a pile of sand—I'd say at least a pickup truck full of sand. And at the bottom of the pile of sand I found a couple of these." He pulled out two large brown beads.

"Those are Asmina's!" Sari exclaimed.

"That's what I thought. But what the heck is sand doing in a forest?"

No one had any ideas.

"Anyone else?"

Katja shifted her legs to kneel on them, making her appear taller. "Bol, you gotta hear this."

"Go ahead."

Her eyes were wide with excitement. "We were having our theology lesson with George, some crap about the ten lost tribes of Israel migrating to the Caucasus, near where I'm from, so they became the Caucasian race, when we heard someone yell, 'Fire!' George told us to stay put, but as soon as he was gone, Daud and I made a beeline for the computer."

"Did you get a look at it?" Bol leaned forward.

"We couldn't get past the password. We tried a few, but we gave up and hurried back to our seats before George returned."

Bol sat back and sighed, clearly frustrated.

Katja continued, "However, back in the study room, Daud picked up George's Bible, and inside he found a piece of paper that he showed me. Guys," she looked around the circle, "this is where it gets freaky."

Sari held her breath waiting for Katja's big reveal. Her Bosnian friend tortured them with a pregnant pause.

"This paper was headlined, 'Ten Sins of ISIS.' The list began with beheading, then there were other horrible things like burning alive, rape and beating, car-bomb, something else with a bomb, I can't remember them all. I wish Daud was here, he'd remember better than me.

"But here's what grabbed me: the first four sins on the list were crossed out, some with black pen, some with blue. And number five on the list was crucifixion."

A shock wave swept around the room.

"I don't get it," Nadia said. "What are you saying?"

"So what?" protested Danilo. "So he watches the news, what's the big deal?"

"But why are four lines crossed out?" Katja argued. "It has to mean something."

Lotanna looked like she'd seen a ghost. "Four of our members are missing. Four Muslims."

Sari heard some gasps. But she didn't want to get sucked into Lotanna's fatalism again.

Rebecca's face was red. "They're at the hospital. We would have got to see them today too if Sari hadn't messed everything up."

"They're not at the hospital," Lotanna objected. "Now we finally know what happened to them. And what's happening right now to Daud."

Sari stifled a cry. "I thought maybe Henry was just testing us to see how we would respond when one of our own is threatened. You don't think Henry's really beating him, do you?"

"No," Lotanna answered, "I think he's being crucified."

Several people protested. It took Bol a while to calm everyone down.

"Look, we don't know anything yet. But there are some more clues to discuss, and then we'll come back to Daud, okay?" He glared everyone to silence. "How about the digging crew—did you find out anything?"

Jolly looked at Imam. "Dude, we were too busy rescuing the opera-screamer."

Ismail made a rare comment: "Something unusual—Curt took me into the trees to dig today—to dig a hole."

Bol leaned forward again. "What kind of hole?"

"Just a hole. He wanted it deep as my mid-thigh and just wide enough to stand in."

Sari knew right away what Lotanna was thinking. She shook her head. *It surely cannot be...*

"Hmm," Bol mused. "Anyone else? Kitchen crew?" Lotanna and Nadia shook their heads. "Cleaning crew?"

Taj spoke up. "I took the chance to look around the storerooms. There is one that was locked, but I found a screwdriver in another closet and forced the lock."

Bol's eyebrows raised in surprise. "What was inside?"

Taj looked sad. "Guns, rope, hand grenades, several small round black items that looked to me like maybe landmines, at least two items that looked like they could be bombs—basically an arsenal."

Next to her Zoe said something in French. Nadia started shaking and biting her long blond hair. Katja swore under her breath. Lotanna tilted her head to the ceiling and closed her eyes, but Sari noticed she looked like she was gaining strength, not losing it. Sari didn't know what to think. She had wanted so badly

166

to trust Henry, to see the good in everyone. *Am I nothing but a blind fool?* She blocked out the barrage of doubts to focus all her energy on not crying.

"You didn't tell us yet what you found, Bol," Taj continued calmly.

Bol looked at Alex. "Remember how Larry had us spreading ashes on the new plot of land he's preparing? Well, I found where the ashes came from. West of the barn in the forest I found a wooden post in the ground as tall as me, blackened from burning, with a pile of ashes around it.

"There is no logical explanation to me for why you'd have ashes around a pole unless you were burning something tied to it."

Nadia's hands trembled violently. Lotanna got up and moved over to put her arms around the Jordanian girl. Katja swore again, louder this time. Nandita stumbled to the toilet where Sari could hear her wretching.

"No way, dude," Jolly shook his head. "Don't...no...I can't believe..." He stood up abruptly and walked away from the group.

Bol started to speak, then hesitated. "Guys, I think we..."

"Shut up," Alex groused.

Bol closed his mouth and there was an eerie stillness in the room for a few moments before the muttering and whimpering started again.

Sari was really fighting to keep the tears back now. Her eyes were moist, and one started to fall but she quickly wiped it away. Panic was tearing her stomach into shreds, rapping incessantly at every surface of her brain.

Eventually a few people resumed talking, but she had a hard time focusing on what they were saying. Imam said they had to do something. Ismail wanted to get the weapons and fight their way out. Fatimah objected strongly. The room began to buzz in her ears, and the stabbing pain in her chest she thought she'd left behind her, she felt penetrate right through her back.

She needed something to focus on, some whisper of *hope*.

Jesus. She pictured her Savior, her Comforter. But the image of a cross transformed, and there was her friend Daud with nails being pounded into his palms.

Sari couldn't keep it in any longer. She buried her face in her hands and began to sob loudly.

Chapter 30

It had been an exhausting day for Louis. He was working the phones from his Atlanta hotel with Selena and Aliyah, while his staff in Washington D.C. had put all political business on hold to help him contact every Muslim organization in America, warning them to close religious schools and mosques, postpone events, and generally stay indoors if possible. They had finished that round of calls by about three in the afternoon. Then Louis had assigned them to contact every major peacemaking organization to ask for their help calling the vast number of Christian denominations and organizations in their networks, begging them to step up and provide care and protection for the Muslims in their cities. He was grateful that there were a lot more peacemaking agencies out there than there used to be before 9/11.

Every time he got put on hold, he'd turned his attention to CNN. The beheading video already had over seven million views and was climbing fast. Meanwhile, nearly every hour CNN was reporting a new attack against Muslims in America. There was a student beaten almost to death at a university in Texas; a mosque that got its ornate stained-glass windows shot out in Phoenix; a Muslim elementary school in New York City pelted by rocks and bricks; a Muslim member of the U.S. Air Force found dead in his barracks; and a Sikh taxi driver murdered in Seattle—most likely mistaken for a Muslim.

Mixed in with the American tragedies were reports of random attacks against Americans in Muslim nations around the world. In airports, hotels, and tourist traps, Americans were being chased, beaten and killed simply because of their nationality.

With each new report coming in, Louis's heart sank a little deeper. Muslims in America had been for the most part ignored until 9/11. As the twin towers toppled to the ground,

Islamophobia's trajectory erupted in a contrasting rise. But it also served to bring this minority out into the light forcing Americans to decide whether or not they should be included under the age-old axiom to "love your neighbor." Muslim-Christian understanding and peacemaking initiatives had exploded across the nation. Louis thought they had made tremendous progress—now it could all be undone by three minutes of viral madness.

Louis glanced out the window at the lights beginning to twinkle on the Atlanta skyline, and took what he hoped would be his last phone call of the day. When he hung up he turned to his wife.

"Selena, honey, are you up for another visit to the FBI?" he asked his wife as she was hanging up her own cell phone.

"Have they got good news for us?"

"Agent Durak didn't say. But he wants us there before the president's press conference at eight."

"Let me shower and change. I'm with you all the way."

He knocked on Aliyah's hotel room door. When she opened it, he could see the redness around her eyes, the slumping of her shoulders. Gently he made the offer for her to come along, and she answered with a nod.

But no matter how bad they felt, Louis reflected, it was but a drop in the bucket compared to the pain of Kareem's parents right now.

Agent Durak ushered them into the empty conference room at seven-thirty. Selena looked like she was dressed for a funeral, with a black knee-length dress. Aliyah had changed too, but Louis noticed she hadn't bothered with any makeup.

Durak was sipping from another one of his brown-green health drinks. "Have you had any dinner yet?" Louis asked the agent. He grinned and took another sip, motioning for them to sit.

"We've made good progress today," he began.

"Have you found the kids?" Selena asked.

"No, ma'am. But let me tell you where we're at." He put his drink on the conference table and pulled out his notebook.

"We are pretty confident that we know who made the video."

170

"Who?" Louis leaned forward eagerly.

"Remember the extra security that Jack Porter hired? Jack testified today that two days before the event, he bumped into two men at the hotel who told him they were from a private security firm and had received a tip from us at the FBI, obviously a lie, that terrorists were gathering in the area to target some international event, but they didn't know which one. Jack made a couple calls, believed their story, and immediately asked if they could send two of their special forces guys up to protect the camp.

"Jack told us the name of the security agency. We found they had been threatened with death and dismemberment if they didn't back up the two men's story.

"Both Jack and the security agency were able to describe the two men. One we have no name for yet, but looks ex-military. The other we believe we have identified as one Heinrich Christenson, a well-known white supremacist. He was raised in Alabama by a wealthy grandfather who was a member of the Ku Klux Klan. When granddad died, Heinrich put his inheritance into real estate, and owns property in Alabama, Georgia, South Carolina and Idaho. He's married, with one son killed in Iraq. He's a member of several different Christian Identity and white supremacist groups, and once ran for public office in Alabama but failed. This man—"

"Hold on a second," Selena interrupted. "You said, 'Christian Identity.' What about this guy is remotely Christian?"

"Christian Identity is a belief that whites are the true lost tribes of Israel and chosen race. They're anti-Semite, anti-minorities, anti-homosexual, anti-government, and have over fifty thousand known adherents across America and several other nations. I don't know much about their theology, just that the FBI frequently gets called in to deal with their crap.

"Anyway, all that to say that Christenson has a racist ideology, wealth, political connections, and most likely a powerful grudge against someone.

"After the description and the profile led us to Christenson, we found one of his old political speeches and compared it to the voice on the video. Tech says it's a ninety-six percent match, which is good enough for us."

Durak took another swig of his health drink, turned a page in his notebook, and continued.

"Christenson was last seen back in January as a speaker at an Aryan Peoples seminar in Idaho. Within hours of his speech, there was an attack on a local mosque, but when the authorities tried to bring in Christenson for questioning, he had disappeared. His status is still a hate crime suspect. But no one has managed to trace his whereabouts until this appearance in Atlanta. We can't find any phone records, credit card transactions, or bills of any kind dated this calendar year. He's hidden himself well.

"Right now we're investigating his various properties and examining all those associated with him over the past forty years."

Louis interrupted him. "Does this man have any history of violence?"

"Actually, no, which makes us wonder if the ex-military man with him or a third party could be the mastermind behind the perverse viciousness of these videos."

"Wait," Aliyah put her hand on Selena's knee to steady herself. "You said, 'videos'?"

"You haven't seen them yet?" Durak asked, puzzled. "They must have not made it onto the evening news."

"Oh, no," Selena gasped. "Don't tell us there are more!"

Agent Durak swallowed and looked grim. "I'm afraid so." He turned to the laptop on the table under the large screen TV and searched through some files. "We haven't been able to trace the first video yet, as it seems to have been forwarded through several servers including some in Germany and Australia. The next two videos were sent through different channels altogether, one we traced back to Norway, the other to Argentina, before we lost the trail."

"Two?" Aliyah looked like she was going to be sick.

The image of Asmina's lovely smile appeared on the TV in front of an American flag. Durak continued, "Once we had the photos you provided us of the participants, we've had our tech team scanning everywhere for their faces showing up online. So even though this was sent from a different IP address, we caught the face and immediately saw the similarity to the other video."

He pushed play. The picture stayed frozen on Asmina's face, framed by a white satin cloth, with three strings of large brown beads around her neck, her brilliant white teeth contrasting with her radiant dark skin, while that same ominous voice from the first video spoke.

This is our second message for all the enemies of America—ISIS, Al Qaeda, and all Muslim terrorists everywhere—listen up!

You treat your own women worse than animals, restricting their movements and education, forcing them to cover their bodies with hot black blankets for clothes, mutilating their genitals—you are not true men, you are nothing more than beasts.

However, when you kidnap and rape Christian girls, and subject them to such horrors, you have gone too far. For the sake of all women of the world, this murder will be on your heads.

Let me introduce you to your second victim.

Asmina's voice spoke, and like the first video, jumped between words:

Hi, I'm Asmina. I'm nineteen. I'm from the South Sudan. I'm a Muslim…I'm…in…pain…conflict…with… no…hope for survival.

Louis hadn't really gotten to speak with each of the participants much yet. He had been hoping to do that up at the camp over the two days he had committed to helping Aliyah. But he remembered reading Asmina's file, and his admiration for the young entrepreneur.

Just that morning he had finally gotten through to Asmina's older sister who lived with her in Khartoum. Her sister had been shocked, but had commented on how strong Asmina was and how anything she faced in America couldn't possibly be as bad as the civil war they'd just come through in South Sudan.

Now he'd have to call her back and tell her that yes, evil could be just as devastatingly cruel in America as it could be in Africa.

The scene changed on the screen. There was a black woman wearing a white bikini stretched out on a pile of sand. The camera moved closer, and Louis could see it was Asmina's face, still wearing her head covering and necklaces, eyes closed, her bare chest rising and falling slowly as if in a deep sleep. She looked so *vulnerable.*

The voice continued its tirade: *As I said, brutalizing your own women is one thing. But when you open fire with your Kalashnikov on our white Christian women sunbathing at the Sousse resort in Tunisia, where you killed thirty-nine tourists, you have aroused a sleeping giant. The white people of the world will no longer be your victims—we will rise up to drive you out of our nations and water the earth with your blood.*

For the victims of Sousse!

From off camera an automatic weapon opened fire, peppering Asmina's body with bullets. Her body jerked at each shot, blood spurting from her wounds. Louis had to look away and found the two women with him had done the same. Selena shuddered, eyes tightly shut. Aliyah had even covered her ears with her hands to block out the *rat-a-tat-tat* of the gun that seemed to go on forever.

We applaud those who have begun to restore the proper order of society in America with your bold acts against the cursed Mohammedans. Our time has come!

We call upon the righteous, the chosen, the white Christians of America to cleanse our land of the Islamic plague. We are ANTSA—Act Now To Save America.

Selena wrapped the sobbing Aliyah in her arms. The young Persian was babbling incoherently. Agent Durak clicked on another file, then paused and turned to the congressman.

"There's a third. Do you want to see it?" Both men glanced over at the women.

Louis shook his head dejectedly. "Maybe not. Can you just tell us who is in it?"

Durak looked down at his notes. "Muhammad Usman, from France. He was...uh...burned alive."

The pit of his stomach was wrenching in pain. He'd have an ulcer or two before this was over for sure. "Three of them, dead. How many more might die if we don't find them?" Louis wondered.

Durak nodded. "We're doing the best we can, sir." He glanced at the clock on the wall. "See what you can do with those two before everyone appears for the press conference."

The agent picked up his plastic cup and took a loud slurp of the last few drops, tossed it in a trash can, and exited the room, leaving Louis and the women drowning in their ocean of grief.

Chapter 31

Louis, his wife Selena, and Aliyah were surrounded by even more agents than they'd seen that morning, crammed into every inch of the conference room, mirroring what they saw on the television screen, where journalists both foreign and domestic were packed like sardines into the White House's East Room. The air was electric in both places, wondering how the president would respond.

The White House Press Secretary stood at the podium.

"Good evening, Ladies and Gentlemen. Before the president and his special guest of honor take the platform, we will hear a brief statement from the director of the FBI."

Louis had met the elderly director before, and knew that his slightly hunched back and use of a cane in no way impaired his brilliant mind. The director reached up and angled the microphone down towards his mouth.

"Many of you have seen a YouTube video portraying the beheading of a Muslim young man by someone claiming to be a white supremacist, this same video calls for other Americans to perpetrate acts of violence against Muslims in America.

"This is, in fact, the first in a series of videos, with at least two more discovered today, all of which carry the same basic message.

"The victims in these videos are not American citizens, but are young Muslims from various nations assembled for an international peace event. The ten Muslim and ten Christian youth participants have been missing for five days now. The FBI has been working around the clock in partnership with all other government and law enforcement agencies to find these young people.

"If you have any information regarding the missing youth, or any information concerning suspicious behavior by those who may be the white supremacists behind these videos, we ask you to contact the authorities immediately."

The FBI director ambled off stage and was replaced by the Press Secretary once again, who adjusted the microphone for the president's tall frame.

"Ladies and Gentlemen, the president of the United States."

A hush fell over the crowd as the president took the stage. Louis couldn't help send up a few words of prayer under his breath for his leader in the face of this crisis.

"My fellow Americans, one of my predecessors in this office declared a 'War on Terror.' Since then, America has taken the lead around the world in defeating the forces of violent extremism in the Middle East, in North Africa, in Central Asia, in Southeast Asia. We have allied ourselves with like-minded administrations working together with us for peace.

"Today, the 'War on Terror' has come to America. In the words of Walt Kelly, 'We have met the enemy, and he is us.' The terrorist is no longer the foreigner across the seas, or the hidden cell of hate in our midst, we have found that terrorism also hides in our own hearts.

"We Americans have a history of violence toward minorities—toward the American Indians, toward the African-American slaves, toward the Japanese-Americans forced into internment camps during World War II, and toward many other minority groups—not only those differentiated by the color of their skin, but by their beliefs, their culture, their gender, or their sexual orientation.

"Today our prejudice has reared its ugly head once again, with random attacks against Muslims across our nation. This prejudice feeds on anger and fear—anger at atrocities committed by ISIS, for instance, and fear that allowing religious freedom in America, one of our constitutional rights, could open the door to ISIS-type attacks in our land.

"Yet it is the defense of this freedom for all religions that separates our nation from those controlled by ISIS. It is the honor and justice that we show all our minority colleagues, customers and classmates that make our nation great. Hurting them will not stop ISIS; it is the equivalent of stabbing ourselves, of cutting off our own arms. Our enemies rejoice when we bleed; but they will tremble when we rise above their violent ways with the nobility of truth, peace and love.

"It is time that we stop pointing the finger at other countries, at other religions, and examine our own hearts. These scenes on the screen reveal our dark side. But they don't tell the whole story. They don't speak of the many whites who operated the 'underground railroad' for blacks escaping the horrors of slavery; or of the human barricades of Christians, Jews and atheists protecting threatened mosques after 9/11; or of the countless volunteers who every day sit beside AIDS patients and hold their hands as they take their final breaths. These glimpses of unadulterated goodness are also in the American heart.

"Today we have a choice to make. Hatred has raised its rifle and taken aim at one particular minority in our midst. Is our American value of 'Love your neighbor' strong enough to become a shield for the defenseless?

"I call upon every American in our great nation who knows a Muslim personally to go to them and pledge your support. I call upon every American city that boasts even one mosque or Muslim school to organize your citizens to stand guard and protect our neighbors' property. I call upon every American man, woman and child who lives in the blessing of an unthreatened life to consider those now hiding in fear, and to take their hands, and welcome them out into the wide open spaces of a nation of freedom for everyone, a nation that still believes that all men are created equal, with the right to life, liberty, and the pursuit of happiness."

The president's crescendo made way for a standing ovation. Louis put his arm around his wife and found both her and Aliyah in tears.

America's commander-in-chief continued, "Because the nature of this terrorism has tragically taken the lives of several international young peacemakers, the brightest and best, those who would lead us to a future of greater hope for peace, I've invited a leader I highly respect to speak now to the international community."

There was a buzz among the journalists as the president's surprise guest took the stage—a middle-aged, bearded man dressed in a suit and tie.

The president introduced him. "My fellow Americans, I give you my dear friend, the king of Jordan." The two men embraced warmly.

Louis had met the king twice at peace events. He was one of the most humble and gracious people Louis had ever known. *If the Middle East produces the best terrorists, they also produce the best peacemakers—and this guy is at the top of the list.*

But Louis knew something the journalists did not, and he knew that listening to the Jordanian leader was going to break his heart in two.

"Peace be upon you," the king began, "and peace be upon us all." He held the podium tightly with both hands, as if he needed the support. Next to Louis, Aliyah started weeping again.

"I share my heart with you today, not as a head of state, nor as a peacemaker, nor even as a Muslim leader. Today I speak to you as a father."

Louis watched the Arab man's face muscles contort, trying to keep control. The East Room was quieter than a funeral, wondering what this show of emotion could mean.

"I have endeavored to raise my children to love and respect all men, for the leading of a nation requires such a posture. For this cause, I suggested to my son that he attend the Youth for Peace Fresh Start Initiative here in America. For the past five days, I have heard nothing from him.

"Then last night, the organizers of the event informed me that my son, and his friends, had been kidnapped. This morning I learned that three Muslim youth from the group had been brutally murdered, and the authorities fear the killings may continue."

The king turned away momentarily in obvious distress. Louis noticed that the president, who was standing just behind the king's right shoulder, was biting his lower lip. Louis couldn't help the tears that began to run down his cheeks. He ignored them, focusing on the burning questions in his mind—*what if the kidnappers didn't know they had captured a prince? If they saw this report on the news, what might they do to the boy?*

And what did the king think he could gain that would be worth taking that risk?

The bearded sovereign continued. "My white Christian brothers of America, I implore you, are you not also fathers? Do you not long for your sons and daughters to enjoy their childhood, to grow into strong and beautiful youth, to fall in love, to pursue their dreams, to bear you sweet grandchildren, to redeem all the mistakes we've made and make this world a better place? On this, can we not agree, to let the children live?

"My Muslim brothers around the world, I implore you, are you not also fathers? Do you not long for your sons and daughters to enjoy their childhood, to grow into strong and beautiful youth, to fall in love, to pursue their dreams, to bear you sweet grandchildren, to redeem all the mistakes we've made and make this world a better place? On this, can we not agree, to let the children live?

"And to my son, Imam, I want to say—" the king choked and looked away, his shoulders jerking. The president reached out a hand to steady him. Louis noticed some of the journalists were fighting the tears back as well.

"My son...my precious son...if you can hear me, take heart. Show your courage to your brothers and sisters in captivity. Show your courage to your captors. Whether you live or die...this is your moment to be a champion for peace."

The king turned, his shoulders heaving again, and was instantly wrapped in the unabashed embrace of the president, who then helped him leave the stage.

The Press Secretary emerged. "Thank you for your attention. We regret there will be no opportunity for questions at this time."

Louis embraced both Selena and Aliyah, who were crying unashamedly. As he did, he reflected on the disturbing reality they faced.

What if we can't find those kids before they all die? What if the only solution rests with them alone?

Chapter 32

The afternoon passed like an impressionist dream for Sari, her flood of tears reducing her sight to blurry shapes and colors, her sobs reducing the sounds around her to indistinct noise.

She vaguely remembered Fatimah's arm around her at some point. She had asked Fatimah how she could be so strong, and the girl had answered something about doing it every day in Palestine.

She was aware of other voices crying too, and once she had heard people yelling, but she couldn't distinguish who it was, nor did she care. She was of no help to them now.

She was mourning her own guilt—for doing nothing as her friends were led like lambs to the slaughter, for not listening to Lotanna and being strong for the others, for not praying enough, and now, for being a burden to the others. Why was she even here? Surely someone better could have been chosen.

If she hadn't argued for everyone to trust the staff, maybe Lotanna and Bol could have planned an escape. Maybe her friends would still be alive.

Henry had asked for her help and she had agreed. She had helped a killer. She wasn't just a foolish girl playing at peacemaking—she was *guilty* of murder.

Stop it! Sari, you've been to that dark place and you're not going back. Would Jesus condemn you, or lift you up?

No food or water all day long wasn't helping either. She felt weak of body, mind and spirit. Vague images danced through her head: of her friend Bali coming to save her from the *jihadists* that were hiding in her home; of her adopted father Abdullah throwing himself into a burning church to save her mother; of Abdullah staggering home a bloody mess after being captured and tortured by ISIS.

They never gave up. They'd rather die than give up.

I made a decision, that I would not be afraid.

She breathed an unspoken prayer, and stirred up her courage to reengage with the world around her. Looking around, she spotted Ismail, Imam and Fatimah bowing in their *sholat* prayers. Danilo and Nandita appeared to be asleep. She could barely hear Rebecca humming a tune with her eyes closed, sitting in the corner. The others were gathered around Bol talking intensely.

The South Sudanese young man saw her watching, and with a forced smile, motioned for her to join them.

Sari crawled over to the group and squeezed in between Lotanna and Zoe.

Jolly welcomed her. "You look a little sick."

Zoe stood up for her. "She still looks much too good for you."

Sari began to apologize, "No, I'm okay. Look, I'm sorry, guys, I've been no help—"

Lotanna interrupted her. "It doesn't matter," she said gently. "We're all in this together. We'll get through it *together*." Lotanna squeezed her hand, and Sari felt the faintest trickle of strength travel up her arm and penetrate her heart.

"Guys, let's hear what Sari has to say about our dilemma," Bol suggested.

Sari was pretty sure she'd be of no help whatsoever, but she nodded.

"Here's where we're at," Bol continued. "Some of us want to take our first chance and make a run for it. But Taj here believes that whatever horrible deeds Henry is doing, he's uploading to the internet, and thinks we should disable the computer."

"That's right," Alex jumped in. "Take away his audience, there's no motivation."

"Take away his victims, there's no show," Zoe countered.

"Meanwhile," Bol said, "Ismail over there wants to lead an armed revolution. But Lotanna thinks that's a big mistake." He looked at the Nigerian girl.

"We fight force with force against someone military like Curt, we'll lose, and they might kill us all."

"Not if we take him out first," Katja argued.

Everybody started speaking at once, which was exacerbated by the arrival of Ismail, Imam and Fatimah. Eventually Bol got them to quiet down.

"Come on, everybody, you've all had a chance to speak. We haven't heard from Sari yet."

They all stared at her. Sari blinked rapidly, unsure how to say what was in her heart.

"Didn't you have some encounter with terrorists?" Lotanna prodded.

Sari breathed out deeply. She wanted to honor her adopted father, but didn't want to lead the group astray once again. She was determined this time not to say too much. "Yeah, I did. My adopted father was tasked with infiltrating a *jihad* cell and turning them non-violently."

"No way, dude, that's crazy!" Jolly scoffed.

"Did he do it?" Bol leaned forward intently.

"Yeah, sort of," she answered. "Out of seven, he turned four of them, arrested one, and two were sadly killed, but not by my father."

"How did he do it?" Bol asked.

Sari took another deep breath. Her memories of Pak Abdullah treating the bombers with dignity and kindness deserved to be shared. "He treated them as human beings, tried to understand what motivated them, and give them a stronger motivation."

"The strongest motivation is a gun to the head," Ismail interjected.

"It's a powerful motivation for that moment," Sari explained. "But as soon as the threat of death is lifted, the person's desire for vengeance, for instance, actually increases. My father tried to find motivations that would replace that vengeance permanently."

"Like what?" Fatimah asked.

"Like the honor of the family name, the desire to see your family again, a place of love and belonging—you know, the common longings of every heart that Katja shared about."

The room was quiet for a moment as Sari's words sunk in. This time they could draw their own conclusions without her opinions.

"But some couldn't be turned?" Katja asked.

"Yeah, sadly that's true. My father saw it not just as rescuing our city from terrorists, but also rescuing as many of the cell members as he could from a future filled with only death."

Nadia offered in a quiet, skeptical voice, "You want *us* to rescue the *staff*? They're…they're *murderers*!"

"I get it," Zoe nodded slowly. "Like with Jeremy the other day. You told me to get to know him, to invite him here, because you wanted him to have, what do you say, access to a place he could belong more than with the staff."

"I wasn't thinking about rescuing him at the time," Sari admitted. "I just wanted us to see him as a person, as a friend, rather than as a staff."

"We could turn Jeremy," Zoe declared. "I'm sure of it."

"That would provide us interesting options," Taj considered, "having someone on the inside."

"Anyone else we could turn?" Bol asked.

"Maybe Abagail," Fatimah suggested. No other names were mentioned.

Sari wanted to tell them that sometimes the person who looked the hardest could turn the fastest if they knew which buttons to push, but she bit her tongue.

In her heart, a still, small voice reminded her of how her overconfidence earlier had caused her to reject the wisdom of Lotanna's experience. She turned to her friend, "Lotanna, did you ever try or see someone else try to turn a captor when you were a prisoner? What happened?"

Lotanna ran her fingers through her long wavy hair. "When I was new there, one of the older captives warned me about this. She told me that if we convinced one of them to help us, that man would most likely pay for it with his life. She said that sometimes it was better to have a sympathetic advocate behind the scenes than to ask him to take a big risk and die."

"So what did you do?" Sari asked.

"We tried to always act in a non-threatening way, letting the captors feel that they were in complete control. But we also looked for opportunities to communicate that we were human beings—by calling people by their names, telling simple stories common to us all, saying 'please' and 'thank you'—some girls went too far and were brainwashed into joining the captors, but the rest of us did our best to keep our dignity and let the captors see it too."

"So you're saying we shouldn't try to turn anyone?" Bol wanted a clear answer.

"No, I'm just saying, if we turn one against the other, we could be signing their death warrant, so be careful what we ask for."

Alex looked at Ismail, "I think it'd be easier to take them down if we could turn some of them to our side."

"Takes too long," the Indonesian boy protested. "You're a Christian. You're not next in line for some horrible death."

Sari realized the truth of his statement. She could have fun building relationships, but Ismail, Imam, Fatimah, Taj and Jolly might be spending their final hours on earth. And she certainly didn't want to get Jeremy killed.

Bol had an idea. "What if we don't allow them to take anyone else out of this room? What if the next time they pick a person, the Muslims link arms around that person, and then the Christians link arms around the Muslims? I don't want to see anyone else leave this room alone no matter what they say."

Several people nodded.

"What if they threaten to kill us all?" Nadia's voice quavered.

"All for one and one for all!" Jolly raised his imaginary sword to several confused looks.

Taj said, "So far they've wanted us one by one. I think they're filming our executions. If we stick together, they will have to kill us all and their show will be over."

"We'll be over," Ismail objected.

"We're over anyway," Lotanna said. "They'll kill the Muslims one by one, but don't think for a minute they'll let the Christians go to tell the world what they've done. We've seen them all. When the last Muslim dies, there will be a mass grave waiting for us. So sooner or later, we'll all die."

"Sick bastards," Alex mumbled.

With this sobering thought, the lights went out. Everyone searched under pillows and mats until they found the candles. Fatimah still had the matches in her pocket, and lit them both. Jolly went to get the toilet tank lid to be their candelabra. They sat in silence for a while watching the dancing flames.

Eventually Bol spoke up. His voice sounded tired, even defeated. "We're all processing a lot. Maybe we should just sleep on it and make a plan in the morning," he said. "Henry said we had twenty-four hours, so at least we don't have to worry about anyone dying tonight."

The room returned to its deathly silence. Nadia had stopped whimpering. No one was cursing. Even Rebecca's humming had died. Perhaps they were all in shock. *I mean, really, how could this possibly be happening?* Sari wondered what her five Muslim friends were thinking about, knowing how little time they may have.

No one moved to put out the candles. Their flames, once a source of cheer, served only to project ghostly shadows dancing on the walls that surrounded them. It was almost as if Henry had sent them to mock the youth with images of the hell he had planned for them tomorrow.

Sari followed a few of the others as they left the circle for their mats. She lay on her side, staring at the wall, completely exhausted. She had given all she had and it wasn't nearly enough. *Whatever happens tomorrow, will I have anything left to give?*

She was tossing and turning, unable to sleep, when into the depths of their silence intruded a scraping noise and the bright beam of a flashlight.

Chapter 33

liyah was weeping on the bed, her cell phone lying where she had dropped it on the carpet.

"I can't do anymore. Please don't make me," she pleaded pathetically.

Louis and Selena had overheard her conversation with Zoe's parents, who were understandably upset and had told Aliyah exactly what they thought of her.

At this point, all the families but two had been notified. There had been a variety of responses. Louis went through the checklist in his head: two threatening to sue, three threatening bodily harm to himself and Aliyah—one of which was on a plane to Atlanta that night—one parent had collapsed and had to be taken to the hospital... Surprisingly, many of the families had been understanding, they just tended to call every hour day and night asking for news.

He had taken it upon himself to call the families of those who had died. Usman's extended family apparently was full of revolutionaries, all of which felt they should call and threaten Louis personally. Perhaps he'd remove France from any travel itineraries for the near future.

Selena was stroking Aliyah's shoulders and whispering calming words.

Louis's cell phone rang. He wondered which parent was needing assurances this time, but was surprised to see Agent Durak's name on the screen. *This late at night? Maybe a breakthrough?*

"It's the FBI," he told the women.

Aliyah wiped her tears with her head covering. "Did they find them?" The hope-against-hope etched in the Persian woman's face made him even more desperate to hear some good news.

"Agent Durak," he answered.

"Congressman. Sorry to bother you so late."

"Please, call any time. We're not sleeping much anyway. Please tell me you found them."

"That call is coming, just not today," Durak informed him. Louis frowned and shook his head 'no' for the women. Aliyah put her face back in the pillow to cry again.

"Sir, we've discovered a fourth victim posted online. I'll text you the link."

"Just tell me who."

"Yasmin Ali, Philippines. She was thrown off a building."

"My God." Louis was silent for a moment. He cleared his throat, his voice coming out a bit hoarse. "I'll notify her parents." He mouthed Yasmin's name to his wife, who shook her head. "Are you making any progress?"

"Yes, actually. The more video footage our tech guys get to examine, the more clues we have to their whereabouts. We're analyzing the background trees, grass, sky, bushes, and now we have a building, looks like it could be a barn. Our tech guys are pretty certain they're still here in this region of the country. We didn't get a complete shot of the building—the camera was on the roof tracking the girl being pushed toward the edge, then a shot of her lying on the ground about thirty feet below—but it was enough for us to put up a fleet of choppers tomorrow scanning for the layout we have so far.

"We also have an ID on the ex-military accomplice—we believe him to be Curt Jansen, thirty-three, veteran of Iraq with a medical discharge due to his PTSD. He served in the same platoon as Christenson's son. Jansen's younger brother, Jeremy, eighteen, reportedly didn't show up to high school about two weeks ago and hasn't been seen since. They're both Alabama boys, and Henry is originally from Alabama, so my bet is we find them in some backwoods hideout there."

"Did you ever find the policeman, Ted Olsen?"

"Georgia state, county and local police forces have no cop by that name currently on duty; however, a Ted Olsen did retire about ten years ago. Most likely a case of stolen identity."

188

Louis didn't feel like this was going to end any time soon.

"Please, Agent Durak, find them before another child dies."

"We're working twenty-four seven, sir. Pritz has already mobilized SWAT teams, anti-terrorist units, Special Forces, you name it, to take these dirtbags down once we find them."

"Are you sure that's the right tactic?" Louis asked skeptically. "Might that not galvanize more support for white extremists against our government? Are these the president's orders, or Agent Pritz's?"

"Unless we receive a direct order from the higher ups, this is Pritz's call as the Special Agent in Charge. Trust us, sir, we've done this before, and we'll be in and out with maximum speed and minimum bloodshed."

Louis made a note to make one more phone call. He needed to get through to the president.

"Thank you for the update, Agent Durak."

"We'll let you know when we've got them."

Louis hung up and shared the gloomy news with Selena and Aliyah. He tried to call the White House, but was informed of a four-minute time slot he could squeeze into the following morning. Dejectedly, he stretched out on the bed.

"I wish I could sleep," he mumbled, eyes closed. "Too many other parents out there who aren't sleeping tonight."

Selena took one hand off of Aliyah's shoulder and rested it on her husband's thigh. She started to sing softly, "There is a light that shines in the darkness, there is a light that shines in the darkness…"

"You singing me to sleep, honey?"

She shook her head. "You can't sleep just yet, dear."

"Why not?" he mumbled, eyes still closed.

Gently she ran her fingers along his jawline. "You have to call Yasmin's family, dear."

Louis had felt the weight of the world in peacemaking before, when he'd tried to negotiate a cease-fire in north-west India where hundreds had died; or when he'd tried to help an Indonesian peacemaker who would later become president, and nearly gotten the man assassinated; but the weight he felt crushing him now every time he picked up his cell phone surpassed all of those put together. His had always been the voice of hope—until now. His voice had become the public announcement service for the Grim Reaper.

He opened his eyes and stared at his cell phone on the desk just three feet away, willing it to suddenly explode with spontaneous combustion so he wouldn't have to make that call. But no matter how viciously he glared at it, nothing happened.

Thanks for sending your daughter to America. We threw her off a roof.

His dream, Aliyah and Jack's dream, the twenty participants' dreams—they'd been sucked into the black hole of a nightmare.

Selena was staring at him. After thirty years of marriage, he knew what every one of his wife's looks meant—this one was telling him he'd better man up and he'd better do it now.

Slowly he rolled to a sitting position, swallowed hard, and picked up his cell phone.

Chapter 34

"The candles!" Bol hissed.

Jolly knocked the candles flat on the toilet tank lid and threw a pillow on them, then he sprawled on top of the pillow. The flashlight bounced around from face to face and caught Sari right in the eyes, blinding her for a moment.

The voice behind the light spoke. "Uh…I brought you some food."

"Jeremy!" Zoe exclaimed, jumping up and heading toward the door. She took the flashlight out of his hand and pointed it up at his face. "I'm so glad you came!" Then she shone the light on the box in his arms, the word EVIAN printed on the side. "Bring it here," she directed him.

Sari felt the collective sigh of relief, and in a moment the candles were lit again just in time to see Jeremy open the box.

"I brought some bottles of water, crackers, peanut butter—the kitchen was locked, but the storeroom wasn't. I thought you might be hungry."

Bol passed the bottles around, and Katja opened the crackers and peanut butter. Sari felt bad for those who were asleep. She went to Nandita, Danilo and Rebecca, gently shook them, and told them to come get the food and water. Eventually, all three joined the group.

"Dude, you da man!" Jolly praised the American boy. Several others expressed their thanks.

Sari watched as the friendly gesture, and the sight of food and water, breathed fresh life into their group.

With a mouthful of peanut butter and crackers, Jolly continued. "You dudes should have seen this guy rescue Sari! Fearless, man! Leaping through the flames like a circus act. A regular Luke Firewalker."

"I wish I could have seen it," Zoe sighed. It looked to Sari like Jeremy blushed.

Fatimah gushed, "Oh, he was wonderful! If Sari had been burned, I couldn't live with myself. But Jeremy saved the day."

Some of the guys shook Jeremy's hand or patted him on the back. Sari smiled. *This* was the breakthrough with the staff she had been hoping for. *Maybe I wasn't completely wrong after all.*

"Thank you for saving my life," she smiled at Jeremy. "But I'm curious, why did you bring us food and water tonight?"

"Uh, I don't know, I just didn't think it was, uh, fair, you know?" the boy stammered. "That guy getting beaten, you guys getting no food, just 'cuz of an accident?"

Bol asked quietly, "Did you see Daud get beaten?"

"No, they've kept me underground all day cleaning by myself."

"But maybe you saw them bring him back inside? How did he look?"

"No, I didn't see him at all. I hope he's okay."

The group all looked at each other. Bol flickered his eyebrows at Zoe.

The French girl touched Jeremy's arm. "You've been so kind to us, it's like you're part of our group. You know, I was wondering if you could maybe take a message for us to the others at the hospital...?" She left it open.

"I could give it to Curt. They don't let me go out much. After work they lock me, and usually Larry too, in our quarters. I think maybe they're doing stuff they don't want us to know about."

"What kind of stuff?" Zoe asked innocently.

"I don't know, but my brother doesn't like it. He comes back mad a lot. He wakes up in the night screaming too. Do you think it's from the war? He's never been right since the war."

Lotanna tried to comfort Jeremy. "Seeing death can really scar a person on the inside."

"What was he like before the war?" Sari asked.

"We used to have great fun. He loved taking me fishing or hunting, or just swimming in the creek. I was just a kid, you know. I called him 'Brother Bear' and he called me 'Little Bear.' We did everything together, especially after our parents divorced. I miss those days," he sighed.

"I hope you get them back again," Zoe said. "Now, I want to make sure you know everyone's name and something funny about them." She introduced each person and made them share something humorous. Sari learned that Fatimah once got her head stuck in a bridge railing; Taj once got such a bad electric shock that not only did his hair stand straight up, but his face muscles twitched uncontrollably for nearly an hour; Danilo's mom had taught him several nonsensical words that he thought were English until he wrote them in a paper in college; Zoe as a little girl had been on a televised talent show where both she and her poodle wore pink tutus and danced—Jolly volunteered to play the poodle's part and they reenacted the whole routine; the stories got funnier and funnier and soon they were all laughing, even Ismail and Rebecca.

"See, aren't you glad you came?" Zoe elbowed Jeremy.

"My gosh, what time is it?" He looked at his watch. "I better get back before they miss me. My two-hour guard shift is over soon."

There was a collective, "Awww..." Sari could tell Bol wanted to say something, but Lotanna was shaking her head at him, and Bol remained silent.

Taj held up the Evian box. "Everyone please put your empty water bottles inside, as well as the food. We don't want Jeremy to get in trouble."

Jeremy and Zoe stood. "Thank you," she smiled warmly, holding his arm. Then she whispered something in his ear. Sari saw the boy's eyes widen.

He nodded, grabbed the box, then exited the room.

Sari noticed Lotanna mouth the words, "Thank you," to Bol, who grimaced. She turned to her friend.

"What was that about?" she whispered.

"Bol wanted to ask Jeremy for help, but it's not the time," Lotanna whispered back. "Jeremy doesn't know anything, and may not believe us. It's more important that he likes us than that he knows."

"Oh," was all Sari could think of to say.

"Don't put the candles out yet," Zoe announced, "I have a surprise for you."

Sari wondered what her devious, flirty friend was up to. In a few moments she had her answer.

The door opened again, and this time the flashlight shown on a beautiful maroon guitar.

"My baby!" Alex yelled, jumping and running to his travel companion. He was too moved to say anything to Jeremy, but Zoe took care of that.

"From all of us, thank you!" Zoe planted a kiss on Jeremy's lips.

"Ooooooo…" several people teased.

Sari couldn't see Jeremy's face, but she could imagine its bright redness as the boy turned and stumbled out the door, drunk with love.

Alex sat down and began caressing the strings. "Zoe…" He got choked up and couldn't finish. She flashed him her talent show smile and sat back in the circle.

Everyone was quiet, enjoying the soothing guitar tones. Alex seemed to be practicing a series of chords and a melody, and no one wanted to interrupt him. The chord progressions were unlike anything she'd ever heard before. She scooted over to Katja to ask about them.

"Mostly Alex plays rock music. He's very popular with the youth," Katja explained. "But he also re-recorded one of his albums in the traditional style of *Sevdalinka*, which is a kind of melancholic folk song often about sad subjects such as love and loss, the death of a dear person or heartbreak. This is a *Sevdalinka* melody."

Sari found it hauntingly beautiful, and wondered what was Alex's inspiration for this piece.

She didn't have to wait long to find out.

Alex stayed on one chord, while speaking to the group. "You know, I was thinking…Daud had a good look at that list of ISIS sins, right Katja?"

Katja nodded.

194

"When he first jumped out of his seat to take Imam's place, I thought to myself, 'That's not like Daud.' I wonder if he came to the conclusion that we all did when he read that list. I kind of think he knew exactly what he was doing. He knew what Henry and Curt were planning to do to the next person they took. He knew what they would do to him, and he knew he wasn't going to ever see us again. I mean, the way he said good-bye? He knew."

Sari thought back to Daud's breaking free of Curt's grasp to take one last mental picture of the group. She shot a glance at Imam, who had gone white as a sheet.

"This song's for Daud."

Alex's fingers flew expertly over the strings, pulling at the sadness deep in Sari's heart and giving it a voice. Then he started to sing.

Just a boy from Bethlehem
Raised with guns and war
But he chose a better path
By helping feed the poor

He tried to understand their lives
Find the courage in their pain
He put their stories on the screen
So the world won't look away

He lived a life of sacrifice
Right to the very end
Believing it an honor
Dying for a friend

Now we release him with our love
That his soul may find its rest
Of all the people that we know
His story was the best

Tears wet Sari's cheeks. She glanced at Katja, whose face was also glistening in the candlelight, and she took the girl's hand.

195

Katja reached for Nandita's hand, and she took Jolly's hand, and on around the circle until they were all holding hands in sacred silence.

Imam broke the stillness with a choked voice. "I swear to you all, if I make it home alive, the whole world shall know."

"Sing it again," Katja pleaded.

And Alex did.

DAY 6

Chapter 35

The morning master-planning session had not gone well. Too many people had divergent opinions about what to do. Ismail had still lobbied for obtaining weapons. Rebecca and Danilo, in the light of a new day, were again unsure that the others weren't over-imaginative and wanted to give the camp staff one more chance. Taj was adamant they needed to take out the computer. Only Fatimah supported Sari's idea to try and turn their captors. The most common solution was to find a way to escape.

The only thing everyone had agreed on was that no one should be allowed to leave the room alone.

The guitar safely hidden away in the bathroom, everyone sat nervously waiting Henry's arrival and what he might say about Daud.

True to his word, he didn't appear at the usual morning time slot, but waited until something like twenty-four hours after the fire incident.

The five white men and Abagail filed in as usual and stood at attention as Henry launched a new day.

"Well, well, well," he began, grinning widely. "You all look positively eager to start the day, don't they, Reverend George?" The older man soberly nodded.

"Your foolish friend of yesterday has been appropriately punished. It'll take a day or two to recover from the beating Curt gave him. But I'm willing to put that unfortunate lapse of judgment behind us." He smiled broadly again.

"In fact, I'm restoring the privileges for the three of you who have shown the good sense to join us in the staff quarters—showers, clean clothes, as much food as you can eat, and we trust, guidance from us that is stimulating both intellectually and physically. If you three would please step over here." He motioned with his hand to Rebecca, Danilo and Katja to join Abagail. Katja shot a nervous look at Bol, but joined the others.

"Would any of you other Christians like to join?" Henry waited, but again the invitation was rejected.

"No matter," he smiled. "For the rest of you, you've worked so hard this week, and it's such a beautiful day out there, I thought perhaps you'd like to go for a hike."

Sari's jaw nearly dropped through the floor. *Is he tempting us to attempt an escape?* They all looked back and forth at each other, unsure what Henry was up to.

"All of us?" Jolly asked, incredulous.

"Of course, unless someone needs to stay behind. How is our Indian princess doing?" He looked sympathetically at Nandita, who still was clearly weak.

Lotanna answered for her. "She's much better, thank you. I'm sure some fresh air and exercise would do her some good."

Sari was surprised Lotanna would force the poor girl to hike, but remembered their agreement that no one be left alone.

"All right then! I expect we'll have a memorable day. Curt, Larry and Jeremy will prepare water bottles, etcetera, and be back for you momentarily. You three," looking at Katja's group, "just follow Abagail to the showers."

Sari waved a timid good-bye to Katja, praying under her breath that she'd see her friend again.

The door remained closed for only a few moments before the three younger men reappeared and ushered them up the stairs and into the barn.

Sari surveyed the animals. All of them seemed content with their food and water. Her eyes were drawn to the hay bales upon which she had nearly been barbecued. The burnt edges had been trimmed away, and the bales restacked in a different formation. Taj must have seen her puzzled expression, because he looked up at the bales with her.

Fatimah whispered in her ear, "Remember this, not as a place of near death, but as a story of courageous rescue." Sari flashed Fatimah a weak smile.

Curt swung open the large doors and they filed out into the barnyard. Henry was right—it was a beautiful day. Sari took a deep breath of the fresh air, and let the bright blue of the sky and greens of the forest wash the anxiety from her heart.

When everyone was outside, the muscular man barked instructions.

"We'll be hiking south," he pointed towards the left of the barn door. "Everyone grab a water bottle from Jeremy's box." Immediately the box was surrounded. Sari decided to wait for everyone else, which allowed her to notice Curt talking to Jolly and pointing toward a green Army jacket hanging on a post in the garden to their right. Jolly nodded and set out for the garden.

But he wasn't the only one separated from the group. Sari noticed that Taj had also wandered off toward the garden side of the barn, but was gazing up at the structure. *Such a curious boy.*

Lotanna handed Sari a bottle of Evian, and whispered to her, "Something's not right." So many times Sari had mistakenly doubted her friend that this time she did her best to listen.

"What should we do?"

"Stay alert."

Suddenly Taj's high-pitched voice echoed across the yard. "Jolly, stop!"

Jolly slowed his pace and turned, surprised. "'Sup, dude?"

Taj screamed it this time, "FREEZE!"

Jolly stopped in his tracks, just a step shy of the ditch they'd been digging all week. Sari noticed for the first time that the ditch had been filled in. Everyone was staring at Taj and Jolly, faced off in the north barnyard grass.

Bol stepped out from the group. "Jolly, don't move! Listen to me. You need to carefully turn around and walk straight back here the way you came."

"Dude, I was just going to get that jack—" He swiveled his head toward the garden.

"NO!" Bol and Taj cried together.

Jolly started to feel scared. "Is there like a snake behind me?"

"Just walk straight back to us, now!" Bol said.

Jolly's eyes were wide with fright. He slowly pivoted and started walking back to the group. Taj also approached them, picking his way along the barn's face.

"What are you doing? I told you to get the jacket," Curt snapped.

Jolly looked from him to Taj and Bol and kept coming.

"Relax, bro, I'll get it." Jeremy started jogging toward the garden.

"NO!" Bol and Taj screamed again. Bol added, "Jolly, stop him!"

Jolly looked really confused, but stepped to block Jeremy's way. Jeremy dodged to the left.

"Grab him!" Bol shouted, and Jolly showed everyone once again his football tackling skills, bringing Jeremy down hard on the ground.

The younger boy punched the surfer angrily. "Get off me!"

But suddenly Curt was there, tossing Jolly aside like a bag of rice, and picking Jeremy up off the ground.

Jeremy tried to shake free of his brother's grip. "I could've taken him." But Curt just marched him back to the group and dumped him unceremoniously at Zoe's feet, Jeremy's face beet red.

"I'll get it myself." He turned toward the garden.

"That won't be necessary," Bol said. He pointed to a spot along the filled-in ditch farthest from them and sent his water bottle skidding toward it along the grass.

When it reached the ditch, a blinding light erupted from the ground, and a deafening blast hammered their eardrums.

Chapter 36

The hotel staff had been incredibly accommodating. Of course, a phone call from the White House, with a promise to foot the bill, was an effective motivator. One entire hallway, with its own lobby for gathering, was reserved for the families of the kidnapped youth, who had been flying in over the past twenty-four hours. Louis counted representatives of six families huddled together in the lobby around a large screen television, and he knew at least three more were on the way.

The fifth execution video had been the most macabre yet—Daud, the Palestinian boy, crucified. Louis knew the video had shaken these families to the core, and judging by their body language since, they had lost all hope. Each was waiting not for rescue, but for the last chance to see their loved one's face on television before he or she died.

Selena was a rock. He watched her holding the weeping mother of Zoe, whose eye makeup had left long black streaks down her cheeks. Aliyah was back in her room. Louis was concerned that his peacemaking partner was having a breakdown every bit as devastating as the families' around him.

His cell phone beeped, and he stepped out into the hallway and dialed the number given him at the White House.

"Hello, Louis?" the president answered.

"Mr. President, thank you for your time."

"Of course. I watched the crucifixion video. It was the single worst image I've ever seen in my life."

"Me too." The moment demanded silence, but Louis knew the clock was ticking.

"Mr. President, the FBI said they've narrowed down the search via satellite to seventy-two locations. Agent Pritz wants to hit each one with overwhelming force. I called to appeal to you that different tactics be considered."

"Go on," the president prodded.

"First of all, the world needs to see some of these hostages walk out alive. If threatened, the kidnappers may kill them all.

"Second, the kidnappers' goal seems to me to want to force America to answer Islamic violence with violence. Your administration has worked hard to change that cycle. Here's your crucible—will you respond to these brutal murders with brutality or with restraint."

The president had a reputation as a decisive man, and it didn't take him long to consider. "Negotiate with the kidnappers? The American public won't like it."

"The international community will. And at the end of the day, what people will consider a victory is the youth walking out alive. We have to make darn sure somebody survives."

"I'll have my people make the calls."

"One more thing, Mr. President, please tell them to send in a friendly, white, southern negotiator, not some uppity D.C. robot."

"Right. Give my love to Selena."

Louis paused at the doorway to the lobby. The television was covering this around the clock. All over the south crosses were popping up in yards in solidarity with the killers. Meanwhile, there had been more attacks against minorities of all types, and riots by blacks in St. Louis, Baltimore and Florida.

But the news coming from overseas was worse. The crucifixion video had mentioned Daud's ethnicity but not his religion. Now thousands of Palestinian Muslims were attacking American tourists in the holy land, and proclaiming a new *intifadah* against the Zionists and the West. Daud's parents had been trying to get a flight out of the country, but couldn't even get to the airport safely.

Selena caught Louis's eyes, silently signaling that he was needed by the parents to her left. He sighed and approached them, sitting on the sofa with their heads in their hands. He knew they were Jalil's parents from San Diego. He knelt next to Jalil's father.

"I just spoke with the president. They're doing everything they can."

Jalil's father couldn't speak. His mother wiped the tears from her round cheeks and looked pleadingly up at Louis.

"This is why we leave Iraq," she said. "This is America. Everyone get along famously. Everyone can make friends. Jolly friends with everyone. No war in America. Why? Why?" She twisted her dark blue rayon head covering in her hands like she were untying invisible knots.

"Tell me what makes your son strong," Louis encouraged.

The woman looked at her husband, who still couldn't speak, so she answered. "Jolly is boy, he very selfish. But Jolly is man, he is so kind—kind to neighbors, kind to children, kind to poor on the street. When he go surfing, he always take extra bag of my *arooq* to give food to bums of beach. Jolly is big heart. He—" She started weeping softly.

Louis put his hand on the father's shoulder. "You have a remarkable son. You have raised him well. In this terrible situation, those youth who are afraid or weak will be grateful that Jolly is there to look out for them. I have no doubt he's displaying the big heart of a hero right now."

The man muttered something in what Louis guessed was Arabic. He looked enquiringly at the woman.

"He say, 'Please, boy not die.'"

Louis's already broken heart was getting ground to fine dust. "Yes. We pray so."

He patted them both on the shoulder, then approached Alex's family. Nothing in Washington mattered to him anymore. All he could think about was the survival of these kids.

A thought struck him. *Maybe if politics were focused on the survival of our children, on the survival of the next generation, we could stop all our foolish bickering and posturing and gain some perspective.*

Chapter 37

The entire group stood rooted near the barn door, staring at the site of the blast, a shallow crater over a meter in diameter and slightly deeper than the original ditch. Jolly was visibly trembling.

Bol spoke first. "Taj, how did you know?"

The slight Indian adjusted his glasses and explained calmly, "When we were in the barn I saw Sari staring at the hay bales. I noticed they had been stacked in such a way as to create steps along the wall leading to a barricaded platform at the top.

"Once we were outside, of course we all noticed right away the ditch was filled in. Yet we hadn't seen a pipe anywhere all week. I returned to the puzzle of the hay, wondering if it might be situated around the window overlooking the garden. Sure enough, from outside I caught the sunlight bouncing off a metal object in the window, unseen from within the barn, and it all made sense."

Taj wasn't making any sense to Sari. "I still don't understand."

"A camera. There's a camera in the window, obviously to record one of us dying. Ditch...land mines...trip wire..." Taj looked from face to face.

"That was supposed to be me," Jolly hoarsely whispered.

"And it nearly killed Jeremy," Zoe said angrily, hand on the sitting boy's shoulder. "If Jolly hadn't saved him."

Larry headed for the ditch. "No, Larry!" several of them shouted. "Come back!"

"I want to see," he called back. Larry knelt down near the ditch and peered closely at it. "There's a wire just above the dirt." He walked cautiously along the freshly covered ground that encircled the barn. "Looks like it goes all the way around." Then he started back toward the group, confused. "A circle of death!

Someone made a circle of death all around us!" He jumped from foot to foot nervously. "Who would do that?"

Jeremy stood up and faced his brother. "Yeah, who would do that, Curt? You did this, didn't you? You nearly killed me!" Jeremy was livid.

Curt glared down at him. "It wasn't supposed to be for you."

"Oh yeah? Then who? Him?" He pointed at Jolly. "He's an American citizen. I thought you went to war to *defend* Americans—now you come back here and try to kill them? What has he ever done to you?"

"Shut up! You don't know what you're talking about."

"Then explain it, big brother, explain why he deserves to die." Jeremy's rage was scaring Sari, but she figured it needed to come out. Everyone's attention was riveted on the two brothers.

"We'll talk later," Curt barked.

Jeremy put his nose right up to Curt's chin. "We'll talk now. What are you hiding from me—you and Henry and George—you think I'm not man enough to know?"

Curt slapped Jeremy so fast the boy never saw it coming. Lying on the ground, Jeremy touched his mouth and saw the blood on his finger. Slowly he scrambled to his feet, standing a healthy distance from Curt this time.

"I should have never listened to you. I should have never come here. The war changed you, man." Angry tears dripped down Jeremy's cheeks. "You used to be my hero. Now you're blowing up American college kids?"

"The war never ends!" Curt retorted. "There's always an enemy."

Jeremy pointed to the youth around him. "That's your enemy? Unarmed kids? What, just because they're a different religion than you?" Jeremy spit in the dirt and turned to walk away.

Fatimah quietly interjected. "The boy he killed yesterday was a Christian."

Jeremy froze, then slowly looked back. "You killed that boy who started a fire?"

The hatred in Curt's eyes spoke for him.

"You…killed him?" Larry asked, confused. "Henry said to beat him. Henry didn't say to kill him."

"Shut up, Larry, if you know what's good for you," Curt threatened.

Jeremy started to turn away, but spun back once more and faced Taj. "Wait, you said there's a camera?" Taj nodded.

Jeremy burst past everyone into the barn and scrambled up the hay bales. Everyone followed him inside. At the top he had to navigate a narrow slit along the wall to reach the window. Seconds later he emerged holding aloft a video camera on a tripod.

"What kind of twisted, sick, perverted…!" he yelled. He snapped the camera from the tripod and sent the three-legged stand into the heart of the pig pen, eliciting several offended oinks. Then he held the camera over his head, and with an angry roar, smashed it on the barn floor.

"Big mistake," Curt snarled.

"Oh, no," Larry started rocking back and forth, "he'll be mad, he'll be really mad."

"I don't care," Jeremy replied, scrambling back down the hay bales. "I never want to see you again."

"You're not going anywhere," Curt ordered.

"Or what, you gonna kill me too?" Curt didn't move to stop Jeremy as he flung open the barn door and marched off, jumped the ditch, and disappeared into the forest.

"Oh, no," Larry was beside himself. "This is not good, not good, not good." He pulled out his knife. "You want me to stop him, Crush? I know how to make him afraid."

"Shut up, Larry, and don't tell them anything. I'll take care of it," Curt growled.

Then he barked at the rest of them, "Everyone back downstairs."

Lotanna whispered to Sari, "I agree with Larry—not good, not good, not good."

Chapter 38

Larry ran ahead of the group and was first down the stairs, chanting loudly, "Not good, not good, not good."

"Shut up, Larry!" Curt yelled from the back, but he had to wait to make sure everyone passed through the trap door before he could descend. Sari was in the middle of the group, trying hard not to be fearful about what was coming next.

At the bottom of the stairs, Larry pulled out his knife and ran along the hall scraping it against the steel wall. Everyone covered their ears at the shrieking sound. But perhaps it achieved its goal, as Henry, George and Abagail all burst into the hallway.

"What's going on?" Henry snapped.

"Did you…?" George queried of Curt.

"No," Curt admitted. He pointed at the group. "And they broke the camera."

"Beelzebub!" George swore, the eyes behind his glasses blazing.

Larry started bouncing and waving his hands. "Liar! Liar! Jeremy broke the camera. Then he ran away."

Henry glared at Curt. "Is this true?"

Curt's face showed nothing.

"Beelzebub!" George said again. "Son of the devil!"

Henry wasn't done with Curt. "You told me he could be helpful. You said he would learn our ways. Now he could ruin everything." His near-bursting blood vessels made his large nose look even bigger.

"Well, what are you still doing here?" Henry yelled. "Get that boy!"

"Then what?" Curt's eyes narrowed.

"That's not your concern. You just get that boy back here, dead or alive, soldier!"

George added, "No one who puts his hand to the plow and looks back is fit for the kingdom of God."

The two large men faced off, and Sari wondered if Curt would obey this order or not.

Henry added, "And take that idiot with you." He waved vaguely toward Larry.

"Hey, I'm not an idiot." Larry retorted. He started toward Henry angrily, but Curt grabbed a wad of Larry's shirt in his hand and jerked him toward the stairs.

Henry turned to say something to George and Sari saw her chance. As Larry passed, she softly spoke: "Larry, you're not an idiot. You're smart." He shot her a look but was stumbling to keep up with Curt.

Fatimah noticed this exchange, and stepped in front of the stairs blocking Curt's exit.

He growled, "Step aside."

Fatimah slowly pivoted, but as Curt's face passed hers, Sari heard her say, "Be gentle. Jeremy's just a lost little bear in the forest."

Two steps up, Curt turned back. "What did you say?"

Fatimah continued. "He ran from a killer, but he still hopes to find his brother."

Curt's icy blue eyes stared at her. Then he followed Larry up the stairs to hunt for Jeremy.

When the trapdoor had closed, she saw Bol whisper something to Zoe, who dramatically collapsed, screaming and writhing in pain, right at Henry's feet.

"What the—" Henry jumped.

"Oh, my stomach," Zoe moaned loudly. "I'm going to be sick." She rolled on the ground and grabbed on to George's ankle.

"Let me go!" He shook his leg.

Henry looked for help. "Abagail! And you," he pointed to Nadia, "take this girl to the bathroom. Get her some medicine. Do something! The rest of you, back to your quarters!" He made shooing motions with his hands to herd the group back into the common room, where they heard the door clang shut and the metal bolt slide into place.

Everything had happened so fast, it wasn't until Sari looked to see what Bol wanted them to do next that she realized their leader was not in the room. Neither was Taj. Or Ismail.

A sinking feeling hit her stomach. *If Ismail convinced them to go for the weapons...* She didn't want to imagine what might happen.

They weren't supposed to get separated. Now there were at least four groups of them scattered about, with no way to know if another death was imminent. Their "inside man" had abandoned them and might even be the next to die. She hugged her knees to her chest and began to pray quietly for God to protect each one, including Jeremy.

"Everyone, would you be willing to come together?" It was Imam taking leadership in Bol's absence.

Sari joined the others, their group now down to seven. They sat in a circle.

Imam cleared his throat. "Ahem. Well, if perhaps we sheltered any doubt as to the nefariousness of these pseudo-camp staff, at last we are assured of the truth. And thanks to Taj, our American brother Jolly is still in one piece."

Jolly swallowed hard, all the usual care-free spirit sucked out of him by his near death experience.

"It would seem that our sister Zoe's theatrics were a ruse for our friends to disappear. Let us hope they are not discovered."

Several people nodded agreement.

"Now here we are, incarcerated once again. Any ideas as to our most expedient use of this time?"

For a few moments no one answered. Finally Fatimah spoke up. "Can we pray together, like Sari taught me the other day?"

No one objected. There was no point in arguing about it—they all knew they needed divine intervention desperately. Fatimah asked Sari to explain it again, so she did. Then Fatimah volunteered to be the first to voice her heart's cry to her Creator. Lotanna went next. Then Nandita, Imam, Jolly and Alex each prayed—even if only a sentence or two—before Sari concluded their prayer time, and their unified chorus of "Amen" echoed around the steel room that held them captive, but that could not imprison their prayers.

When she opened her eyes, she realized that the sharp chest pains that had plagued her were gone. In their place was a quiet trust in the Almighty. She wondered if the others felt it too. As she gazed into the eyes of each one in the circle, she saw fresh strength, courage and peace.

In the midst of the incredible anger, hatred, fear and pain swirling around them, Sari felt that perhaps they had found the peaceful eye of the storm. She knew that no matter what happened next, this moment would be one she would never forget.

Chapter 39

They didn't have to wait long to be reunited with their friends. It was only a few minutes after their prayers that the door opened for Zoe and Nadia to return. Abagail stood in the doorway pointing with her finger to count heads. *Henry's figured out some of us are missing...*

Zoe begged the older woman, "Please, we could be your children. Don't let Henry kill any more of us, please!"

Abagail didn't respond, and the door bolt clanged shut once again.

"Zoe, are you okay?" Sari went straight to her friend.

"Sure, I was just acting. Bol's still out there?"

"Yeah." Zoe sat down with Sari, while Nadia squeezed in next to Imam.

"Sari, I tried to get Abagail to help us, but I don't think it was, what do you say, effectual?"

"Do you think she knew about the deaths?"

"I don't think so," the French girl frowned. "But she feels her duty is to support her husband no matter what."

"I'm not sure what she could do anyway. Boy, your acting sure fooled me! I thought you were dying!" Sari laid her hand over her heart.

"Works with my parents, my boyfriends—so why wouldn't it work on psychopaths?" Zoe joked.

" *'Boyfriends'*?"

"Not all at the same time," Zoe explained. "I just get bored quickly, that's all."

Zoe's attempt at light-heartedness had little effect on the others. It felt like they were all holding their breath, waiting for the end to come.

When the door opened next Ismail staggered in and collapsed on the floor. Sari managed to stifle her cry more successfully than Nadia and Nandita did. George pointed a long, bloody screwdriver at them and counted heads again before slamming the door.

Sari and Zoe rushed to help Ismail lie back on a mat. He was holding his thigh. Once they got him on his back, Sari could see why. His black dress pants were covered in blood still seeping from a deep cut about half-way above the knee.

"We need to stop the bleeding," she said. "We have to tie it off above the wound."

Feebly, Jolly offered, "You want my shirt?"

"Now that sounds like our Jolly," Zoe smiled kindly. "But no, ego-boy, this pillowcase will do just as well." Sari asked Alex for help to tie it tightly around the upper thigh. Then they propped Ismail's leg up on several pillows. He groaned in obvious distress.

"What happened?" Alex asked the words on everyone's minds.

Ismail twisted and grunted while he talked. "Bol and Taj went for the laptop. Taj told me where to find the screwdriver. I went for the weapons. I promised Bol I wouldn't use them to hurt anyone—I just wanted to grab some dynamite or something to blow a hole in this door so we could escape." He wiped the beads of sweat off his forehead with his sleeve. "I couldn't get the door open, though. I almost had it when George hit my head with something and I dropped the screwdriver. He picked it up and jammed it in my thigh."

"It's imperative that you receive professional care in a hospital," Imam pronounced.

"Whatever happens," Lotanna cautioned, "don't let them take him to a hospital. I've seen people recover from worse injuries. He'll have to endure a few days of pain, but we can't let him out of our sight." Ismail nodded and groaned again.

George opened the door again for Katja, Danilo and Rebecca to enter the room. After the old man had gone, they gathered around Ismail to hear the story once again.

"How do we know he's telling the truth?" Rebecca protested to the Christians.

"Shut up!" Katja rebuked her. "Don't tell me you still believe all their lies? They're killing us, girl!"

"So you say, but George warned us that…I mean, where's the proof?"

Zoe stood up. "You want evidence? Look at Jolly." The surfer was still pale and subdued. "While you were soaking in your hot tub, we all watched as Curt tried to blow Jolly's body to bits with a, what do you say, land bomb? Land mine? Taj saved his life. And George was filming it! We all saw the camera. There is no hospital, there is no Jack, there is no pizza at the mall—it's all been lies to hide their murders!"

"Then where are the bodies?" Rebecca's voice was high-pitched.

"Buried, which is where we'll all be if we don't get out of here."

"We heard Henry tell Curt to bring back Jeremy, dead or alive," added Fatimah. "He's willing to kill his own team."

"That's just an expression," Rebecca objected. "You're delusional."

"And you're the one who told Henry we took the candles, didn't you?" Katja accused the redhead. "Bitch."

Rebecca tossed her hair and stomped off, locking herself in the bathroom.

Sari shuddered. She reflected sadly that unity was like a cool breeze, bringing great refreshing one moment and slipping through your fingers the next.

"I wish we had some water," Lotanna sighed. Sari saw her concerned eyes directed at Nandita, who was getting weaker. All they'd had for two days now was the peanut butter and crackers Jeremy had smuggled in.

Alex heard her and produced a bottle of Evian. "I guess I never let go of it during the bomb blast."

Lotanna smiled gratefully and held it to Ismail's lips, then to Nandita's. She poured about half the bottle on Ismail's wound mumbling something about tetanus, then what was left she lay beside his pillow for later.

"Where are Taj and Bol?" Alex wondered. "The suspense is killing me."

Imam came to Sari and Lotanna. He stroked his beard thoughtfully. "Our potential for a hurried escape seems to have vanished," he said quietly. "It appears we must make the best of it until help arrives."

"Will anyone come?" Sari asked.

"Oh, yes, they're searching for us even now." Imam assured her. "We must keep the group together and endure with dignity."

Sari was surprised. Imam had seemed so reluctant to engage the others at first, but now he acted both confident and determined. Perhaps he was all that Nadia had claimed and more.

The door swung open and Sari saw Taj and Bol, their hands in the air, march into the room. Behind them came Henry, holding a pistol, and George.

"Sit!" Henry barked, and the two boys sat on the floor, hands still up. "All of you, sit!" Henry screamed at them, waving the pistol around the room. Sari dropped to the floor, her heart pounding.

"Count them," he ordered George, who went over the group twice. "One still missing."

Henry's eyes widened in panic. Gone was the calm, controlled demeanor Sari had wanted to trust. Henry's neck veins were bulging, his movements indecisive and jerky. He pointed his gun wildly at people around the room, finally settling on the nearest person, Bol, and demanded, "Who? Where is he?"

Imam cleared his throat and pointed at the bathroom. "Ahem. She's just using the toilet."

"Get her out here now!" Henry looked like a volcano ready to explode. Lotanna rose slowly and walked calmly to the bathroom, knocked on the door and requested Rebecca come out. It seemed to take some convincing, but the American girl emerged, stunned to see a raging bull with a gun pointed at her.

"Sit!" The two girls sat right by the bathroom door.

Henry started pacing, waving the gun around. "You wretches are ruining my schedule. Order! That's what's needed in a world of chaos."

216

"O faithless and perverse generation…" George's gravelly voice echoed.

"You imbeciles know nothing of what is at stake here. I am trying to make you famous. You will become household names. You have a chance to change the course of history. And you want to run around starting fires and breaking into locked rooms. Idiots! Morons! Cretins!"

George mumbled, "In the last days perilous times shall come. For men shall be lovers of their own selves, covetous, boasters, proud, blasphemers, disobedient to parents, unthankful, unholy—"

"Silence!" Henry roared. George's beady eyes narrowed, but he closed his mouth.

"You think you're so smart," Henry wagged his gun at Bol and Taj. "You destroyed our camera. But we still have the webcam on the laptop. Our crusade shall continue. When Curt and Larry return, another one of you will die."

Sari stole a glance over at Rebecca, but the girl's head was down, her face hidden by her red hair.

"How do our deaths further your cause?" Imam asked boldly.

Henry stopped pacing and approached Imam, glaring fiercely down at him. "Since tonight is most likely your appointment with the hereafter, I shall not disappoint your need to understand. You are visitors to the strongest nation on earth. However, America has a weak government, pandering to special interest groups, playing to the polls instead of wielding its power with purpose. We will have a second revolution!"

Their captor began pacing again, punctuating his points by jabbing his pistol at them. "The majority of Americans are white, many of them already armed. All they need is a leader with vision, one whose actions speak louder than the politicians' words. I am that leader. I will restore America to the world power that makes other nations tremble. No one will dare attack our people abroad, or invade our sovereign shores. I will be the one to accomplish this!

"And you will go to your grave bearing the satisfaction of having contributed to our nation's rebirth."

Henry gazed around the room. "The rest of you, don't get too comfortable. I may change my mind about who dies tonight. Perhaps it will be you," he pointed the gun at Taj. "Or you," he swung it around to Jolly. "Or the cripple," he pointed the pistol at Ismail. "Or you," he pointed it at Fatimah.

George flashed a creepy sneer. "Let's do the girl next."

"Oh, I know who you all are." Henry's eyes narrowed as he pointed his gun towards Imam. "Especially you. And I have very specific plans for each of you. Your disruptions will only hasten the inevitable.

"When all has been prepared, we will come for you."

George and Henry left the youth to contemplate their end.

Chapter 40

Nandita's parents had just joined the growing group in the lobby that afternoon when Louis received a text message from one of his aides in Washington instructing him to check out Fox News.

He showed the elderly Indian couple to an empty red velvet love seat, then found the remote and changed the station. There in all his punk glory was Alex's handsome face, with hair like red tongues of fire on top, shaved on the sides, and multiple rings through his ears.

"That's our son!" Alex's parents nearly fell off the sofa.

The newscaster was doing a biographical profile of the boy that included his current work with the International Multireligious Intercultural Center in Sarajevo to develop a new "peace through the arts" youth initiative, mentioned his two peace-themed albums, and played a clip from one of his recent concerts.

Louis texted his aide: *How did they get this?*

The answer came: *Don't know, but since this morning they've been running profiles on all the participants non-stop.*

Louis looked to the heavens, filled his cheeks like a trumpet player, and let the air blow out slowly over his lips. He wasn't sure whether this was positive or a disaster.

Alex's mom was crying loudly, "My baby! My baby!" she blubbered, reaching out toward the screen. Alex's dad wrapped her tightly in his long, thin arms, tears trickling down his face too.

The next profile was of Bol Hol Hol from South Sudan. It had taken Louis two days to contact one of his distant relatives, who seemed unconcerned about the plight of his cousin. The newscaster only had a grainy photo of a dirty gray-shirted teenager on a run-down playground, backed by colorful graffiti, looking unhappily at the camera.

The announcer explained: *Bol's story began like any other poor kid in South Sudan. His entire family was killed by Sudanese troops when he was in junior high school. He had to live on the streets, but somehow found a way to finish high school and enroll in college as a Psychology major. To pay his tuition, he wrote and published comic books about the life of the youth in Sudan. His comic books became quite popular, making him a voice for his generation. This earned him a scholarship to study for his Master's Degree in Diplomacy in Peace and Development at the University of Juba, where his research project has been on rebuilding communities post-genocide. You can see a sample of his comics at his blog: www.theregenerates.com.*

Now this street-smart survivor faces his toughest challenge yet—will he make it through the ANTSA gauntlet of death?

Louis found the newscaster's conclusion distasteful, something more appropriate for the dystopian movie *The Hunger Games* than for reality.

He blinked his eyes several times. The strain of hardly sleeping for four days was getting to him. His back ached, his feet ached, his head ached. An envious thought flickered past his consciousness of his wife now taking a nap back in their room. But every time he'd lain on the bed, he'd done nothing but toss and turn. When this was over, he'd have to take a week off just to catch up on sleep.

When this was over...

The newscaster had segued to the social media reporter—what looked like a teenage girl with an iPad and a perky disposition.

Here's what's trending today—it's all about the Peaceniks! Those international youth held captive somewhere in America have taken captive the attention of the world. Their Facebook pages are exploding with comments. Jalil Saibi, the surfer from San Diego, leads the pack with over nine million likes. Their blogs and Instagram accounts are also flooded with curiosity-seekers and well-wishers. The Bosnian rock star, Aleksander Lukic, we've been told, has one English song on his new album, entitled "Crumbling Walls," and it's now up to number six on iTunes downloads today. Whatever message these youth hoped to get across, the world is

220

hearing it now! Join the conversation at #Peaceniks, #OneWorldOnePeace, #StopTheHate, and #SetOurGenerationFree.

Louis was stunned. Aliyah had showed him some of the musings on these youths' websites, words that held such maturity, understanding and hope that they had been chosen to represent their nations. Through this tragedy they had been given a platform of unprecedented influence. Alive or dead, their voices were being heard.

Alex's mom mumbled through her tears, "They're listening to his song!"

The lead news anchor took over: *Flags are flying at half-mast today for the five victims so far from the youth peace event...*

Nandita's father interrupted Louis's thoughts. "Excuse me, what's the latest update?"

Just then the Fox News reporter mentioned the president's name, distracting Louis. "Just a moment," he told the stooped, burdened man. He pointed to the screen.

...an interfaith prayer vigil tonight at nine p.m. Eastern Standard Time at the White House for the safe release of the survivors of the Youth for Peace Fresh Start Initiative. He has also encouraged every city hall and state capitol building to hold similar vigils.

The death toll from prejudice-related attacks across America has now grown to one thousand, two hundred and forty-one victims, with those injured...

Louis turned away from the television to Nandita's father. "Forgive me, sir, you asked for the most recent update. At noon the FBI told me they had completed half their searches of suspected sites without finding the kids. They believe it is only a matter of hours now."

"And what will the FBI do when they find them?" The old man's aged brow added more wrinkles between the wrinkles.

"The president has instructed them to negotiate rather than engage with force. The primary goal is to bring home as many of the youth alive as possible."

Nandita's father scratched the last vestiges of white hair ringing the sides of his bald head. "Our daughter has not always handled stress well," he shared. "We're not just concerned for her being murdered, but also for her physical health."

Louis gently put his hand on the frail man's shoulder. "The FBI has assured us that they'll have emergency medical personnel with them at every site they search. They're doing all they can for our kids."

The Indian man nodded solemnly and slowly made his way back to the love seat to share Louis's words with his wife. The congressman surveyed the room. They were up to ten families at the hotel, though only eight were here in the room at the moment, including the family of Yasmin. The wealthy Filipinos had arrived with a lawyer threatening to sue, but after Louis introduced them to all the other parents, they had found a seat next to Jalil's family watching the news and hadn't made a peep since.

Only a few more hours till they would be found. But that would begin the most difficult task of all—negotiating their freedom from murderous zealots.

On the one hand, Louis couldn't wait; on the other hand, he desperately dreaded what that confrontation might bring.

Suddenly Aliyah burst into the room waving her cell phone. "Look at this!" she shouted. "It's not much, but maybe…?"

Louis examined the two lines of text. "Maybe…" he answered, the slightest flicker of hope teasing his broken heart.

Chapter 41

Once again no lunch came, but it was doubtful to Sari that anyone felt like eating anyway. There was a palpable gloom in the room. They had tried everything they could think of to change their situation, but if anything, they had exacerbated it.

And another one of them was about to die.

After Henry and George had left, Bol and Taj shared how they'd tried to get to the computer, but Henry was using it. Bol had yelled and set off running down the hallway to distract him so Taj might slip in, but Henry had pulled the pistol from a desk drawer and caught them both. The unusual sag in Bol's shoulders showed how defeated he felt.

Katja had also made an attempt at the laptop earlier when Larry had called George and Henry out into the hallway. But once at the keyboard, she was so panicked it took her too long to locate Aliyah's or Jack's emails. Finally she found Aliyah's and began to type: HELP! UNDER OLD RED BARN, GARDEN, WELL— She'd heard footsteps in the hall and quickly hit SEND, closed her gmail, and scrambled to find a piece of paper and pen that she told Henry she needed to take notes on what George was teaching.

Sari hoped Katja's message got through, and that it helped someone find them soon, because time was running out.

She stretched her arms above her head, then swung them back and forth to loosen up her back. How she hated these four steel walls. She missed the crowded, polluted, noisy streets of the Kelayan district in her home town of Banjarmasin. Kelayan was filled with beggars, prostitutes, thieves, drug dealers, and more than a few murderers. But it also boasted many wonderful people, both Muslims and Christians, who were just trying to live honorable lives, provide for their families, and hope for a better future for their children.

There had been a time when she saw the world as either part of her Christian group, or outside her group. But after everything that had happened over the past three years, and especially after this youth camp, she had come to the conclusion that anyone could claim to be a member of any religion, those labels really meant absolutely nothing. Muslims killed Christians and Christians killed Muslims; while other Muslims loved Christians and Christians loved Muslims. Using religious labels could lead to negative prejudice or positive expectations that may not be met. The only way to ascribe "goodness" to anyone required getting to know them first as individuals.

She surveyed the room. Lotanna, her Nigerian Christian friend, was tending to the wounded leg of Ismail, her Muslim Indonesian compatriot. Meanwhile, Fatimah, her Palestinian Muslim friend, was giving water to Nandita, her Christian friend from India. They had lived this week together, laughed together and endured suffering together. Perhaps it was only fitting that they die together.

With curiosity she watched Imam making the rounds, speaking for a few moments privately with each person. She wondered what he was saying. Eventually he reached Sari and knelt on her mat.

"Sari, am I disturbing you?"

She smiled warmly. "Of course not. What is it?"

"I wanted to thank you for your unique contributions to our group. Both your innate trust in humankind and your leadership in praying together have been an inspiration to me personally, and I trust to others. I believe there is significantly more I could glean from you. However, I may not receive that privilege; thus, I wanted to express my feelings before it is too late."

Sari started to thank him, but the implication of what he was saying caused her to abruptly clamp her mouth closed. Her eyes moistened, and she reached out to lightly touch the back of his hand.

"I wish you all the best." Imam nodded, then moved on to Jolly, who was uncharacteristically subdued, lying on his side on the next mat over.

Zoe returned from the bathroom with Alex's guitar and asked if he would sing. He took it and began to pick a doleful melody.

Lotanna came to sit beside her.

"How's Ismail?" Sari asked.

"Feels to me like he has a fever. Could be an infection; hopefully not tetanus. He really needs medical help soon." Lotanna looked deeply into Sari's eyes. "How are you doing?"

Sari wasn't sure how to answer. "I think I'm still struggling to believe this is real. It feels like a dream…" She didn't know how to continue.

"I remember that feeling in the Sambisa Forest. The older ones forced us to bathe, comb our hair with sticks, and chew on green willow twigs until they were frayed enough to brush our teeth. At first we couldn't understand why—we'd likely be dead or rescued any day. But I learned from those women that you have to live each moment like you have a future, or soon you won't."

Sari took a deep breath. "Are you telling me I need to do something?"

"Yes. Sari, I see the strength in you. Find someone who needs it and go pass it on."

Sari glanced around the room again. It looked like everybody needed encouraging. The task was too great for her, a voice inside was saying. But another contradicted it: *Just do something.*

Her eyes fell on Rebecca, in her familiar corner, red hair covering her face. Rebecca's attitude had at first surprised, then annoyed her. But she looked different now. She looked *broken.*

Sari gave Lotanna the slightest of smiles, and went to sit by Rebecca.

"Becky?" she touched the girl on the arm but got no response.

"You want to talk?" Again no answer.

Sari had no idea what to say. She heard a cry across the room and looked up. Imam was kneeling in front of Nadia, who had thrown her arms around his neck and was sobbing.

Imam is preparing to die, while Lotanna wants me to prepare to live.

She began stroking Rebecca's soft red hair. She could still smell the shampoo—was it coconut and apricot?—from this

225

morning. With her other hand she touched her own filthy matted black hair.

"Hey, when we get out of here, we should go straight to the salon! I want to get my hair cut like yours, it's sooooo beautiful."

She kept stroking, hoping for a response, but seemingly in vain.

"You know, any time you like, I'd love to have you come visit me in Indonesia, and share about the children you teach."

A mumble from under the wall of hair: "You heard Lotanna. We're all gonna die."

"But don't you believe in miracles?"

The American girl didn't answer. Sari stroked her hair some more.

"Can I pray for you?"

She took the absence of a rejection to be acceptance and began to pray softly, for peace, forgiveness, strength, courage and hope to fill her friend's heart.

When she finished, Rebecca's head lifted slightly, allowing her hair to part just enough for Sari to get a glimpse behind the curtain. The girl's eyes were red and puffy, with a haunted look, but they met Sari's eyes and held her gaze for a moment. Rebecca's lips formed a silent "Sorry," then the girl lowered her head and returned to her self-made prison.

Sari kissed the top of Rebecca's head and ambled over to check on Zoe. She wasn't sure if Rebecca felt any better, but she would follow Lotanna's lead and keep *living*.

Chapter 42

There was a lull, for maybe an hour or so, when most of the youth returned to their own mats as though it was where they belonged. Some were lost in their own thoughts. Others wept quietly. Some stretched out on their mats, but no one slept. Sari thought about trying to encourage others, but didn't want to intrude. Besides, there were too many thoughts swirling around in her brain demanding her attention too.

What if it's not just one of us who is about to die? What if, as Lotanna claims, the clock is ticking for all of us?

She thought about Pak Abdullah back in Indonesia. She'd never get to tell her adopted father this story, never even get to say good-bye. Twice now someone she loved had died and left her behind. This time she'd be leaving him to face the pain of loss once again.

Oh, how she wished she had a pen and paper to write a final message for him! Or a phone to hear his voice one last time. What would she say? *Thank you. I love you.* There were no words capable of expressing how much he meant to her anyway.

She thought about her dreams—of studying abroad, of opening a home for child victims of religious conflicts, of marrying and having a family of her own—what if this was the end and none of those dreams would come true. Was there even any purpose in living without dreams?

So many emotions battled inside her. She realized that the only way she would get through the next few hours or days was by choosing to focus on just one thing.

Help me, Jesus!

She tried to still the storm inside her and *listen.*

After a few moments, it came, in the form of her mother's voice: *"...as long as you love well."*

227

She prayed it back to God, yielding herself to His ocean of love.

A loud bang on the door jolted Sari from her quiet place and she opened her eyes expecting to see Henry, but it was Alex.

"C'mon, there has to be way out of here!" he yelled and smashed his fist against the steel door again. "Bol, Jolly, help me! I'm sick of waiting around just to die."

"We've been over the whole room," Bol shook his head dejectedly.

"Then let's go over it again!" Alex prodded. "Maybe we missed something."

"I've been over every inch of this room several times in my mind," Taj interjected calmly. "The only way out is through that door."

Alex didn't seem to want to accept Taj's verdict, pounding the door once more before approaching Bol.

"If that's the only way out, we have to jump them the next time they open it."

"You want us to fight our way out?" Katja asked skeptically.

"If someone has to die, better them than us."

Imam cleared his throat. "Ahem. Resorting to us-versus-them violence is exactly what Henry is promoting and we are supposed to be standing against. This test will reveal whether our belief in non-violence is real."

"Then what do you think we should do?" Alex retorted.

"Die with dignity," the bearded Jordanian answered.

Nadia's crying intensified. Sari left her mat to go put her arm around her friend.

"C'mon, Bol," Alex urged. "We can't just roll over and die. We've got to do something."

Bol scratched his chin. "All right, everyone, let's sit in a circle. Right here, around Ismail." Slowly each person moved to a position near Ismail. It looked to Sari as though her Indonesian friend was locked in his own private room of physical pain. She wasn't sure he could even hear them, but it felt right to keep him in the circle. They waited for Bol to begin.

228

"We're facing a seemingly impossible situation here," their Sudanese leader summarized. "We can't get out of this room without help, the only member of the staff likely to help us has run off, even if we could overpower the staff—which is doubtful— most of us are unwilling to attempt it, and we are now all completely convinced that Henry's agenda here is to kill us." He glanced at Rebecca and Danilo. "For the last few days I've tried to lead you in understanding our situation and finding solutions. Well, I've failed. I've got nothing. I'm open to whatever any of you has to say."

No one spoke. The gloom was palpable. Sari wondered if the dying process had already begun even before whatever Henry had planned.

Jolly spoke up, but in a wavering voice unlike Sari had ever heard from him. "Hey, guys, I don't have any ideas what to do. But I wanted to say that if I had known what was going on here, I wouldn't have been joking around. I had no idea my country had this kind of sick…I don't know what I'm saying. I just wish I'd…done more with my life, you know?" It looked like he had more to say but he stopped.

"Thanks, Jolly. Someone else?" Bol asked.

Nandita's faint voice spoke up. "I just want to say thank you for taking care of me." She looked at each of the girls especially. "And thanks for being my friends. I'm so grateful."

The room fell silent again. Bol started calling names.

"How about you, Katja?"

"This sucks. We don't deserve this. Alex, if you decide to jump Henry, I'm with you."

"Danilo?"

The Filipino boy shook his head.

"Taj?"

"I see no options for us at present except to be vigilant. Our captors do have weaknesses, which may present us with opportunities. We should be ready."

"Zoe?"

"I don't have any ideas, but I, too, am grateful for all of you. From you, I have learned a, what do you say, deepness, that I've

never experienced with my friends in Paris. And I'm not ready to
give up hope. Anything can happen."

"Rebecca?"

The girl's swollen eyes revealed she'd spent most of the day
crying. She looked at the floor. "I'm sorry. That's all."

Bol paused before calling the next name. "Lotanna?"

The captivity survivor spoke with strength and authority.
"Some of us may die, but some of us may get out of here alive—"

"I thought you said we were all going to die," Danilo
interrupted.

"Henry's plan is undoubtedly to kill us all," Lotanna
continued. "But things don't always go according to plan. For
those who will die, do it as you lived, with honor. For those who
survive, never give in to the desire for revenge. Do your best to
contact each of our families and tell them what happened here. Tell
them that in our last moments we were thinking of them and that
our lives stood for something greater, for peace. Promise me this!"
She gazed intently at each face around the circle.

"Yes!" interjected Imam. "If I can't tell Daud's story, one of
you must ensure its proclamation."

Sari watched as heads nodded solemnly.

"Anything else, Imam?"

"After what Daud has done, I would rather die than use
violence to escape, or have others use violence to try and save me.
I hope I am clear on this."

Imam looked pleadingly at Alex, who looked down. Bol
answered for everyone. "We understand."

He continued, "Fatimah?"

Her Palestinian friend looked so calm to Sari, just like the first
day they met.

"This is the world many people deal with every day, in
Palestine, in other places. Some people die, and others live. I
expect I'll die soon. But for those of you who live, don't let our
deaths be in vain. Whether you live or die, let the best you be seen
even by your enemies. That's the you that will inspire those who
live to give everything for peace."

"Nadia?"

Through sniffing and tears, the blond Jordanian girl whispered, "I don't want to die. And I...don't want any of you...to die either." She buried her head in her hands. Sari stroked her hair.

She knew she would be the last to speak. Oh, how she longed for words of comfort to flow from her for each of these precious people she'd come to care for so deeply. *What should I say?*

Bol looked from the weeping Nadia to Sari.

"Sari?"

She felt love swell up within her for everyone in this circle of life. Death would have to wait.

As she opened her mouth to speak the scraping of the opening door jerked them back to harsh reality.

It seemed Death was impatient to claim its next victim.

Chapter 43

"**F**ear God, and give glory to him; for the hour of his judgment is come!" George's raspy voice pronounced as he entered the room. Following George and Abagail were Larry, Curt and Jeremy, with Henry bringing up the rear.

Curt set down the small table he was carrying, and George placed upon it the laptop. Then as was their custom, they stood at attention across the front of the room facing the seated youth.

Jeremy was red-faced and refused to meet the eyes of the youth. He kept his glowering directed at Henry.

Abagail was also looking at Henry, but there was no life evident in those sunken eyes.

Larry's eyes flitted wildly around the room, but kept returning to George with an odd expression Sari couldn't read. He was more nervous than she'd ever seen him. And she could see his fingers twitching over the knife hilt protruding from his belt.

George's body movements were jerky, his jaw clenched, his eyes burning with intensity.

In contrast to those two, Curt looked icy calm. It dawned on Sari why Henry had waited for him to return—*he's the executioner.*

And Henry, well, the large man was rubbing his hands together in excited anticipation, his eyes dancing with delight. *If he'd worn a red suit and beard, he could have passed for Santa Claus passing out presents to children.* Sari shuddered at the thought.

"Good afternoon! The moment of truth is upon us—the moment when the die is cast. Who will die, and who will live?" He took a moment to make eye contact with each of the youth.

"This will be our most dramatic demonstration yet, for today we have a live audience. Reverend George, make sure the webcam can pick up the reactions of the other kids in the background."

"Only with thine eyes shalt thou behold and see the reward of the wicked," George rumbled ominously.

"You all are a privileged group, for few Americans ever get to see up close what you will witness today. This device is a particularly ingenious testament to the perversity of the Mohammedans. I tip my hat to your people." Henry mimed lifting the brim of a hat in the direction of Ismail.

"Curt, go arm the collar," the big man ordered, tossing a set of keys to his lieutenant.

"The collar," George echoed gleefully. Curt roughly pushed Jeremy ahead of him out the exit.

Sari had no idea what the collar was, nor did she want to find out.

Henry's face softened momentarily. "Rebecca, Danilo, Katja—what is about to happen could cause you some distress, although it serves both as justice against our enemies and a necessary shock to our culture of passivity. Would you like to wait inside the bathroom so you don't have to see this?"

"I'll stick with my friends," Katja said boldly. "Becky, Danny, do what you want."

"Me too," Danilo choked out the words. Rebecca nodded and stayed put.

Henry shook his head sadly and shrugged. "These," he pointed to the Muslims, "are not your friends. You will learn this in time."

"While we wait," he continued congenially, "I think it is fitting that you should know that your sacrifices have not been in vain. The desired effect of our endeavors here has been achieved. America is in chaos. Christians are hunting Muslims, blacks and whites are fighting in the streets, the homosexuals are back hiding in their closets—and our pretentious, pathetic president sits powerless in his Oval Office. Soon the good citizens of this country will succeed in cleansing our land and restoring our nation's original greatness. All this will happen in just a few short days. The Reverend George has foreseen it."

Next to her, Fatimah hissed to Sari without moving her lips, "Sounds just like my delusional uncle."

George intoned dramatically, "I have surely seen the affliction of my people and have heard their cries. I have come down to deliver them from the cursed Egyptians and all those who profane my name."

Imam cleared his throat and spoke confidently, "Ahem. There is a flaw in your logic, namely your lack of historical awareness of the psychology of your own people."

Everyone turned to look at the bearded Jordanian. *Was he trying to pick a fight? Or trying to make sure he was the one chosen next to die?*

"Please, enlighten me," Henry smirked.

"As a nation, it is true that the white majority has a history of oppressing minorities. However, each succeeding generation from the Pilgrims to Thomas Jefferson to Abraham Lincoln to Martin Luther King Jr. to this generation has clamored for *more* freedom, not *less*, and this generation is also looking for a subsequent hero. You, sir, have positioned yourself in such a way as to make it impossible for you to become that hero."

Henry snorted. "You impudent imbecile! Presuming to understand *my* nation, *my* chosen race, with your inferior mind? You have just signed your own death certificate!"

"But you told me we could kill the girl," George protested.

"Him first," Henry pointed at Imam. "After that pathetic begging we saw from the White House—the whole world will pay attention to us after his death. You can do what you will with the girl tomorrow."

The White House? Sari's head was spinning.

George grinned wickedly at Fatimah. "Oh, the plans that I have for you..." Sari watched the Palestinian girl raise her chin and stare right back at him, not showing the slightest fear.

Larry's brow was furrowed, and he began dancing from foot to foot. He cocked his head at George. "What are you going to do to her?"

"That's none of your concern." George turned his back on Larry, but Larry wasn't finished.

"Are you going to strip her naked?" he asked.

George turned back to glare at him. "What are you talking about?"

Larry hopped faster. "Crush said you stripped that black girl naked before you killed her."

"Crush is a liar," George retorted.

"Shut that idiot up!" Henry barked.

"I'm not an idiot!" Larry yelled at Henry, then turned back to George. "Is Crush a liar, or are you a liar?"

"You want me to lock you in the closet?" George's eyes narrowed as he stepped menacingly toward Larry.

Sari saw a tremble pass through Larry's shoulders, but he didn't back down. He whipped out his knife and put it to George's throat. Henry jumped back from them.

"Tell me the truth!" Larry screamed.

"Henry, help me!" George choked out.

Larry pressed the tip of the blade against George's neck, drawing blood. "What did you do to the girl?" he demanded.

Sari could see beads of sweat form above George's glasses. The old man stuttered, "It was nothing. She was drugged. I just changed her clothes, that's all."

Shivers ran down Sari's spine. She didn't know what the men had done to Asmina, Yasmin, and the two boys before Daud, but she got the horrible impression that it was something awful. To her right she heard Nadia crying.

"Crush told the truth, you liar!" Larry's feet were really dancing now. "You've always lied to me about girls, haven't you? They're not evil. You like them. You want them."

"Henry…?" George sputtered, terror in his eyes.

"I told you not to bring your idiot project here," Henry shrugged.

"I AM NOT AN IDIOT!" Larry screamed at Henry, then lowered his chin to look eye to eye with George.

"See, today I figured it out. I'm smart. Songbird said so. And I figured it out. You told me the closet would protect me from the seductress. But I'm not an idiot. You didn't want me to see what you were doing with those girls. YOU are the seductress! No, you are the snake in the garden. You said, 'the serpent seduced the woman.' And God cursed the serpent. That means he cursed you."

Larry was leaning harder on the knife handle, and George's blood was steadily dripping down his white collar shirt. The reverend mustered all his courage to wrest control back from his crazed protégé.

"I took you in, orphan boy! I taught you everything you know! You owe me your life!" George screeched.

At that moment the door scraped open. Startled, Larry turned his head. George grabbed Larry's arm and shoved the knife back at Larry, stabbing him in the stomach.

Larry's feet stopped fidgeting. He stared down at the hilt of the blade protruding from his abdomen, his face contorted in pain. Then he raised his eyes to George's face. "I was right," he said calmly this time. "I'm smart. You're the snake."

He slowly forced the blade out of his heavily bleeding wound in spite of the weight of George's whole body pushing desperately to stop him. Then, with the reverend's hands still gripping his right hand on the hilt, he brought the knife back up toward George's throat.

The old man strained and groaned in his attempt to keep the blade away. At about a finger's distance from his throat, the knife progressed no further, and trembling, George looked up from it to meet Larry's glassy gaze.

In the blink of an eye Larry's left hand came up behind George's head and thumped the old man's neck down on the blade.

George was bent over, head resting on Larry's chest, bleeding like a firehose and choking on his own blood. Above his bald head, Larry glared at Henry. With blood bubbling from his lips, he said his final words.

"I'm not...an idiot. And you...are not as...smart...as you think."

With that, his eyelids fluttered and he leaned forward into George until they both toppled to the floor, connected in death by Larry's knife.

236

Chapter 44

Sari's hand leapt to her mouth to prevent a scream. Her heart was pounding like the *rabbana* drums her neighborhood used to celebrate Muhammad's birth.

The grisly sight before her affected the others too. Abagail turned away, as did several of Sari's friends. Nadia's crying was bordering on hysterical. Imam wrapped her in his arms and whispered something in her ear. Katja was swearing quietly.

But her eyes quickly returned to Henry. The large man's brow was furrowed, lips frowning at the bodies lying at his feet. "Complications," he muttered, shaking his head. He stepped around their bodies and touched the laptop's keyboard.

"The show must go on," he mumbled. There was silence in the steel cage while he searched with trembling hands for what he wanted. Then he moved the table back against the wall and spun the laptop around to face them all.

"We are now recording," Henry announced, straightening his back, seeking his place of calm control once again.

Imam interrupted. "Wouldn't it be more appropriate to bury your friends first? At least I assume they were your friends. Will you not honor their deaths?"

Imam's interference pushed Henry back over the edge. His nose practically radiated his face was so red with anger.

"I am in control here!" he raged. "We will follow *my* plan! What I have—"

Now Bol interrupted. "But if you don't show any concern for your own people, why should the others follow you? Why should anyone follow you?"

"Silence!" Henry thundered. "Today we take revenge for what ISIS has done. Seven men accused of helping the Americans had a collar like this," he pointed to the explosive collar in Curt's hand, "wrapped around their necks. Then the Muslims detonated it, severing the heads from the bodies. Today, America will take a stand against such barbarianism by subjecting one of Islam's own people to the same fate."

The obscene hatred, the unadulterated evil in Henry's face terrified Sari more than looking at the bomb. How had she trusted this man? She remembered her adopted father's experience trying to turn the *jihad* cell in her city—"Not everyone can be saved; some will only be stopped by death."

Then she remembered something else he had taught her: "There is always a 'why'."

She had not the least ounce of courage inside her, but the words came out of her mouth before she could take them back: "Is this how your son died?"

Henry stared at her. Abagail turned around to see who had encroached on such a personal issue.

"Who told you I have a son?" Henry rasped as though the wind had been knocked out of him.

Sari avoided looking at Abagail. The elderly woman had told Sari stories of when their boy was young, but nothing about his death. She was really sticking out her neck here, and she knew it.

"Was he killed in the war?" she asked gently.

Henry ran his hand quickly over his face. "Fine, you want to know? *They* killed him." He pointed at Imam, "And our precious government wouldn't even let us bring the body home for a decent burial. Do you know why? They don't care. They *want* our young men to die. Then they can get a bigger budget from Congress and fatten some politicians' and contractors' pockets. They don't fight to win—they fight to keep the money flowing.

"And if someone doesn't land a fatal blow and put a stop to this war, my son has died in vain."

Sari risked a quick glance at Abagail, who had tears streaming down her cheeks.

Imam jumped in. "Ahem. Sir, I am sorry for your loss, and the injustice with which—"

"SHUT UP!" Henry roared. "You think I want more *words*? Words don't change what happened. Only *actions* can do that.

238

Only purposeful, intentional, radical *actions*. YOU WILL NOT deter me from my course!

"And today you will suffer what my son suffered. Bring him here!" He looked at Curt while pointing to Imam. The Jordanian man slowly rose and willingly walked forward before Curt reached him. Imam looked completely calm, as though that afternoon he had already made his peace with death.

As he reached the front of the room, he nodded to Henry. "May I be permitted a few last words?"

Henry looked at the laptop. Satisfied it was still recording and that Imam was well inside the picture frame, he agreed. "One minute."

Imam looked around the room and offered a brave smile. "My friends, all of us here," he waved his arm to include both his fellow peace participants and the American staff, "have lost something, or someone we care about because of war, prejudice and hate. But for those with eyes to see, like Daud had, we have gained something greater, we have gained *someones* greater. I end this week a richer man than when I started. The true legacy of peace is friendship. It is my honor to die with such as you."

He turned back to Henry. "I am ready."

Nadia began wailing, "Noooooo…"

Curt brought forward the explosive collar.

Sari turned her head away, too horrified to watch.

Chapter 45

The hotel restaurant had an extensive menu, something that normally would have tempted Louis to overeat, but frankly, he didn't even want to be here. Selena had coerced her husband and Aliyah and Jack to leave the television screen and mourning parents behind to eat some dinner. In the end, he'd closed the menu with a sigh, and his wife had ordered asparagus soup for him.

Louis flashed back to the last time he'd eaten out with both Aliyah and Jack. Just a week before the international participants were scheduled to arrive, he'd taken them to one of his favorite places, the 1789 restaurant near Georgetown. The Federal-era building and colonial antiques had sparked a spirited conversation about why immigrants found the New World of America so attractive, from the pilgrims to the present day. Aliyah had shared about her parents' immigration from Iran during the rise of Ayatollah Khomeini. Though famous for his quote, "America is the great Satan," her parents became convinced that their chances of a peaceful, prosperous life would be better as Muslims in America than as moderates in their own home town. In spite of a few occasions of persecution over the years, their decision had proved correct, and Aliyah was raised with a tremendous appreciation for the freedom of worship upheld in her country of birth.

Now this same young woman, who barely two weeks ago was bubbling over with visions of world peace, looked but a shell of that enthusiast. She picked at her tandoori chicken and rice with her fork, but never managed to lift it all the way to her mouth.

Jack was the only one getting his money's worth out of the meal, having eaten very little the past few days.

"The FBI will let us know when they find them, right?" he asked Louis, who nodded.

"With those clues from the email, it could be any time now, right?" Jack asked again.

"They should be narrowing in on the site any moment," Louis nodded again, glancing out the window at the approaching sunset. "I'm sure there are thousands of sites with a barn, garden and well in this region, but if they can trace the email it should narrow those down fast. However, once they find the location, negotiating with the extremists could make for a long night ahead."

"Those poor kids," Jack sympathized as he stabbed another bite of steak. "I hope they're getting enough to eat."

That'll be the least of their worries.

"Eat your soup, dear," Selena prodded. Louis took another spoonful. They hadn't let Jack watch the internet videos of the executions. Louis had finally watched all five, and dreaded number six more than his own death.

"You, too, Aliyah," Selena cajoled, "please try to eat at least a little bit. You need your strength for what's to come." Aliyah made a pretense of lifting the fork near her mouth, but it returned to the plate still carrying its cargo.

"What's to come…" the young Persian echoed. "What's to come for me is going home. I'm so sorry, but when this is over, I want to go help my parents with their tax consulting business. I just can't do peacemaking anymore."

"But what about our plans for the internship at Georgetown this fall?" Jack asked. "You're the coordinator—we can't do it without you."

"You can lead it, Jack. I just don't have the heart for it anymore."

Selena put down her fork and put her arm around Aliyah. "You do whatever you need to do, right, honey?" She glanced at her husband.

"Absolutely," Louis agreed. "Being near family sounds like the best thing for you. You've already accomplished so much, it's time others stood on your shoulders."

Aliyah began to cry softly into her napkin. Selena wrapped her arms around the woman. Louis and Jack exchanged glances, then Jack went back to his steak and potatoes.

After Aliyah had wiped her eyes and taken a sip of water, Jack started a new topic. "Are you guys going to the prayer vigil at City Hall tonight?"

Louis looked at Selena and knew her answer. "I think we'll stay here with the parents tonight. But you go ahead, we'll be joining you in spirit."

"How about you, Aliyah?" Jack queried without looking at her.

She shook her head. Dabbing her eyes once again with the napkin, she apologized to Selena. "I'm so sorry I'm ruining this dinner. May I go back to my room?"

"Oh, goodness, my dear, you don't need to ask permission, of course! Go get some rest. I'll check on you later."

Aliyah left her meal basically untouched and hurried out of the room.

"I hope she changes her mind," Jack said. "She is really, really good at what she does."

Louis agreed. "She's a tremendous bridge-builder, networker, organizer and visionary. I'm sure she'll be back. She just hurts so much right now because she cares so much."

"Like someone else I know." Selena smiled at her husband fondly.

"When you stop caring, you're done," Louis continued. "Aliyah hasn't stopped caring. She'll be back."

"For her sake, for the parents, for the poor kidnapped youth and for our fallen world, I hope this ends soon," Selena sighed.

Jack polished off his last bite of steak and patted his sculpted stomach with satisfaction. "That was good. Hey, my family is Christian and all, but I don't really go to church. What am I supposed to do at a prayer vigil?"

Louis answered. "Some people will light a candle or bring some flowers. There should be people of various faiths praying from the front you can listen to, or songs you sing together. And when you feel something well up inside of you that you want to express, just look to the heavens and let it out. God will hear."

Jack nodded. "Okay, that's cool I guess. Can I ask you something? Are you guys praying people?"

Louis smiled. "All the time. Couldn't do this job without it."

"Like what do you mostly pray for?"

Selena answered this one. "Right now, we're praying for a miracle."

Chapter 46

"**N**o!" Bol jumped up. "This is my brother, and he will not die alone." He grabbed Imam in a hug, locking his arms around Henry's intended victim.

"Get away from him!" Henry yelled. "Curt!"

Sari could see Curt hesitate. Before he could decide what to do, Fatimah had grabbed on to Imam from behind. Then Taj and Jolly leaped forward and locked arms across Imam's chest from the right and the left. Sari realized this was what Bol had suggested earlier, and she stood to join them. Alex and Katja were ahead of her, starting another layer around the group in spite of Henry's roars.

She turned to Rebecca. "Come on, we've got to all do this together." She held out her hand and Rebecca took it, standing to join the group.

Lotanna pulled Danilo in. Zoe helped Nandita. Through glassy-eyed sobs Nadia completed the circle of protection around her beloved.

"I hired you for action, you useless maggot! Separate them! Do something!" Henry railed at Curt. The executioner ignored him, his eyes glued to the circle of youth, the collar still dangling from his hand.

Sari craned her neck to catch a glimpse of Jeremy. He started to take a step toward them, then stopped, shot a glance at Curt, then at Henry. Sari saw the desperation etched in his clenched jaw.

"Fine. Jeremy, get my pistol. You can help me send these senseless fools on to hell."

Jeremy froze.

"Go on! Our global audience is waiting for an execution!" Henry glared at the boy, waving him toward the door.

Sari clung tightly to the youth around her, but kept her neck turned to see what Jeremy would do. *Please, God, help us!*

"Curt?" Jeremy asked hesitantly, but his older brother didn't even turn to look at him. He was transfixed on the young people before him.

"Go, boy!" Henry's shout echoed off the steel walls.

Jeremy looked back at his towering commander, then made a sudden lunge for the laptop. He spun it around so the webcam was on Henry.

"Stop!" Henry threw one hand up to cover his face, and with his other reached for the laptop. Jeremy took a step back leading Henry closer to the center of the room.

"You little brat! I'll shoot you too!" Henry let his furious face be exposed to the camera while he grabbed for the laptop with both hands. For a moment there was a tug of war, accompanied by surprised gasps from the youth.

Just as Henry raised a foot to push Jeremy away, Curt exploded into action. He jumped on the bigger man's back and in an instant had the collar wrapped around his neck. Jeremy released the laptop and fell backward, sending Henry crashing to his knees. He couldn't break his fall or fight Curt without releasing the computer. The big man cried out in pain as his elbows absorbed the weight of his toppling, just as Curt clicked home the final connection and stepped back.

Henry stared into the computer screen at his own face— bulging red veins, flaring nostrils, wild eyes—and a black box tucked neatly under his chin like a bow tie.

"Arrrrrgh!" he growled, slamming the laptop's lid closed and pivoting on his knees to look up at his lieutenant. "What is the meaning of this?" he raged. He appeared to Sari like a rhino about to lower his horn and charge.

Curt took two quick steps away from him, and from out of his pocket whipped a small cell phone-sized black box with a short antenna and a red switch.

"Stay where you are or I'll blow your head off," Curt said icily.

"I trusted you! You filthy Judas! You're digging your own grave, and his," he pointed at Jeremy menacingly, "and everyone else you've ever known or loved."

Curt motioned with his chin to Jeremy. The boy opened the squeaky door and stood awaiting his next instructions.

"Everybody out!" Curt ordered. "Except you," he glared at Henry.

At first they were all too shocked to move. Finally Lotanna released her grip on the circle and repeated for them to start moving. One by one the youth released each other's grasp and headed for the door. Imam and Bol put their arms around Ismail and helped him hop out. Sari saw Fatimah and Lotanna do the same for Nandita. Zoe grabbed the still hysterical Nadia and propelled her forward. Alex turned back, rushing to the bathroom to grab his beloved guitar before joining the exodus. All the while Sari could hear Henry growling and cursing and threatening them as they passed.

"You're dead! All of you! I'll show no mercy. Torture, rape, agonizing deaths..." Henry railed on and on, but Sari tuned him out.

At the door she paused. "Abagail, come with us?"

The old woman had slid lifelessly down the wall and was crumpled in a heap, but she lifted her head at Sari's call. Sari stared at the wrinkled pug-face, beaten down by years unloved.

"A woman's place is with 'er husband." Abagail dropped her head to her breast once again.

Curt saw that Sari was the last one in the doorway, nimbly snatched up the laptop, and followed her out.

Henry's scream echoed around his prison: "You'll all die, die, DIE!"

Curt slammed and bolted the door behind them, and not even the screams could escape.

The clang of the door bolt was a sound that had first puzzled, then concerned, then haunted Sari; now it was the sweet resonance of freedom.

Chapter 47

Sari turned to Curt. "Thank you for saving—"

"Don't thank me," Curt retorted. "I'm a killer." He tossed a set of keys to his brother. "Get these kids supplies and let's get them out of here. Everybody keep moving."

Jeremy led the group down the hall and into the staff quarters, stopping to unlock the door to a large closet.

Zoe, who was nearest the door, exclaimed, "Our suitcases!"

Alex and Jolly jumped forward to help Jeremy get all the baggage out into the hall and matched up with their excited owners.

Curt sucked some of the joy out of the moment. "Everyone grab only one change of clothes—warm, long-sleeved shirt, long pants, walking shoes, and if you have it, a light jacket. You have a long hike ahead of you."

"What about the rest of our stuff?" Danilo asked.

"Leave it. Once you're found, someone else will come back and get it for you. Jeremy, grab a box of water, some food, and all the flashlights we have."

Sari rummaged through her suitcase as though meeting old friends. She pulled out a fresh pair of dark blue stone-washed jeans and chose both a white t-shirt and a thin black pullover sweater. She found her hair brush and tried once to run it through her hair but the tangles were too much. She tossed it back in the suitcase. No watch or cell phone though. She asked Curt about them.

"Destroyed." He pointed at two opposite doors. "Men, change in the room on the left, women on the right. Get moving."

There was so much she wanted to ask Curt, but followed his orders with the others. When she finished changing, she joined Lotanna to help dress Nandita.

"Listen up, everyone," Lotanna got the girls' attention. "What just happened back there stays back there. Right now you need to get dressed and focus on escape. No whining or crying, you hear me? Help each other to keep going, because we're getting out of here."

Transformation began to happen all around her. They had left the common room in a daze, but the change of clothes was helping them alter their focus. None of the girls bothered with their hair or makeup. Nadia pulled out a hairbrush, but her hands were shaking too badly and, like Sari, she dropped it back in her suitcase. *At least her hysterics are under control.*

Someone knocked on the door. "Let's go," Curt's voice barked.

By the time the girls emerged, the boys had already closed and stacked the suitcases and guitar case in the hall. Curt laid the laptop on top of them. Jeremy passed out a bottle of water for each person and three flashlights for the group, keeping one for himself. He hitched a backpack up on his shoulders and led the way up the stairs to the surface.

Imam and Bol had a terrible time getting Ismail up the stairs. Curt watched this, then disappeared down the hallway, returning with a long, thin sofa cushion and two four-inch diameter pipes. He left once more and brought back three lengths of clothesline. Jolly helped him get the extra supplies up the stairs. Once they were all in the barn, Curt threw a hay bale over the trap door.

When Jeremy opened the barn doors, Sari could see the sun had almost set. There were beautiful purples and pinks softening the western sky over the forest. It wasn't the most gorgeous sunset she'd ever seen, but she knew it was one she'd never forget.

With expert speed, Curt lashed the clothesline around the head, the middle and the foot of the firm sofa cushion, attaching the pipes underneath, explaining as he worked.

"This will have to do. Grip the poles from the sides of the cushion, letting your wrists prevent the poles from sliding too far in or out. The rest of you, march in tandem, flashlights spaced out evenly."

Imam and Bol laid Ismail on the makeshift stretcher. The poor Indonesian boy looked like he was barely conscious.

"I don't have to tell you to be extremely careful stepping over the tripwires surrounding us. Once you get past the perimeter, head south-east," he pointed away from the sun. Looking at Jeremy, he continued, "In about a quarter-mile you should come to a creek. Follow its flow for another two miles or so and you'll see a corn field on your left. On the opposite side of the cornfield is the nearest house in these parts. From there you can get help."

Jeremy nodded and gave his brother a quick masculine hug.

"You mean you're not coming with us?" Fatimah asked.

"They'll be looking for me, after what I done. For what it's worth, I'm sorry." He gazed back at Jeremy. "When they ask you questions about me, just tell the truth." Jeremy nodded.

"Be strong, Little Bear. One day I'll find you." Curt pulled out his own small flashlight and set off at a jog into the sunset.

"Let's go," Jeremy called. Sari could see a new confidence in the boy.

He straddled the tripwire bravely making sure each person stepped across it safely. Then he appointed Jolly and Alex to take one flashlight and bring up the rear, while he led the procession. Everyone paired up, the girls agreeing to take turns helping Nandita walk, and the boys taking turns carrying Ismail's stretcher.

Sari grabbed Zoe's hand and pulled her to the front of the line behind Jeremy. She was dying to find out the story behind Curt's change of heart.

She kept her eyes on Jeremy's flashlight as it flitted across the ground, picking out a safe path for the group, but stayed close, wanting to talk.

"Jeremy, you know how grateful we are for you rescuing us, don't you? Can you tell us how you convinced your brother to help you?"

The American boy focused on the ground and kept moving, but angled his face slightly towards them to tell the story.

"After I stormed off mad, I realized I couldn't leave you all there, and I was on my way back to help you when I met my brother and Larry. I told him I wanted to know what he'd been hiding from Larry and me. Oh, he was angry at first, but I think it wasn't really me he was mad at. Finally, he told us the whole story, about how Henry made him kill the others, but now he was having doubts." He paused. "I just want to say I'm so sorry for what happened to your friends. I'm ashamed to have been part of it."

"It wasn't your fault," Zoe responded gently. "But why did your brother do it?"

"He said after the war he came back to no job, and nothing he was good at except killing people. Henry convinced him he could still serve his country by waging a secret war against our enemies. I think he liked having someone else to give the orders so he didn't have to think too much, he could just *act.*

"But I argued that you guys weren't our nation's enemies, that Henry was using him for something evil. My brother sat there picking at the bark of a tree stump until it was completely bald. Eventually, he looked at me with eyes like a lost child. 'Tell me what to do,' he said.

"I told him we had to stop Henry and save you guys. Larry agreed. Curt asked me how. I told him we would follow his lead. I don't think he really had a plan. And then Larry...I never thought he'd freak out like that and get himself killed. Poor Larry."

"That was terribly sad. We'll never forget what he did, standing up to Henry and George like that." Zoe agreed. "What's Curt going to do now?"

"He'll have to hide, I don't know how long. I'll miss him. But at least I know I have my brother back again."

Sari smiled in the dark. The brooding, anti-social boy they'd met the first day was now more confident and friendly, the evidence of a healing heart.

"And what will you do next?" Sari wondered.

"I don't know. I'm just a high school dropout." The boy's shoulders drooped slightly.

"No you're not," Zoe objected in her lilting French accent. "You saved our lives. You're going to be hailed as an international hero."

Chapter 48

They found the creek as the last traces of sunlight were fleeing. Lotanna called out to Jeremy asking for a brief rest. She sat Nandita down on a rock. Imam and Bol carefully lowered the sleeping Ismail's stretcher too, and all of them drank some water. Jeremy passed around some granola bars from his backpack. To the hungry hikers, these bars were more precious than gold.

There was a rustling in the trees near Nadia. She squealed and grabbed on to Imam. "Are there w-wild animals in this forest?" she stammered.

"Nothing to be afraid of," Jeremy told them. "We might run across a deer, fox, opossum, badger or skunk, but nothing likely to bite us."

"What about snakes?" asked Nandita weakly, remembering the trick Larry had played on them.

"Nah, we make so much noise I'm sure the snakes are giving us a wide berth. Relax. Remember these animals are more scared of us than we are of them."

Sari felt fairly safe in such a large group. But she imagined if she'd been out here alone at night, she'd have been terrified.

It was a lovely clear night. Occasionally through the treetops they could catch a glimpse of the moon smiling down on them, and brilliant stars twinkling across the sky. She breathed in the crisp, cool mountain air and felt her skin tingle with pleasure.

"We'll follow the creek that direction," Jeremy pointed with his flashlight. "I'll try to pick the easiest route, but there is no path, so bear with me."

"We need a bit slower pace with the stretcher." Bol looked up from his hands on his knees.

"Okay. Everyone ready?"

Danilo and Alex grabbed the stretcher, and Sari heard them grunt as they lifted Ismail from the ground. She put her arm around Nandita and was surprised to see Fatimah do the same from the other side.

"Lotanna told me Nandita won't make it with just one person helping her, she needs two."

With the frail girl's arms on their shoulders, they were practically carrying her. Several times one of them caught a toe on a root or rock and they nearly all tumbled to the ground. *At this pace we'll be walking all night long. In the condition we're in, will we even make it?*

Zoe called out to them all from the front. "Hey, Alex, you want to sing us a song?"

Alex was breathing hard. "Can it wait till I'm done with this stretcher?"

"Anybody else?" Zoe asked.

There was no answer for a while. Then Sari heard from far behind her a low melody arise. At first she didn't recognize the voice. The clearly American accent finally helped her deduce that it must be Rebecca.

The redhead girl's voice cracked with nervousness, but it was on pitch and clearly trained to sing. Sari didn't recognize the song, nor could she hear all the lyrics plainly, but she heard the chorus: *With you I am brave / With you I am brave...*

Sari's spirit drew strength from the words. God had heard their prayers and rescued them, and he would surely be with them all the way home.

Taj and Jolly were on their second shift carrying the stretcher when the small Indian boy cried out and Sari heard a crash. Taj had stepped on a loose rock and turned his ankle. He sat in the dirt holding his foot and whimpering. Ismail had taken a spill off the stretcher and was groaning in pain too. Jolly and Bol helped Ismail get situated on the cushion again while Sari checked on Taj.

"Why don't we take your shoe off and see how bad it is." She started to untie his basketball sneakers.

252

"Wait!" Danilo crouched beside her. "If it's a sprain, it will swell less if you keep the shoe on. At least, that's what my coach said when we were doing a cross-country run."

"Oh, I guess that makes sense," Sari yielded. "We could ice it in the cold stream, but there's no way to elevate it until we get to safety. You think we should keep going as is?"

Danilo shrugged. Taj looked up at them both. "We should keep going."

"Can you stand on it?" Danilo asked, offering his hand to help the boy up. Taj tried to stand but couldn't put weight on the foot at all.

Jeremy reached a decision. "All right, I'll take Taj's place with the stretcher, and we need the other guys to take turns carrying Taj on your backs. He doesn't look that heavy."

Alex bent forward and Taj hopped up on the Bosnian's back.

"Think of it as a skinny Indian guitar, Rock Man" Jolly joked.

"Who's going to lead?" Nadia asked.

Jeremy moved to the front of the stretcher. "Any of you have forest experience?"

Lotanna took the flashlight from his hand. "I do. Follow the creek to the cornfield, right?"

"And keep the pace slow." Jeremy and Jolly lifted the still groaning Ismail.

Lotanna moved to the front. "Come on, everybody. We've got warm baths, hot food, and soft feather pillows waiting for us, not to mention hugs from the people we love. Keep those feet moving."

Chapter 49

When Louis's cell phone rang, the entire room turned to face him—gaunt, tired faces, some aged with despair, others still clinging to the slightest wisp of hope.

Louis looked at the caller ID. "It's the FBI," he announced. His heart was so high in his throat it was hard to choke the words out.

"Staunton. Did you find them?"

Agent Durak replied, "Well, sir, yes and no. A dozen different teams were covering the final sites on our list today, but once we traced the email we honed in on their location right away—an old barn, a garden, a well—in northeastern Alabama. Our intel was confirmed once we discovered the barn was surrounded by landmines. Fortunately, our new ground-penetrating radar device picked them up before we stepped on one of them. After that, it took us a while to find the entrance to the underground base used by the extremists, but we found it, and like you said, we called down to negotiate rather than overwhelm them with force."

"And? Did they negotiate?"

"No one answered," Durak explained. "So we went in quietly to search the place. We found the kids' suitcases. But the kids were gone."

"I don't understand."

"Our first thought was they'd all been killed, but we searched through the rather extensive underground facility and found no bodies inside. What we did find was an arsenal befitting a small army. Eventually we discovered a locked room with four people inside—two dead American men, and the suspect Heinrich Christenson with his wife. Christenson had an ingenious bomb strapped around his neck. He claimed that he and the others were forced into helping the ex-military Curt Jansen kidnap and kill the kids, and that when they refused to cooperate any more, Jansen killed two of them, nearly killed him, and took the kids outside to execute them."

"My God. Do you believe him?"

"Who knows? We've taken him into custody. After that we searched the grounds around the barn and did find some graves, but not enough space to bury twenty people, and we also spotted several tracks leading into the woods. Most likely the kids left here alive with Jansen. No telling what weapons he might be carrying."

Louis breathed a sigh of half-relief, half-dread at what still might be to come.

Durak continued, "It's possible there's another explanation, but for now our orders are to find Jansen and shoot to kill."

Louis rubbed his temples, but the aching pain only increased. "Whatever you do, don't scare him. If he's as unstable as those videos portray, he could gun them all down."

"We're with you, sir. Having them in the open is to our advantage. They're somewhere in the forest, so using choppers with floodlights is out. We'll pursue on foot. We'll have the dogs ready to go momentarily. We've got snipers. If the dogs get us within half a mile the snipers will try to determine which of the group are extremists and take them out before they know we're there. We'll let you know when we've found them."

"Thank you, Agent Durak. Godspeed."

Louis hung up and tried to explain to the desperate families around him. "Everyone, the FBI is closing in. Some of the perpetrators are captured or dead. The kids have left their underground facility and are on the move, most likely still under the control of the remaining captors. The FBI is in pursuit."

There were gasps, tears, hugs, then everyone returned to their previous places around the room— sitting…pacing…praying…waiting…

But the worst of it, Louis knew, was the *imagining*. Imagining what their children might be suffering right now, or what they were about to suffer.

And imagining what life would be like if they never saw their children again.

Chapter 50

Their pace had slowed to nearly a crawl, with stops every few minutes to change carrying responsibilities, when they finally reached the cornfield. The moon was almost straight above them now, and the night sky was the most glorious Sari had ever seen. In spite of the cold wind causing her to shiver, she wanted to just lie down right there and spend the night. Civilization could wait until morning.

But Lotanna was a slave driver. "Change carriers!" she called out. "Two minute rest."

Danilo collapsed on the ground. "Let's just sleep here."

"Can we at least have fifteen minutes rest?" Sari begged.

"I know you're all tired," Lotanna sympathized, "but Ismail and Nandita, maybe even Taj, need to get to the hospital *tonight*, not tomorrow. So call on God or your hunger or missing your family or whatever motivates you to keep going. We just walked two miles through a forest—we're not letting this little cornfield stop us when we're so close!"

"She's right, come on, guys," Bol agreed. "Time to push through."

Imam came over to Rebecca and Fatimah who were huffing and puffing and barely holding Nandita up. "Put the girl on my back. I shall bear her from here." He knelt in front of them, and too tired to protest, the girls obeyed. Imam slipped his strong arms under the anorexic girl's tiny thighs and locked his hands in front.

Seeing Imam carry Nandita jarred the others into action. Jolly turned to Taj. "Jump on, bro, my surfboard weighs twice as much as you anyway." Bol and Alex grabbed the stretcher. But Katja could see Alex was exhausted from carrying Taj and offered to help Bol with the stretcher. Alex looked too tired to argue.

"No more stops," Lotanna demanded. Then she gave the flashlight to Jeremy. "Lead us home."

The first few minutes were discouraging, as the corn seemed to go on forever. But soon they could see the roof of a barn peeking above the stalks, then the roof of a house. Sari could hear Imam and Jolly breathing heavily in front of her, but they kept moving forward.

Suddenly the cornfield ended and they were in a small patch of vegetable garden behind the house.

"Watch out for tripwires," Danilo joked to no response.

A dog barked. Jeremy held up his hand and everyone paused. A golden-coated dog as tall as Sari's knees appeared, blocking their path to the house, legs spread, barking loudly. Sari wondered if he would attack them and tear them apart. But Jeremy reassured them, "It's all right, retrievers are friendly dogs, just keep walking and make no sudden movements." He began talking softly to the dog, taking a few steps forward, then stopping, then repeating the process.

The dog stayed put, its bark echoing off the surrounding hills. Sari saw a light come on in the house. The door opened and an old woman in a nightgown and cap stepped out on the porch cradling a shotgun.

"Who's there?" she cried out without the least bit of tremor in her strong voice.

Jeremy held up his hands while shining the flashlight toward her. "Excuse us, ma'am. We need an ambulance. Can we borrow your phone?"

The porch light revealed a leathery face squinting through the darkness at them. "Land sakes! How many of you are there?"

Jeremy took three steps closer. "Sixteen, ma'am, three injured."

The old woman lowered her shotgun. "Bindy, heel!" The dog stopped barking and joined its master on the porch. "Well, come in, come in!" Jeremy led the group forward. As he climbed the stairs, she asked, "How do ya'll get to be a way out here at night?"

"If you don't mind, ma'am, I'll tell you while one of these folks makes that phone call?"

"Land sakes! Follow me."

Everyone filed into the living room. It was filled with paintings of cows, wooden carvings of cows, and small porcelain cows. The patchwork quilt draped over the wooden couch had a cow design cleverly sewn into it. Imam laid Nadia there. Jolly dropped Taj into a brown leather recliner and manipulated a lever on the side so that the chair leaned back and propped Taj's feet up. Sari's eyebrows shot up at this—she'd never seen such an ingenious contraption. Bol and Katja carefully lowered the unconscious Ismail to the floor. Everyone else collapsed on the floor as well.

"So, which of ya'll wants my phone?" the woman asked.

The group all looked at each other. Imam cleared his throat. "Ahem. Bol has been a brilliant leader thus far. He deserves the honor." Others nodded their agreement, unless they were just nodding off to sleep.

"Anyone remember Aliyah or Jack's phone numbers?" Bol asked, hands on his knees to catch his breath.

From the recliner Taj spoke with his eyes closed. "Mrs. Aliyah—202-555-4528."

"How does he do that?" Nadia whispered to Sari, who shrugged.

From the hallway, they could hear Bol's voice, tired but triumphant.

"Mrs. Aliyah? This is Bol. We're all safe."

Chapter 51

The eleven o'clock news that night focused primarily on the prayer vigil. Though a few of the parents had retired to their rooms, Louis, Selena, and five of the families remained in the sitting room, finding the meagerest of comfort from being together.

An estimated twenty thousand people are still here at the White House...

Louis watched the television cameras span across the crowd of people holding candles, people of all different races and cultural dress, arm in arm. A heavyset African-American woman about his age was leading the crowd in singing *We Shall Overcome.*

The newscaster then flashed up similar scenes from across the nation. *All fifty capital cities and hundreds of thousands of cities across America are holding similar prayer vigils tonight, at city halls and other public places. The police have presented a strong show of force at most of these events to prevent any disturbances, and thankfully to this point we have none to report. The reports of random acts of violence have also dropped today. It seems the consciousness of America has chosen these missing youth, dubbed the "Peaceniks" by social media, as the new flashpoint of peace.*

In Los Angeles, a prayer vigil at the Hollywood Bowl just kicked off, offering celebrities a chance to express their prayers or words of support. Turner Field in Atlanta, where the Peaceniks were last seen alive, exchanged their usual rendition of "Take Me Out to the Ballgame" during the seventh inning stretch of the Braves game for a prayer led by the mayor of Atlanta. And other events across the nation from junior high basketball games to rock concerts began with a minute of silence for the people of our nation to offer their prayers for the safe return of the kidnapped youth.

Meanwhile, earlier today other parts of the world also expressed their support with prayer vigils. You can see this crowd at London's Westminster Abbey drew about three thousand. And here's Paris, where over five thousand gathered outside the Notre Dame Cathedral. Lagos, Nigeria had the largest turnout so far, nearly fifty thousand. Do we have footage of that? Right, here it is. This is Tinubu Square on Lagos Island. Nigeria was the home of the first Peacenik to be executed.

More vigils are scheduled in a few hours to begin in Honolulu, Seoul, Manila, Jakarta, at the Sydney Opera House, and in many other cities as the sunset moves across the Pacific Ocean.

The most remarkable thing about these vigils is that they are intentionally multi-faith. In fact, with our estimations at over twenty-five million attending American events alone, it is already being recognized as the largest inter-faith prayer event in history.

Louis nearly dropped his glass of water. He turned to his wife. "Did you hear that, honey?"

Selena's eyes were closed, her head resting on the back of the couch. "Uhuh," she grunted.

"They did it," he whispered. "Those kids did it. We wanted to challenge them to go back to their nations and bring people together who had a common desire for peace. Well, it only took them a week, and martyrdom, but they accomplished more for our nation, and surely for theirs as well, than we could have ever dreamed of." He shook his head in wonder.

"But at what cost?" Selena mumbled.

Louis was well aware of the cost. The video images would haunt him until he died. But those deaths had not been in vain. He hoped it would be of some comfort to the devastated families around him.

The newscaster was explaining about prayer vigils being planned across the Middle East as well when Louis heard his name being called.

Aliyah had just entered the room dressed in gray silk pajamas, holding a cell phone to her ear and looking white as a sheet.

He stepped toward her inquisitively. She just handed him the cell phone and crumpled to the floor in tears.

260

"Hello?" Louis began. "Who is this?""

"This is Bol. Where's Mrs. Aliyah?"

"Bol?" Louis couldn't believe his ears. "Bol Hol Hol?"

"Yes, you know me?"

"This is Congressman Louis Staunton. What's going on? Are you all right? Is this a ransom demand?"

"No, I mean, yes, we're all right. All fifteen of us, we've escaped."

"No kidnappers there with you?"

"No, sir. We're safe now."

Louis hurried to the couch to shake Selena awake, the weight of the world drifting up off his shoulders. "Thank God! Hold on." He covered the receiver and announced loudly, "Everyone! The kids are all right! They escaped!"

The previously subdued room suddenly burst into life, as family members jumped up with questions or started hugging each other. Louis signaled for them to keep it down.

"Bol, where are you?"

"We're at a farmhouse. We need an ambulance. Ismail's seriously wounded, and Taj and Nandita aren't doing so well either."

"Don't call an ambulance. We'll have a chopper pick you all up in minutes and take you all to the hospital and we'll meet you there. Can you give the phone back to the farmer?"

"Yes, sir. Thank you, sir."

Louis covered the receiver again and handed his own cell phone to Selena. "Call Durak for me, okay?"

"Hello? This is Congressman Louis Staunton. Who am I speaking with?... Mrs. Whitaker, you don't know how happy I am to meet you. Did you know those kids in your house are some of the most famous people in America?... Yes, that's right, the very ones on the news. Now I need you to give directions to the FBI so they can get a helicopter over to pick those kids up right away. Hold on a second."

Selena handed him his own phone. "Agent Durak?"

"Congressman, glad you called. Jansen appears to have them holed up in a farmhouse. Our snipers are in position. Pritz is about to—"

"Tell your snipers to stand down! Do it now! The kids just called us from that farmhouse. They escaped! They're in no danger now. They need a medical evac though."

"It could be a trick, sir," Durak countered.

"You can check it out for yourself. Write down this phone number and call the owner of the house."

He spoke into Aliyah's phone. "Mrs. Whitaker, what's your phone number?" He repeated it twice for Durak to write down. "Now I'm going to hang up, and the FBI will call you right back. Please stay calm and answer their questions… That's right, God bless you."

He hung up Aliyah's phone and spoke to Durak. "Tell me which hospital you'll take them to and I'll bring the families there… Got it. See you soon."

All the families were already practically smothering him trying to eavesdrop on every word. When he hung up, they took a step back waiting eagerly for the news.

"All fifteen are alive. They escaped to a nearby farm. I was told they need medical help for Ismail, Taj and Nandita. The FBI will fly them to a hospital to be determined momentarily. Please grab what you need and we'll meet in the lobby in ten minutes and get the hotel to bus us over to the hospital together." He met the eyes of Rebecca's father. "Mr. Heath, please knock on every door so no one misses that bus."

"My pleasure," the large redheaded man grinned.

Nandita's parents looked anxious, but thanked Louis and bustled out. Several others hugged everyone in the room before departing. Selena helped Aliyah to stand and she and Louis put their arms around the weeping woman.

"Come to the hospital with us?" Selena pleaded. "The kids will want to see you."

Aliyah nodded, drying her eyes with her pajama top. Selena took her back to her hotel room to change.

Louis dialed his cell phone once again. "Congressman Louis Staunton. Listen, I don't care what the president is doing, he'll want to hear this."

Chapter 52

The rest of the night was a blur to Sari. She remembered the deafening *thucka-thucka* of the helicopter that had landed near the farmhouse, drawing them out on the porch to watch, then a bunch of men in all black with guns shouting and motioning, herding the kids into the chopper. Finally there were stronger arms to help the weak, and Sari could stop worrying about Nandita and Ismail and Taj, and let someone take her hand and help her inside.

Once seated, she'd fallen asleep with her head on Jolly's shoulder and he had to wake her up and push her out the door to stumble from the helicopter into a hospital. The hospital had looked so close, but felt so far away. She had never realized how heavy feet could be. If it weren't for Jolly's hand in her back, she would never have made it.

Everyone was whisked to separate rooms right away. Sari remembered the insane pleasure she'd felt climbing up onto the white bed with a soft pillow. The room smelled like lemons. She was just about to drift off to sleep when the first needle stabbed her arm, and she had opened her eyes to watch a chubby male nurse draw some blood. She had closed her eyes again, then the second needle stabbed her, and she saw a tube attached to her arm near the wrist. She had asked the nurse if she could sleep, but a man wearing a black outfit and black cap with FBI written on it in gold had barged in to argue with the nurse, who had restricted him to only five minutes.

Sari had tried her best to answer the man's questions, but was nodding off so he kept pinching her toe to wake her up. She didn't understand why they couldn't wait until morning to talk to her.

Next a tall doctor with a face like a vulture had come in to argue with the FBI guy. They both left. Last to enter was Mrs. Aliyah and a tall black man Sari recognized but couldn't recall his name. They had hugged her and said something about telephoning Pak Abdullah, but at that point her brain was too fuzzy to care anymore.

Sari closed her eyes and let her mind wind down. Images paraded across her consciousness—grinding corn for cornbread; screaming from the top of the burning hay bales; washing her hair in the back of the toilet; Alex's song; the stars above the cornfield.

The word "peace" floated by in the clouds, and her body rose slowly to float beside it. She floated on her back lifted by a puffy white cloud with her head turned just enough to keep her eyes fixed on the word. It was pulsating, like a heart was beating inside of it, beating slowly, but clearly *alive.* The pulses were hypnotizing.

She slipped into a blissful, peace-full rest.

DAY 7

Chapter 53

The next day Sari felt like she'd been reborn. The nurse removed the IV drip from her arm and allowed her to take a shower. Her suitcase had magically appeared, and Sari picked out her brightest outfit to reflect her mood—red and black checkered pants matching a white t-shirt with a giant red heart between the words "I" and "Atlanta" that she'd bought at the airport when she'd arrived. She fastened her long hair in the back with a white lace hairclip, put on makeup, and almost felt like a tourist again.

Her debrief with the FBI agent took about an hour, but at least he was sympathetic. Even though retelling the events of the last week stirred up many emotions, it felt good to share it with someone. Of course, given the choice, she would have preferred for her first sharing to be with her adopted father, Pak Abdullah. She imagined him smiling at Jeremy's turn around, and hoped when he heard her stories, he'd be proud of her.

At noon, a nurse told her to bring all her belongings, and escorted her down to the second floor cafeteria. The nurse was asking kindly about her home in Indonesia when suddenly a man in a white doctor's coat whipped out a camera and the flash went off in her face. Sari raised her hand in front of her.

"Did they abuse you? Rape you? Tell me—"

"Security!" the nurse yelled. Almost instantly two muscular men dressed in business suits seized the man's arms, confiscated his camera, and dragged him off down the hall, still calling out to Sari for a quote.

"Sorry about that," the nurse frowned. "He must have stolen that coat to get past the security team."

Sari was a bit shaken. "What did he want?"

"Oh, the press has besieged our hospital. You guys are the hottest item in the news, and everyone wants the scoop."

Sari wasn't sure what a "scoop" was. The press wanted photos of *them*? She remembered Pak Abdullah complaining about being hounded by the media in the aftermath of the assassination attempt when her mother had died. But before she could figure out how best to worry, the nurse threw open the door to the cafeteria.

Red, white and blue balloons floated gaily against the ceiling. A giant banner read, "WELCOME HOME, PEACENIKS!" The room was buzzing with happy people.

Mrs. Aliyah came over and grabbed Sari by the arm, steering her into the crowd. "Sari, you look positively radiant! Come join the party."

"Mrs. Aliyah, may I ask, who are all these people?"

"These are the families of your friends! I'm so sorry Mr. Abdullah couldn't be here for you, but most of your friends have parents or loved ones here. You should meet some of them."

The Persian-American woman steered Sari toward Zoe, then left her.

"Sari!" Zoe exclaimed, accenting the second syllable much like she pronounced "Paris" *pay-REE*. Zoe hugged her tightly, then turned Sari's shoulders to face her parents. "*Maman*, Papa, this is my friend Sari from Indonesia."

Sari smiled at the couple. Zoe's mom had poofy blond hair shaped like a conch shell, heavy makeup, and a chic outfit with blue bubbles bursting on a green background. Zoe's father sported a thin moustache, thin eyebrows, but lively green eyes, and was dressed in a brown suit with a gray tie. She figured Zoe got her looks from her father but her fashion sense from her mother.

Zoe's mother grabbed her shoulders and kissed her on both cheeks. Zoe's father took her hand in both of his and kissed it gently.

"It's nice to meet you," Sari stammered. "Your daughter is so brave, so strong. She's just…wonderful."

The parents beamed. Zoe ripped off something in French, and they nodded and beamed even more. Then Zoe's father wrapped Zoe in a hug and whispered more French in her ear. Sari thought maybe it was time to move on.

The doors opened and she saw Ismail being wheeled in on a hospital bed, his parents by his side. She headed for them, longing for a chance to speak her own language once again. A week of only English, she realized, had tired out her brain.

"*Bapak, Ibu,* welcome to America!" she greeted Ismail's parents in Indonesian.

Their faces lit up as Ismail's mother kissed both her cheeks and his father shook Sari's hand then touched his hand to his heart. They asked about where she was from and how she was doing. After the appropriate amount of small talk, she turned to Ismail.

"How are you feeling, older brother?"

The young man managed a weak smile. "Sleepy. These pain meds are amazing."

"What did the doctor say about your leg?"

"Honestly, I don't remember. Just that I'll be in the hospital another week. My parents were starting to panic about it until Mrs. Aliyah told them they won't have to pay for it." He made a feeble attempt at another smile.

More than Ismail's leg, Sari was dying to know the condition of his heart. "That was quite an escape, wasn't it?" She hoped he'd take the bait.

"I don't really remember much, to tell the truth. I remember going up the stairs, feeling the night air, and then getting dumped on the ground in the forest. My next memory is the helicopter and then waking up here in the hospital. What was it like, hiking through the forest?"

Sari filled in some of the details for Ismail, including the sacrifices the others had made to carry him out. He listened quietly.

She wrapped it up. "I know you've been disappointed by Christians. But one thing Henry said that was true: 'We don't need more words; we need actions.' Everyone took turns carrying you, even Danilo and Katja."

Ismail blinked rapidly before answering. "I'll be sure to thank each one."

Sari smiled widely. "Get well soon. And stay in touch with me, okay?"

"Okay," her Indonesian friend replied.

At that moment, the tall African-American man she'd briefly seen the previous evening spoke into a microphone.

"Welcome, everyone! I think we're all here. Would you all please try to find a seat at a table so we can serve you lunch?"

He paused while everyone sat down. Sari searched for a table with an empty chair, and wound up with Jolly, his parents, and Katja.

"Looks like you and me are on our own," Katja murmured.

No sooner did they sit down than bottles of water appeared on their table, followed by plates and utensils, then one after another dishes of food: salad, baked chicken, potatoes, roast beef, beets, green beans, a yellow squash—and the one that brought Sari the most joy—white rice.

Sari's eyes popped at the sight of the rice. She'd never gone a week without rice before, and she never wanted to do it again. She could have hugged that bowl to her chest and died happy, but she realized she wasn't paying attention to what the speaker was saying.

"...and on behalf of the staff of our Youth for Peace Fresh Start Initiative, Mrs. Aliyah Mahmudi and Mr. Jack Porter, I'm Louis Staunton, extending the warmest welcome to all the families of our peace participants.

"Each of you parents made a choice to allow your son or daughter to take a risk and build a bridge of understanding with those from a different background. The risks were real, as the whole world realizes afresh today. The effects of the horrible deeds of the last few days will be with us forever. We have wept together. We have comforted one another. And we will continue to do so until this great shadow over us has passed.

"But with great risk also comes great reward. Your children's stories of courage in the face of this indescribable horror have built for them a uniquely influential platform. Your families will now be sought out by people all around the world to speak for peace. Even as you are still working through your pain and grief, you must prepare yourselves and your children to be a voice in this generation.

"And it starts today. Immediately after this lunch, at two o'clock, we will all step into an adjacent room to hold a press conference. This will be our chance to tell the world what we want them to hear. From the press conference, a bus will be standing by to take you back to the hotel to check out, then directly to the airport so you can return to your homes, if you'd like to leave tonight. During the lunch, you can speak with our volunteer travel agents," he pointed to three young professionals at a table on the right, "who will book your flights home compliments of the president; who, by the way, was planning to be here today before the bombing of the American embassy in Bangladesh required his full attention.

"I know your original flights home are still a week away, so if any of you would prefer to stay in the United States until then, my wife and I are happy to invite you to our home in Washington D.C. We'll give you a tour of the capital that you'll never forget." Louis smiled warmly. Something in his smile reminded her of Pak Abdullah. *A tour of Washington D.C. sounds amazing! Can I take this bowl of rice with me?*

"So after you eat, I suggest you say your good-byes here in this room before the press conference. Be sure to thank the amazing hospital staff who have taken such good care of you." Applause filled the room. "As well as the FBI agents who worked tirelessly searching for, and finally, rescuing you. To my left is the Special Agent in Charge Todd Pritz, with Special Agent Casey Durak and their team." More applause filled the room. Sari had never imagined the FBI would care about them. She wondered why.

Her answer came with Louis Staunton's next words: "To offer a prayer of thanksgiving for the return of our beloved children, I've invited a close personal friend, a fellow peacemaker and a good friend of America. Ladies and Gentlemen, please welcome His Majesty the King of Jordan."

Sari's mouth dropped open as she clapped her hands, even more when she saw the bearded man sitting next to Imam rise from his seat and take the microphone.

"Peace be upon you. It is my honor as a father to join with you all, fathers and mothers like me, in thanking God for the safe return of our children. Let us pray."

Sari watched as some heads bowed and eyes closed, others lifted hands with their palms up before them, eyes also lifted to the heavens.

"*Bismillah ir-Rahman ir-Rahim.* In the name of God, Most Compassionate, Most Merciful, Your throne extends over heaven and earth, and You feel no fatigue in guarding and preserving Your own. Today we thank You for reuniting us with our children. We also thank You for the five peacemakers who laid down their lives that the rest of us might have a better world. We pledge ourselves to honor their deaths by how we continue their struggle for peace. Comfort their families, and receive these five into Your Paradise. May all our children's struggle for peace inspire a new generation that no longer stumbles over the prejudice they inherited from us, but rises to a higher place, to a true reflection of Your great love for all mankind. Amen."

"Amen," Sari joined many others in the echo.

Katja reached for some salad. "So that was Imam's dirty little secret, huh?"

"I guess it's a good thing I tackled Ismail instead of the prince," Jolly agreed.

Sari took a generous portion of rice first, then tried to decide what to eat with it. A thought struck her.

"Do you think anyone else knew? I think Nadia knew. But what about Daud?"

The other two thought as they chewed. "I doubt it," Katja decided. "He had us all fooled."

Jolly's mom cocked her head to one side. "One of your friends is prince?"

"Yup, mind-blowing, huh?" Jolly answered.

Sari's attention was drawn to the cafeteria door, where an FBI agent was talking to someone through the doorway. Louis Staunton joined in, and then shook the hand of a tall, blond, handsome young man Sari had never seen before. She nudged Katja. "Who's that guy?"

"MIJO!" Katja screamed, dropping her fork and nearly giving Jolly's mom a heart attack. The Bosnian girl leaped out of her chair so fast it crashed to the floor. She raced across the room and flung her arms around the new arrival.

Sari remembered her conversation with Katja over a bag of manure and smiled. So this was the Christian guy her Muslim friend was so crazy over.

"Is that Katja's boyfriend? What a stud," Jolly observed. "Just saying…"

"She looks so happy," Sari remarked. Now Katja had someone to celebrate with. It seemed like everyone had someone there except her. She desperately missed her mother, and Bali, and Pak Abdullah.

"Don't look so down, babe, the best boyfriends are surfers, you know." Jolly grinned at her. She smiled back.

Terrorism had taken from her the people she loved the most. But pursuing peace was certainly giving her more people to love. People from all over the world.

Chapter 54

After eating, Sari started making the rounds to say good-bye to everyone. She began with Nandita. The Indian girl stood up from her wheelchair and held Sari for a long time.

"Thank you, thank you, thank you, Sari," Nandita gushed. "I can't believe you and the other girls carried me through the forest." She craned her neck toward her parents. "She *carried* me, Papa, Mummy." The elderly Indian couple bowed their heads in respect toward Sari and thanked her profusely.

"Oh, I know you'd do the same for me," Sari smiled. "How long are they keeping you in this wheelchair?"

"Just another day or two till my strength returns," Nandita replied. Sari was happy to see more color in her friend's face. Just twenty-four hours ago she'd looked a pale shell of herself. "We'll probably go home the day after tomorrow, my parents said. I'll miss you, Sari."

"I'll miss you too. Stay in touch, okay?"

"I will."

As Sari hugged her new Indian friend again, she felt a tap on her shoulder. She released Nandita and turned around to find Danilo's serious face.

"Hey, I just want to say I'm sorry," the Filipino youth began. "I refused to see what I didn't want to be true, and I—"

"It's okay, Danny," Sari interrupted. "At first, I didn't want to see it either. We all struggled to make sense of things. What's important is you carried Ismail through the forest to safety. I know he'll never forget that." She smiled and embraced him.

"I'll never forget all of you either," Danilo promised before moving on. Sari watched him apologize to Katja and get a friendly punch in the arm. She couldn't help smiling.

She paused to survey the room and let the beauty of all that was happening around her sink in. It was fascinating to see all her friends' parents, and how much their children were like them. Alex's parents didn't have punk haircuts or multiple rings in their ears, but their ruddy faces and jerky mannerisms reminded her so much of the young rock star. Rebecca got her bright red hair from her dad and her prim and proper outlook on life from her mom. Lotanna's mom was heavier than her daughter, but had the same gorgeous skin, full lips, and wavy hair. She also spoke her opinions bluntly, but without any hint of arrogance. Meeting her reminded Sari how strong Lotanna had been for the group, and she told her so.

"I'm sorry I doubted you at first, Lotanna. You figured out what was going on long before the rest of us. I should have listened to you. Where would we be without you?"

"Still sleeping in the cornfield?" Lotanna quipped.

Sari laughed. "You taught me that I can choose not to fear. I wish I'd known that years ago. So many days I hid in my home afraid to go outside, afraid of the scary world around me. If only I'd had your strength and courage back then."

"You have your own strength, Sari," Lotanna countered. "You trust people. I once called you 'naïve,' and I'm sorry. If we want to do like Jesus and 'love our enemies,' we have to be strong enough to trust them and get to know them as people just like us."

"Thanks for facing the 'rattle-snake' with me," Sari giggled.

Lotanna laughed too. "Come visit me in Nigeria. You'll always be considered a member of my family." She glanced at her mom, who nodded.

"You will be my own daughter," the older woman smiled through crooked but brilliantly white teeth.

"And you're always welcome to stay with me in Indonesia." Sari's eyes were blurry as she hugged Lotanna again, desperately hoping it wouldn't be the last time.

Fatimah joined in the hug. "Hey, you two!"

They opened their arms to include her in the embrace, their foreheads touching each other. Fatimah whispered conspiratorially.

"I've got a great idea. Sari can stand on this table while I set it on fire, and while she screams, Lotanna and I can slip out the side door and go find some handsome American boyfriends."

All three giggled. "Do you have any ideas that *don't* include fire?" Sari asked.

"Fresh out. Say, Sari, where's your family?"

"Mrs. Aliyah said they were having a hard time getting ahold of my adopted dad. I want to meet yours! Where are they?"

Fatimah grimaced. "The unrest is Palestine is keeping them from getting to the airport."

"That's a shame," Lotanna sympathized.

"So are you going to stay the extra week with Mr. Staunton?" Sari asked.

"Well, Imam's dad offered to fly me to Jordan in his private jet with Imam and Nadia. I've never been in a private jet, sounds fun. But if you stay, maybe I'll stay with you."

Sari bounced up and down holding Fatimah's hands. "Oh, please, please, please! We could have so much fun together."

"Fine, you talked me into it. But you better make it more fun than a private jet!"

"It will be!" Sari felt so much less alone. They gave Lotanna one more good-bye hug and continued wandering around the room together hugging their friends. Sari thought Nadia looked so ecstatic she might pass out. She wondered if it was from meeting the king, anticipating a ride in the private jet, or getting a few more hours with Imam that was making her friend dizzy. Nadia gave Sari an enthusiastic kiss on the cheek and turned her attention quickly back to her handsome prince.

They scanned the crowd to make sure they hadn't missed anyone. "Did you see Bol's family?" Fatimah asked.

"No, where are they?"

"Well, I've been doing some complex algebra, and I see only one African family, Lotanna's. That family he's standing with now looks Asian, but Ismail's is over there by his bed, and Danilo's is over there by Mrs. Aliyah. Don't tell me he was adopted by Asians!"

Sari's curiosity was piqued. "Let's go find out." They approached the middle-aged Asian couple who were dressed immaculately, obviously very wealthy, but carrying a heaviness in their shoulders and faces that the other families had left behind.

"Sari! Fatimah!" Bol hugged them. "I'd like you to meet Yasmin's parents."

Yasmin's father held out his hand, but Fatimah ignored it and threw her arms around him. Sari took the cue and embraced Yasmin's mother as well. She felt the woman's chest begin to heave, then sob. Sari continued to hold her tight without speaking as the woman struggled to regain control. Eventually she released Sari and dabbed her eyes with the lavender pashmina scarf loosely looped over her head.

"I apologize. It's just—"

"Don't apologize," Fatimah answered. "Your wonderful daughter is worthy of every tear."

Sari could see Yasmin's father was swallowing hard, struggling to keep his own composure. She wanted so badly to say something comforting.

Bol coughed. "I was just telling Mr. and Mrs. Ali what a privilege it was to know Yasmin and to face such evil with her pure heart at our side." His penetrating gaze got through to Sari. Though Yasmin had acted like a diva, her parents didn't deserve to remember her that way.

Sari reached out and took Mrs. Ali's hand in hers. "My mother was killed trying to stop a terrorist attack. It still hurts. But what she died for…you know, nothing she could have done would ever make me love her more, but the way she died did make me prouder of her than ever. I mean…she'll forever be my mom, but now she's also a mother of peace." Sari wanted to say more, but the words caught in her throat.

"My daughter, a daughter of peace," Mr. Ali responded thoughtfully. "Thank you, dear girl."

They hugged Yasmin's parents again, then Fatimah grabbed Bol's hand and the three of them wandered on.

"I don't see your family, Bol," Fatimah said.

"They all died in the civil war. Did I forget to mention that?" Bol smiled.

"There's a lot about you that you didn't mention," Fatimah replied.

"Well, since I know that neither of you has family here either, maybe we could get to know each other better at Mr. Staunton's house this week."

"Do you mean it, Bol?" Sari gushed. "Oh, this will be so fun! I can't believe it!"

"You guys are staying?" Bol's eyebrows rose hopefully.

"Yes," Fatimah assured him, "and with you two along for the ride, who knows what might happen!"

Chapter 55

Somehow Sari managed to hug everyone and say her good-byes before Jack had them all line up outside the door to the press conference, behind Ismail on his hospital bed. She hoped no one would put her on the spot and make her say anything. The parents were told to wait in the cafeteria and watch through the open door, to protect them at least a bit longer from the ravenous media.

Her thoughts drifted back to her last press conference, in Banjarmasin, when Pak Abdullah had needed to act creatively and courageously to save everyone's lives. If she could just get through this press conference without a bomb going off, she'd call it a success.

Jack threw open the door and single-file, they all marched into what looked like a lobby and stood along the nearest wall. About three meters away from them, what appeared to be an elastic bandage had been stretched across the room about waist high acting as a barrier to the press. Flash bulbs popped, blinding Sari momentarily. When her eyes adjusted, she could see the media outnumbered them by nearly ten to one. They were packed into every corner of the room, some even squatting on a receptionist's counter, jostling for the best camera angles. *If this is what being a celebrity is like, I think I'd hate it.*

In place of a podium, there was a rolling steel medical cart with a microphone connected to a lone speaker on top of it. Louis Staunton calmly tapped the mike and the journalists grew quiet to hear what he would say.

"Good afternoon, Ladies and Gentlemen. I am Louis Staunton, a congressman from Michigan, but today I have been asked by the president of the United States, who hoped to be here, if I would represent him.

"Today I will make a public statement regarding the kidnapping and release of the participants of the Youth for Peace Fresh Start Initiative, commonly referred to in the media as the 'Peaceniks.' Then you will have a chance to hear firsthand from a select few participants and one of the parents. Afterwards, we will not be answering questions as this is still an ongoing FBI investigation. I would ask that at the conclusion of this press conference, you honor these young heroes by allowing them to leave this room and return to their homes in peace.

"The FBI has allowed me to give the following statement: One week ago, twenty young international peacemakers came to Georgia for a two-week camp on peacemaking. On the first evening of the camp, the regular camp staff were subdued and the twenty youth drugged and kidnapped, and taken to an underground facility some distance away. Their captors began killing the youth one by one, filming their executions, and posting them to the internet in an apparent scheme to provoke other Americans to also commit acts of violence against minorities in general and Muslims in particular. Five of these young peacemakers were violently murdered.

"The kidnappers were planning to continue these executions, but with the help of a brave young American, the youth managed to escape." At this point, Louis looked to the doorway, and two agents escorted in someone Sari had thanked God for at least a hundred times.

"Jeremy!" several young people screamed happily.

The Alabama boy blinked rapidly at the flashing cameras and blushed. Louis stretched the microphone cable as far as it could go and put his hand on the boy's shoulder. "Jeremy Jansen is a true American hero. Not only did he stand up to the kidnappers, but he led the youth on a night march through the forest to a distant farm, where the FBI found them near midnight just fourteen hours ago."

Bol started applauding, and Sari joined him. Soon all the youth were smiling at Jeremy and applauding and many of the journalists joined in. Zoe left her place on the wall and gave the boy a hug and a quick kiss on the cheek, turning his face an even brighter shade of red. The agents then moved him to the end of the youth line next to Jolly, who put his arm over the boy's shoulder as Louis continued.

"All fifteen of the remaining youth have been examined here at the hospital and are in good health, the worst case being a deep stab wound in the leg that is healing well." Louis pointed out Ismail lying on the hospital bed to his left. "Most of them will be released today to return home.

"The last thing I want to mention is that these young people managed to escape without any of them attacking their captors. In the face of hatred and violence, they chose to exhibit their commitment to peace. With them, I would speak to the American people who have been tragically victimized in these past few days. Would you follow their examples, and choose what the Good Book teaches us, to 'overcome evil with good'? Only by taking a stand for peace can we stop the cycle of mutual destruction.

"And now I'll let you hear directly from some of the youth themselves."

Sari wondered who was going to speak. Were they given time to prepare? *I wonder what I'd want to say if I were chosen...*

Her eyebrows lifted when she saw Rebecca was the first to step forward and take the microphone.

"Hi, my name is Rebecca Heath from Dearborn, Michigan. I started a free after-school program helping the children of immigrants learn to read. I knew that some of my friends were racist and Islamophobic and they told me I was wasting my time. I never realized that I could serve those kids and still have prejudice hidden deep within my heart.

"During our captivity, we were often confused about what our captors' intentions truly were. I confess that I wanted to trust the voices of those with white skin, or who claimed the Christian religion, like me, and I couldn't easily trust those participants who were different than me." She looked down and swallowed hard. "Yet in spite of my mistrust, judgmental words, and uncooperative attitude, all of these people," she extended her hand toward her friends, "forgave me and treated me with kindness.

"I guess what I'm trying to say is, even if we think our hearts are free of prejudice, we only really know for sure when we're in relationship with others and things aren't going well. That's when we find out who our true friends are, and what kind of friend we are. Thank you."

All the youth clapped enthusiastically for Rebecca, and again many journalists joined in.

Bol stepped forward confidently and smiled broadly at his audience.

"Good afternoon. My name is Bol Hol Hol. I'm from the South Sudan. I have lived through a brutal civil war that didn't just take our loved ones' lives, but for many, robbed us of our dignity, our courage, and our voice. Rebuilding a school or a home is easy compared to rebuilding the collective psyche of a nation.

"But I believe that if my nation had the quality of young leaders that I met at this peace event, we could succeed in one generation. The young people standing behind me are all outstanding leaders who have represented their nations well, including our new American friend, Jeremy. In the days to come, each of them will be speaking publically and writing about their experiences. Listen to them.

"And there are five of us who won't be speaking publically, or writing, yet their voices cry out to us from beyond, not for vengeance, but for a better world. Kareem, Asmina, Usman, Yasmin, Daud—we will not forget you. This morning in my hospital bed I asked myself why each of them were chosen to die. The first few days of our captivity, these were the ones who spoke out the most clearly for truth, righteousness, and peace. Our captors wanted to silence their voices. We must not let that happen. We must carry their voices, for their destinies are now joined to ours, to bring an end to hate and wage peace across the world, from America to South Sudan. God bless you."

Sari was moved to tears by Bol's passion. She hadn't realized how eloquent he was. *I'm so blessed to have had the chance to follow his leadership.*

Imam was the third participant to speak. *A prince!* It was taking some getting used to, seeing him as a prince. To Sari he was just Imam.

"*Assalamu alaikum.* Peace be upon you. My name is Imam Ghozali bin Abdullah. I reluctantly submitted to my father's wishes that I join this event as a representative of the country of Jordan. My fellow peacemakers were unaware that I was from my nation's royal family.

"I affirm all that my Christian brother Bol has stated—this is a truly extraordinary coterie of young world-changers, and I have learned much from them all. In these few days together, I have discovered a new passion and direction for my life.

"But first I feel compelled to tell you about a participant who is no longer with us, Daud Younan, a freshman at the Bethlehem Bible College, and my Christian Palestinian brother. Initially, when the members of our company began disappearing, we didn't realize they were being killed. After the fourth person disappeared, Daud was the first to deduce correctly that we were being systematically executed.

"Our captors had selected me to be the fifth victim, when suddenly Daud leaped forward and persuaded them to take him instead. None of us understood at the time. But Daud knew that I was to be crucified that afternoon, and he took my place. Because of his sacrifice, I am alive today."

Imam paused to regain composure, but wasn't helped by a loud sobbing near the FBI agents. Sari wiped her eyes and could see Imam's father leaning over, hands on his knees, weeping loudly. Louis Staunton placed his hand on the king's back. *Maybe Imam hadn't told his dad Daud's part in the story yet.*

"This Christian youth fought the greatest *jihad* of all. Wielding the weapon of self-sacrifice, he battled to save my life. Against the diabolical, murderous darkness, he did not confuse peacemaking with passivity, but he resisted the violence of evil with an equally violent light. I've no doubt that history will validate his triumph." Imam paused, head bowed as though in reverence.

"Daud was a filmmaker," the prince continued, "and he taught us that sometimes we have to block out the surrounding environment and focus just on the face before us, like this." He held up his hands as Daud had done, forming a rectangle of vision

284

before his eyes. "We can eliminate all the chaos around—the politics, the economics, the injustice, even the troubles of the past—and just see the person in this moment as a human being like ourselves." Imam panned the audience slowly with his view-box, then dropped his hands to his side. "When we look deeply into someone's eyes, if we're wise, we recognize that this, too, is a child of God."

Now Imam seemed to grow in size before Sari's eyes. His voice rang out with power and conviction as he stared directly into the television camera.

"People of Jordan, brothers and sisters in the Middle East, I appeal to you today, there is no future for any of us in killing one another. Let us lift our eyes beyond our current heroes of military generals or suicide bombers and exalt one who is infinitely more worthy, Daud, the Palestinian Christian martyr, who died for the sake of friendship, giving his life for a Muslim like me. My Muslim, Christian, Jewish, and Western brothers, killing each other dishonors Daud's name. I call upon you to lay down your stones, your guns, your tanks, your missiles. I hereby pledge to you that I refuse to die in the killing of others. When I die, let it be serving others, a whole-hearted sacrifice of love not only for the people of Jordan, but for the people of our world.

"When going to war, my people are often heard to cry '*Allahu Akbar*,' meaning 'God is the Greatest.' How is it we have forgotten another of His beautiful names, '*Allahu As Salaam*,' meaning 'God is the Giver of Peace'? Brothers and sisters, in the midst of great adversity such as we faced in captivity, such as you face bravely every day, let this be our rallying cry."

Imam strode boldly toward Jeremy, grabbed the surprised boy's hand, and thrust it with his above their heads, shouting, "*Allahu As Salaam*! *Allahu As Salaam*! *Allahu As Salaam*! God of all peace, unite us!"

Flashes popped like fireworks capturing this profound moment, yet the journalists couldn't help shouting their cheers along with the peace participants. The entire room was caught up with a fresh vision of what could be. Tears poured down Sari's face even as she screamed with the others.

Imam dropped Jeremy's hand and gave him a bear hug. Sari felt Fatimah's hand slip around her waist and turned to hug her. All the youth began hugging each other. Sari glanced over at the FBI agents at the door and had a sudden urge to go hug them too, but just giggled to herself at the thought.

Imam handed the microphone to Louis Staunton, who stood grinning at the chaos around him. Sari saw him exchange looks with a smiling but weeping Mrs. Aliyah. *I'll be forever grateful to those two for this opportunity.*

When the clapping and cheers died down, Louis spoke, "Ladies and Gentlemen, our final speaker at this press conference is one of the parents. I give you His Majesty, the King of Jordan."

The applause lasted a long time, long enough for Imam's dad to gain control over his heavy weeping, wipe his eyes several times, and take a deep breath. He motioned for his son to come stand beside him.

There they stood, side by side, two bearded men with serious expressions, used to the weight of a nation resting on their shoulders. Sari wondered if today they weren't feeling the weight of the whole Middle East, or even the world.

The king held the microphone in his left hand, wrapping his right arm around Imam's shoulders. With glassy eyes and a choked voice, the king spoke.

"This is my son." His throat constricted and the tears began flowing again. It took him nearly a minute to regain composure. He lifted his eyes to the heavens and tried again. "This is my son," he repeated in a stronger voice.

Then he motioned with his left hand for Rebecca to come forward. The red-headed American girl hesitantly stepped toward the large Arab man. He waved for her to stand on the other side of him. Then switching the mike to his right hand, he put his left arm around Rebecca's shoulders.

"And this is my daughter." He placed the microphone back on the steel medical cart and hugged each of the two tightly.

Louis Staunton stepped forward and took the hands of Jolly and Lotanna, leading them next to Imam where Louis mirrored the king, an arm around each one.

Mrs. Aliyah emerged next to Rebecca with one arm around Katja and the other around Taj on crutches.

Jack Porter grabbed Sari's hand and led her next to Ismail's bed where he embraced the two delegates from Indonesia.

The others linked arms and stepped forward parallel with the king.

"Our children," Imam's father continued, "are our greatest treasure, and our future. Not just my children, or your children, but ALL our children.

"Let us make sure they stay alive to fulfill all their dreams.

"*Allahu As Salaam*! Peace be upon us all."

Chapter 56

Back through the cafeteria and out a back door, Jack led the group to the bus. Sari had imagined it would be a tour bus much like the one that had taken them to the camp; this bus was all black and looked like it was for transporting prisoners. Maybe the FBI had provided it. *Anyway, freedom wasn't determined by what was outside them but by what was within them.*

Sari stood with Bol and Fatimah, a few steps ahead of Louis, Aliyah and Jack watching the other youth and their families board. She thought to herself that if she'd been alone, she wouldn't have been able to bear it. Thank God she had Bol and Fatimah with her.

"Are you missing them already?" Bol asked her.

She was surprised by his perceptiveness. "Yes, I am. How about you?"

"A little. But I can't wait to follow them on social media and see what they're going to do next."

"Do you think we'll ever see them again?" she asked.

Bol shrugged. Fatimah responded, "If we continue to pursue peacemaking for the next twenty or thirty years, I imagine we will. Imam may become one of the strongest voices for peace of our generation, but who knows? Maybe others of us will become that too."

"Yeah, our world needs a voice like Imam's," Bol agreed. "But it's going to take all of our contributions working together for peace. We need Alex's music, Taj's connecting people online, Lotanna's advocacy for victims—"

"And those with extreme courage to sacrifice themselves for others like Daud did," Fatimah interrupted.

Sari gently grabbed each of her friends' arms. "And we need those who can bring diverse groups to work together, like you, Bol.

And those who find a way to redirect their family's path to something beautiful, like you, Fatimah."

Fatimah put her hand over Sari's. "Don't forget people like you, Sari, who choose to see the best in everyone."

"I wish we could all get together and do this again in Indonesia," Sari sighed.

"Or in South Sudan," Bol added.

"Or in Palestine," Fatimah agreed.

"Some of them, like you, Fatimah, are going home to really dangerous places. I hope they'll be all right." Sari's forehead wrinkled with anxiety for her friends.

Jolly had just helped his parents up the stairs and into the bus. Now Taj and his parents were the last ones boarding. The injured youth let go of one of his crutches and reached up awkwardly to grab the railing, but slipped and started to fall backwards onto his petite mother.

A hand appeared, stretching through the doorway and locked onto his wrist, steadying him. Sari squinted to see who it was. She caught the reflection of sunglasses and a wave of long brown hair. Jolly was making sure his Indian friend made it to his seat safely.

Fatimah noticed too. "They're looking out for each other. They'll be fine."

The bus driver jumped in his seat and closed the door and they heard the engine roar to life. All three of them started to wave.

In one of the bus windows there appeared two hands forming a rectangle as Daud had taught them. Pressed into the box were bright green eyes and the freckled face of Rebecca.

Bol, Fatimah and Sari all returned her symbol with view-boxes of their own. One by one the windows of the bus copied them until all twenty-four were filled with Daud's salute.

Sari held Daud's box in front of her eyes until the bus was just a speck driving into the brilliant light of a sunny summer's day.

Louis Staunton had stepped up beside them. "All right, you three, follow me. My wife has a shopping trip planned for you this afternoon and a good night's sleep before we fly to D.C. tomorrow morning."

That evening at the hotel, Sari was just about to turn out the light and snuggle contentedly in her enormous, lavish bed, when she heard a knock at the door.

She opened it and welcomed Mrs. Aliyah into the room. The woman offered her a cell phone.

"I've been trying for days to get ahold of Pak Abdullah for you. He finally answered! I told him I'd call him back in a few minutes so he could talk to you. Are you ready?"

Sari threw her arms around the woman gratefully, then held the phone like a freshly discovered diamond and took a deep breath. She hit the call button.

"Is this my daughter, Sari?" a deep voice answered in Indonesian.

"Bapak! It's so good to hear your voice!" Sari gushed.

"Forgive me, I was in the Sumatran jungle the last few days trying to peacefully disband a terrorist training camp. No internet or cell phone signal. Your friend told me on the phone that you've just been through something terrible and I'd hear all about it on the news. Are you okay? What happened?"

Sari sat down on the rose-patterned comforter, curling her feet up under her, and Aliyah smiled and gently closed the door as she left.

"I'm fine, don't worry. And I have the most incredible story to tell you.

"It all started my first morning in America. All of us youth had these glorious dreams of peace, but first we had to find each other in the darkness…"

The origin story of Sari and Abdullah's path to peacemaking
(Peace Trilogy Book 1)

In the midst of a global clash between international terrorism and an American congressman's peacemaking effort, a poor Muslim-majority neighborhood in Indonesia holds the keys to victory. While some in the neighborhood are making efforts to understand the truth behind the Muslim-Christian divide and build new bridges across it, others are determined to perpetuate and intensify the hatred that has plagued the region for years.

When a tragedy reveals an unexpected villain, it will be up to two unlikely heroes to set aside their differences and save the day. What will it take to keep hope alive? And who will be willing to make the ultimate sacrifice for the sake of peace?

This intense thriller will encourage you to reexamine your understanding of love and forgiveness, and reconsider what it means to be a true peacemaker.

Available at **Amazon** or at **www.jimbaton.com**

Sari's city is being torn to shreds by ISIS
(Peace Trilogy Book 2)

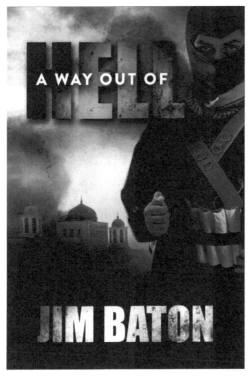

"Just tell me what you want me to do." Abdullah braced himself for the worst.

The Intelligence agent leaned back in the chair with his hands pressed together tapping his lips. "If ISIS is indeed here, I want you to find their terrorist cell and take it down. And I want you to do this…" he paused, "…non-violently."

ISIS is threatening to destabilize Indonesia. In the city of Banjarmasin, Abdullah will need all his experience as a former jihadist and as a reformed peacemaker to save his city. His adopted daughter, Sari, a Christian university student, is one of the targets. She's also the only one who believes Abdullah can succeed in overcoming evil with good.

In this riveting sequel to *Someone Has to Die*, Jim Baton introduces us to the real people caught in the web of terrorism, with their wide variety of backgrounds and motivations, and the possibility that they, too, can change.

Available at **Amazon** or at **www.jimbaton.com**

If you liked the PEACE Trilogy, check out Jim's

HOPE Trilogy

In the HOPE Trilogy, teenagers Kelsey and Harmonie solve mysteries, fight for justice, experience the supernatural, and find their place in God's destiny for their town of Hope, Colorado.

The Hope Trilogy is written for those who are hungry for God's revival and transformation of their communities.

Available at **Amazon** or at **www.jimbaton.com**

Praise for SOMEONE HAS TO DIE

"Where has Jim Baton been all our lives?! This is one of those rare 'first novels' that demands another. There are many academic books outlining the tensions and differences between Christians and Muslims, but beyond a riveting story, this book enables us to enter into the existing deep emotions, convictions, and inherited prejudices which otherwise elude us. The Batons know it because they've lived in the center of it for decades. I couldn't put it down. ...and I don't even read novels!"

Greg Livingstone, World Outreach, Evangelical Presbyterian Church

"Hatred, persecution, fear, terrorism--just daily life for millions around the world. This book takes us through it all to the other side, to the hope for peace. I highly recommend it for peace-lovers everywhere."

U.S. Congressman Mark Siljander (ret) President, Bridges to Common Ground, Author of *A Deadly Misunderstanding*

"SOMEONE HAS TO DIE will make you squirm, cry and smile. You will squirm as you realize that we are all fraught with stereotypes about Christians and Muslims. You will be confronted with the hypocrisy of your own faith, regardless of what side of the chasm you find yourself. You will cry as you are confronted with the ugliness of hate and the gentle power of self-sacrifice. You will smile because love is stronger than hate, and evil doesn't have to win."

Erik Lincoln, Peace Activist, Author of the bestselling series, *Peace Generation*

"It's easy to demonize those different from us. It's a bit harder to research facts in order to understand them. It's even more of a stretch to step into their world and to walk in their shoes. But Jim Baton has gone one step further: he's told their story. The story is about conflicts between Christians and Muslims in Indonesia, a country where Baton has lived for many years, but it is more than that. It's also a story about us, whether Christian or Muslim. It challenges us to look at the truths about ourselves, about the prejudices, ignorance and anger that are in each of us, and that, if left untouched by God's love, can spill out to ravage nations, communities and families. Yet there is hope. God can and does change hearts, as Baton so beautifully testifies to in this warm and uplifting story."

Dr. Rick Love, Founder of Peace Catalyst International

"An incredibly realistic portrayal of relationships between our Muslim and Christian friends with fascinating lessons for peacemakers."

Rob Rice, Executive Director, Community Based Rehabilitation International

"SOMEONE HAS TO DIE shows the real struggle between the major religions of the world, Christianity and Islam, and...demonstrates in a powerful way that reconciliation is possible if people are willing to change. I appreciated that the author did not whitewash the complexities of the two faiths, and the clashes at times had tragic outcomes. The characters were well-developed, and the storyline realistic. I look forward to reading the next book in the series."

Lorilyn Roberts, author of *Children of Dreams*

"Thanks, Jim Baton, for this gift of a book. It's better than a text book in how Christians and Muslims can live together and honor and love one another...or not, as sadly, some of the characters in your book choose to do, causing much pain and heart ache. The very real characters along with their personal dramas, global issues, and the suspense of a terrorism attack make SOMEONE HAS TO DIE a thrilling read. Set in a city village of Banjarmasin, Indonesia, using local language interspersed with details of life and culture in a Muslim majority country not only makes the story really interesting, but also thought provoking, poignant and sweet at times. I laughed at some of the characters' antics, I cried, I held my breath but I couldn't put it down. I've also bought a number of hard copies to give to friends and family as I know it will help many on their journey in 'loving our neighbors as we love ourselves'."

"Chrissy Van," Christian expatriate living in Southeast Asia

"In SOMEONE HAS TO DIE Jim Baton eloquently writes a beautiful story clearly depicting a paradigm-changing message on how relational healing is what will bring Muslims back into the Father's House. I highly recommend this book."

Ché Ahn, Founding Pastor, Harvest Rock Church, Pasadena, CA; President, Harvest International Ministry; International Chancellor, Wagner Leadership Institute

"SOMEONE HAS TO DIE reads like a classic novel like Uncle Tom's Cabin, Ramona or Ivanhoe as it has the effect of changing public opinion. I feel that this is a very important book for our times."

Jill Davis, Frontier Ventures Resource Center

Praise for **A WAY OUT OF HELL**

"Great book for those open to expanding their understanding of complex issues, and serious about building bridges instead of walls. Well-researched. Highly recommend!"

Carl Medearis, author of *Muslims, Christians, and Jesus;* co-author of *Tea with Hezbollah*

"A WAY OUT OF HELL is a fast-paced, multi-faceted thriller with a secret plot underwriting some of today's most frightening headlines. The lead characters, former jihadist, Abdullah, and savage attack survivor, Sari, are great examples of how Muslims and Christians can come together in spite of a history of years of divisive suspicion and work together to foil the plans of extremists who want to unleash a reign of terror in Indonesia."

Dave Andrews, author of *The Jihad of Jesus*

"I am convinced that the fruit of peacemaking is friendship--real friendship between people with real differences who come together to make a real impact in their communities. Jim Baton makes this happen. I have walked his streets, and I have seen firsthand how Jim has fostered a community of Muslims and Christians who live together and work together to overcome intolerance and extremism with love and respect. Not surprisingly, this is the major story line in A WAY OUT OF HELL, an emotion-stirring journey that in the end leaves you inspired and challenged to love more and thus live better."

Thomas Davis, Global Peacemaking Coach with World Outreach, Evangelical Presbyterian Church

"[Jim Baton's] writing is stellar, the story riveting and excruciating and occasionally embarrassingly true when Baton showcases who is willing to risk peace at all costs and who doubts it can be done. This is the ultimate lesson in meeting extreme prejudice head-on and refusing to blink. Baton makes me believe."

Lisa J. Lickel, author of *Understory* and *Requiem for the Innocents*

About the Author

Jim Baton lives in the world's largest Muslim nation, building bridges between Muslims and Christians who both desire peace. Find out more at **www.jimbaton.com**.

Made in United States
Troutdale, OR
03/02/2024

18139235R00176